Salvation
Station

D0761669

Salvation Station

A Novel

Kathryn Schleich

SHE WRITES PRESS

Published 2020
Printed in the United States of America
ISBN: 978-1-63152-892-7 pbk
ISBN: 978-1-63152-893-4 ebk
Library of Congress Control Number: 2019914836

For information, address:
She Writes Press
1569 Solano Ave #546
Berkeley, CA 94707

She Writes Press is a division of SparkPoint Studio, LLC.

*To all the courageous, resilient, and smart
women I've met in my life*

I

Monday, May 13, 2002
Lincoln, Nebraska
University Place Disciples
of Christ Church

Two of them were just babies. Captain Linda Turner had been a homicide detective for over ten years, but this crime scene was still a shock. *Half a dozen murders are considered a bad year,* she mused, striding toward the scene. Three bodies accidentally discovered through an innocent act: an inquisitive dog burrowing deep into the flower garden behind its new home and bringing its master a gruesome prize.

"Morning, Steve," she said. The cop guarding the area raised the yellow plastic Police Line—Do Not Cross crime tape as she folded her body and slipped under. "I understand the owner's dog found the bodies."

"Good morning, Captain. Yes, ma'am, he recently moved to town, the pastor of University Disciples of Christ Church," Steve offered. "He made the 911 call."

"What a welcome."

This was all the information Captain Turner had on this breezy May morning. The smell of freshly turned soil and blooming flowers combined with a stench she knew all too well. Behind the neat limestone house, the flower garden was cordoned off, and evidence flags and numbered photo markers dotted the soil with yellow. A crime scene photographer had finished documenting the shocking scene, and the coroner was directing forensic experts gingerly extracting human remains from beneath the black earth. The bodies were wrapped individually in blankets, fragile from decomposition. The badly deteriorated remains were gently uncovered, revealing two young children dressed in tattered Disney pajamas. One body clad in pink Disney princesses and the other in Mickey Mouse gave Linda pause. The little girl and boy lay on blue plastic tarps spread over the grass, human jigsaw puzzles waiting to be solved. Linda couldn't look any longer and turned away, her free hand covering her mouth, breathing through her nose to keep from gagging.

It had happened before, but the horror of murdered innocent children always had the same effect: Linda couldn't stop until the depraved killer was found and convicted. She didn't have any children of her own because she had invested 110 percent into her police career, but she was a favorite aunt. Linda envisioned the sweet faces of her nieces and nephews, all under the age of ten.

The back door swung shut with a loud bang, snapping Linda into the here and now. A familiar figure strode toward her. Tall and lean, Lieutenant Lyle Dale was a twenty-year veteran of the force. Dressed in a tailored dark suit and cowboy boots—always cowboy boots—he cut a striking figure. Linda met him halfway across the lush lawn.

"Morning, Lieutenant. Bring me up to speed," she said, gesturing toward the vigilant CSI team.

Lyle spoke matter-of-factly. "One adult male and two small children. CSIs are still looking for a fourth body, but no luck so far."

"I assume that would be the mother?" Linda asked, watching the hive of activity.

"That's our best guess. The children make this crime especially heinous."

"Yes, they do," Linda acknowledged sadly. She strolled back toward the partially excavated garden, shading her eyes from the rising spring sun. "Walk me through the discovery."

Lt. Dale cleared his throat. "If it weren't for the Reverend Martin's very large and curious dog, Kris Kringle, the bodies might have gone undetected. According to the reverend, Kris is always dragging home roadkill or what have you. This morning, Kris took to digging in the flower garden and brought his master a human leg." Lyle turned toward the house. "Rev. Martin followed his dog out here," he added, tracing the pastor's path in one motion ending at the garden, "where he discovered additional human remains. At which point, he called 911."

A strand had come loose from the ponytail securing her blonde hair, and Linda casually brushed it aside. "Any idea yet who they might be?"

"That's where it gets intriguing," Lyle replied. "Rev. Martin moved into the parsonage about eight weeks ago, replacing the former pastor named Gregory Hansen, who'd left to pursue missionary work in Africa. Rev. Hansen was married and had two young children. After the Hansen family moved, the national missionary office for the Disciples of Christ contacted the church concerned that the Hansens had never arrived."

Linda glanced toward the corpses and the growing mounds of dirt from the excavated garden. "Three bodies. What are the chances that the Hansen family never left town?"

Lyle nodded, his face grim. "That's my thought—that these are Rev. Hansen and his children. But we'll need autopsies to confirm that."

The sour feeling in Linda's stomach made her think Lyle was right, but she had another question. "Did the church contact us or file a missing person's report?"

"The church secretary confirmed a missing person's report was filed when the national Disciples office called to say the Hansens weren't in Cleveland," Lyle answered, following her gaze.

Linda kept focusing on those tiny pajama-clad bodies. "Start interviewing persons of interest—"

"I've already got staff ready for interviews," Lyle interrupted. "Rev. Martin is very willing to cooperate and has agreed to let police search the house and take prints. Then there's the church secretary, Darlene Jordan, who specifically asked to speak with the person in charge."

Linda removed a small pad of paper and pen from her jacket pocket, scribbling notes. "I'll talk with the church secretary. Once we've secured the house, you and Amy start canvassing neighbors and church members."

"Right. One other thing: both Amy and I detected the odor of bleach throughout the house, as though someone was cleaning up after themselves."

"Captain Turner? Ma'am, there's a reporter from the *Journal Star* asking to speak with you." It was Steve, the strapping, young, uniformed officer assigned to keep bystanders away from the scene.

"I need to give the press a preliminary statement," Linda acknowledged. "We haven't seen a case involving the murder of children in quite a while, so it'll merit extra attention. I'll see you back at the station." Linda strode toward the quickly forming gaggle of reporters with Steve at her heels.

Cases like this were one reason Linda Turner loved her job. Her dedication and tenaciousness had assured her promotion as the youngest person to attain the rank of captain in the LPD. Sifting through the clues of a tangled mystery, discovering which pieces fit and which led to a dead end, then assembling that evidence into a case to catch the perpetrators and bring them to justice were what had made law enforcement so enticing.

But there was an unhappy downside to her meteoric rise. No longer was there anyone to come home to and share a lifetime with.

To preserve her sanity, Linda made the choice to delve deep into her career, personal needs be damned. This case was already tugging at her emotions. Those children's bodies haunted her. Who would savagely murder a pastor and innocent children, burying the evidence in a flower garden? Why? And most troubling, where was the mother? Linda made a silent vow to find out. No matter what.

2

Tuesday, May 14, 2002
St. Louis, Missouri
The Road to Calvary TV set

H is voice was as smooth as good Kentucky sipping whiskey, the southern lilt forceful yet refined. Among the crowd, a few responded, "Amen!" as the Reverend Ray Williams, his body six foot three inches of sinewy muscle, strode across the cramped stage on a mission to save and assessed his sparse flock. The set was tightly confined; on TV, the lighting, color, and camera angles would give the illusion of spaciousness.

"Remember what the Bible tells us in John, chapter eight, verse twelve. Jesus proclaims, 'I am the light of the world! Whoever follows Me will never walk in darkness but will have the light of life!' Believe in Him and I tell you, brothers and sisters, all who accept Jesus Christ will have everlasting life!"

Rev. Ray had done this work long enough to know everything looked better on television, except the numbers. For five years, he'd courted an audience from a low-power cable TV station in St. Louis, confident his message would attract followers looking for salvation. A couple thousand worshippers invited *The Road to Calvary* into their homes, but it wasn't enough. He had spent more of his own money than he cared to admit; however, expenses kept rising, and there was relentless competition for viewers, members, and revenue.

Even now, Ray was conflicted in his decision to close what had seemed a promising venture. He'd never lost his enthusiasm or the feeling he was indeed proclaiming the word of God and news of salvation. Ray knew everyone was a sinner, including himself. He hoped *The Road to Calvary* would spur people to rise above their sins, accept the Good News, and find the true meaning of Christ in their lives. The reverend smiled warmly at his audience and motioned for them to stand. "Let us share our belief in Jesus Christ by praying together our prayer of deliverance."

The congregation rose to their feet and repeated the words they had come to know by heart: "Lord Jesus, I believe in You. I believe You died for my sins and rose again to save me from a world mired in sin . . ."

At the prayer's end, a cheerful male voice yelled off stage left, "That's a wrap!"

The prayerful opened their eyes. Ray bid his flock goodbye. "Thank you for joining us, and see you next week for another taping."

†

The rented studio space had emptied out, and Ray steeled himself as he prepared to break the news to his miniscule staff. Jeff Jones and Buck Neal had worked with him since the beginning and, other than the cable channel volunteers, were his only employees. After Ray's wife died, he'd needed a break from running a church, and low-power cable seemed the perfect avenue to reach a larger audience.

Although the pay was low, it was more than either Buck or Jeff thought Ray could afford, so they had risen to the occasion time and again, working long hours to produce the show. Jeff, a Gulf War veteran who had left the army with a medal for bravery, had taken the cable station's courses on how to run the camera equipment, while Buck, with a background in TV production and IT, handled the lighting, edited the videotape, acted as stage director, and greeted audience members. But in the world of low-power cable, local religious programming was a staple. With limited resources, Ray had underestimated the toughness of that competition.

As he stood on the edge of the carpeted stage with his cohorts, he marveled at their vast differences. Short in stature, Jeff made up for it with his buffed physique that won area weightlifting contests, while, in stark contrast, Buck sported a mullet, a paunch, and a silver earring. He was a recovering alcoholic, and unlike Jeff who had never married, Buck had three failed unions behind him. As a team, they'd worked together in seamless tandem, and now it was going to end.

Ray cleared his throat. "I always promised you'd be the first to know the fate of *The Road to Calvary*, and unfortunately, that moment has come."

"You're ending the show?" Buck asked.

"I don't want to draw this out, but yes. Even with the reasonable cost of low-power cable, we can't pay the weekly rent for the space. We have a small, loyal following, but we can't survive much longer. The money just isn't there, and I can't afford to keep subsidizing us. I'll tell the congregation and cable station next week that we're going off the air at the end of the month."

"Guess it's a good thing none of us quit our day jobs," Jeff said.

"And I thought our faith in Jesus Christ would make this show work," Buck added unhappily.

"Me, too," Ray said, a sad smile across his handsome, character-lined face. "We gave it five years and put all of our energy into this venture." He draped long arms around each man's shoulder. "No regrets. We didn't change the world, but we put our heart into every show, and I'm eternally grateful to the both of you."

A woman's voice startled all three men. "Excuse me, gentlemen," she said softly. They turned and saw a slender woman dressed in a cream pantsuit with chestnut hair in soft ringlets framing a heart-shaped face. "I'm sorry to startle you," she apologized, "but I've been standing in the back. Rev. Williams, could I speak with you for a moment?"

Stepping from the stage, Ray extended a hand. "Certainly, Miss—"

"Baker. Susannah Baker," she replied, shaking Ray's outstretched hand firmly. "But Susannah, please."

"Susannah, it's a pleasure." He paused and recalled the very pretty face from previous tapings. "You're one of our recent regulars, aren't you?"

"Yes, I started coming around two months ago. Wouldn't miss it for anything." She smiled.

"You said you wanted to talk?"

She laughed nervously, gesturing toward Buck and Jeff. "I'm sorry to interrupt. But when you're done, I wondered if we could talk privately."

Ray turned to the younger men. "There's nothing else to add, unless one of you has questions."

"You do what you need to do," Buck said, patting Ray's shoulder. "Jeff and I will put the equipment away and lock up the building."

"Miss Baker, did you want to talk here, or would you rather go somewhere else?" Ray asked. "There's a coffee shop up the block."

"That would be lovely," she said, her eyes lighting up.

"I'll see you gentlemen next week," Ray said, offering Susannah his arm. They left the office building and stepped out into the warm, spring air, chatting casually as they walked. "Are you new to the area or just our show?" the pastor inquired.

"Both," she said. "But you have a wonderful program, Reverend, and I'm sure it's helped many people."

"Well, not as many as I'd like," he replied. If Miss Baker were asking for a sympathetic ear, Ray thought it best not to drive her away with talk of going off the air. His role for now was to be an attentive listener. At the diner, they ordered coffee and took a table near the windows.

She didn't waste an instant getting to her point. As she fortified herself with a long sip, Susannah Baker's dark eyes were bright with anticipation, as though she were going to impart a happy secret. "Not to eavesdrop, but I couldn't help overhearing your conversation. I'm here to give you a message that ending this wonderful program is the worst thing you could do."

Ray cradled the warm ceramic coffee mug in his large hands. "A message? From whom?"

Susannah Baker paused, searching the pastor's handsome face. "God," she said.

He stared at this mysterious woman. Her pronouncement was genuine and earnest, but a career in ministry had taught him some of the world's craziest souls were absolutely sincere and committed to their own warped reality.

"I'm going to jump right in and hope you won't think I'm crazy. Rev. Williams, you don't know me, but I owe my life to you."

As he observed her gulping a drink from her mug, Ray determined that most individuals who were bereft of reason didn't know enough to acknowledge it.

"You helped me climb out of a bottomless pit and find our Lord Jesus Christ, but I know I'm not the only person you've saved. Last week, God spoke to me in a dream, with a clear plan to enrich *The Road to Calvary* and allow your message to be accessed by a much larger audience."

As Susannah stopped for a sip of coffee, Ray posed a question. "What kind of direction, exactly, did God give you?"

Her penetrating eyes never wavered from his face. "God told me that He has chosen you to work miracles."

His response, a surprised chuckle, wasn't mocking her in any way, but the absurdity of a small-time preacher being called upon to work miracles gave him pause. "Miss, I'm just a poor preacher with a small flock. As far as miracles go, that's up to God."

"I'm not talking about walking on water, Reverend. Suppose you were in a position where you could see and hear the needs and prayers of everyone attending *The Road to Calvary*. Those followers need your help, Reverend, and here's the perfect opportunity to give it to them. You choose the audience members with the greatest needs and, using the miracle of technology, lead them toward redemption, while giving others in the congregation hope."

Ray sat motionless, astounded into silence by what he'd heard. Surely, she was joking, or she was completely nuts and masked it extremely well. His voice took on the tone of the Pentecostal preacher that he was, clear in his disapproval. "I think you're confusing *miracles* with fraud, Miss Baker. And that's not something I want to be involved in."

He expected her to back down or at least sheepishly admit this was indeed an inappropriate plan. Instead, she plunged ahead. "I admit eavesdropping with hidden microphones may be an unorthodox approach, but God sees such methods as acceptable for the greater good. You'll be able to help people with their specific problems, and they'll be empowered to help themselves and improve their lives. And I ask you, Reverend, what is wrong with that?"

Before he could further explain his discomfort, Susannah was justifying the tactics. "There are so many other ways the program can distinguish itself. Envision a choir praising God in jubilant song and members witnessing the power of salvation in their own lives. It's a means to accomplishing a much greater good."

Still not convinced this wasn't simply deception, he made his point a second time. "This would not just be unethical, but a breach of trust," he said, crossing his arms.

Susannah Baker leaned back against the slats of the wooden chair, a slight smile on her full lips. "If you could hear the prayers of potentially every member of your congregation, what would you do?"

"I'd pray for them and hope those prayers are answered in a positive way," he replied.

"Exactly my point," she countered with equal force. "The technology is nothing more than an instrument, providing evidence you wouldn't otherwise have. Being able to acknowledge the needs of the congregation, you help get the prayers of greatest consequence answered and set them on the miraculous path to redemption in our Lord Jesus Christ."

Ray pondered Susannah Baker's proposition and found himself very conflicted. On one side of the argument, he felt employing deception could be a huge risk, and members would surely feel betrayed if they ever knew. But on the other side, such an approach might be the very thing that could save *The Road to Calvary* from the television trash heap.

"You think I'm crazy, don't you?" she asked.

"No, but I'm not convinced these ideas are right for us."

"But you said you're planning to end the program, so you have nothing to lose. And neither do I, so I'll throw out another idea of how *The Road to Calvary* can set itself apart from other religious programming." Elbows propped on the table, Susannah leaned forward. "I've always wondered why there is no such thing as Christian makeovers, because a woman who looks good improves her self-esteem and gives her husband something special to come home to. Tell me where it says good Christian women, especially on television, must have big hair, false lashes, and bad eyeliner."

He chortled; this was certainly an idea that had never crossed his mind, particularly in the realm of ministry.

"Go ahead and laugh," Susannah continued, not offended in the least, "but it's another way to set you apart from the competition."

"My apologies," Ray offered. "I wasn't laughing at you; it's just not something I've ever considered." He ran a finger around the rim of the mug. "You really believe God gave you these directions in a dream?"

"I don't just believe it. I know it. God has great faith in you, Reverend, and he's telling you not to give up."

On some level, Ray realized Susannah Baker's passion was reminiscent of his own, and it fired his spirit. But he needed time to process the core element of eavesdropping to save souls, a ploy he still considered unethical and shameful. He had no intention of turning *The Road to Calvary* into a Barnum & Bailey circus act, full of flamboyant miracles and tawdry sideshow freaks.

"I'll consider it," he said finally. "Give me a week to reflect on your suggestions and consult with Buck and Jeff. I can't promise we'll take you up on any of this."

She smiled, clasping her hands together. "I understand your concerns. Do you think you'll have a decision by next week's taping?"

"Yes," he said. "I'll have an answer after the show."

"Forgive me for being forward," she ventured slowly, "but would you mind if I sat in on the discussion? I understand a lot of this sounds crazy, but perhaps it would help if I could clarify any questions you or your staff might have."

"Well, there isn't much of a staff. Buck and Jeff basically do this for the Lord." He paused, tilting his head back slightly. "You sound as though you've done this kind of thing before," he said, not as a question but an open-ended statement.

Her soft smile turned up the corners of a full, inviting mouth. "God has told me everything I need to know."

3

WEDNESDAY, MAY 15, 2002
ST. CHARLES, MISSOURI
RUTH PERKINS'S HOME

"Your yearly physical with Dr. Garland is this Friday at ten o'clock, so what if I pick you up at nine? That should give us plenty of time in case traffic is heavy."

Ruth Perkins knew her daughter Emma meant well, but she had a way of taking over that could be annoying. She didn't answer right away, distracted by *The Road to Calvary* playing in silence, as Emma had hit the mute button on the remote the moment she walked through the door.

"Why do you insist on watching that crap?" Emma said. "The Reverend Bob—"

"Ray," Ruth countered sternly. "It's the Reverend Ray."

Her mother's outburst took Emma by surprise. "Okay, so you enjoy the *Reverend Ray*. But he's a shyster out to part people from their money. You haven't attended church since Dad died, so why this?"

Her mother's voice took on an edge of irritation. "You know why I left the Presbyterian Church. When your father was dying, Pastor Ron couldn't be bothered to visit him in the hospital. And remember, even you thought the funeral was awful. He barely even mentioned the deceased or all he'd done for the church over a long span. I believe Reverend Ray is sincere, and I enjoy his message. Besides, nobody's forcing you to give them money."

Emma furrowed her brow, knowing full well her mother was right. "Mom, there are other churches. Why dedicate yourself to a person who is so obviously a fraud?"

"That's your opinion," Ruth answered tersely. "I'd appreciate you letting me make my own choices as to my religious beliefs."

Her mother's tone left Emma feeling like a berated child. "Forget I said anything."

Ruth stared into the face of her daughter. Her only child had a lovely heart-shaped face, high cheekbones, and hazel eyes. Wisely, she changed the subject. "I do appreciate you wanting to take me to my doctor's appointment, but it's not as if I'm an invalid." Emma started to protest, but Ruth held up an open palm and continued, "I'm only seventy-nine, Emma, not a hundred, and I haven't had so much as a ticket in over thirty years—"

"Mom!" Emma interrupted. "That's not why I'm going with you. I want to hear what the doctor has to say."

Ruth was forty-four when she'd had Emma, and the pregnancy had caught her and Orville by happy surprise. She distinctly remembered holding her daughter in those first precious minutes, marveling that in this new life, she was seeing herself. As a child, adolescent, and young woman, her daughter had a temper to be reckoned with. Ruth shook her head at the memory. "You have my eyes and your Aunt Irene's temperament."

Emma's eyes flashed. "Why are you talking about this?"

Her anger had always festered below the surface, even as a little girl. It had become so bad that Ruth and Orville chose to get Emma into therapy when she started breaking things in unprovoked rages. The therapist thought perhaps her anger stemmed from being an only child.

Ruth said, "It's too bad we couldn't give you a brother or a sister. I've always wondered if you wouldn't be incensed so easily if you'd had a sibling to help care for."

Her daughter rolled her eyes, shaking her head in annoyance. Ruth realized she should have never broached this subject. "Why on earth are we discussing my temper? You and Dad were the ones that thought I needed to see a shrink."

Ruth moved to the edge of her chair and patted her daughter's arm. "I'm sorry, Emma. I shouldn't have said that. But, when you get angry, you get exceedingly upset, which has always concerned me."

Emma shrugged her shoulders in irritation. "I know it has. But my anger is under control now, and there's nothing to worry about." She paused, squeezing her mother's hand. "Can we get back to your doctor's appointment, please? I should go with you and hear what he has to say."

Ruth hated this "reversal of roles," as she thought of it. She smiled good-naturedly at her daughter. "Don't trust me to tell you what the doctor says?"

"No, that's not it at all." Emma paused and grinned at her mother. "All right, I do have an agenda. I thought we could do a little shopping and have lunch. That spring coat of yours has seen better days, and Dillard's has London Fog on sale. It would be my treat because you could use a new coat."

Ruth would give in, but on one condition. "We can do that—although you don't have to pay for a coat—if we'll be done in time for you to pick up Katrina at school."

"We'll have plenty of time. Katrina has her last soccer game as a senior, and Jack's going to meet us there."

Jack. From Ruth's perspective, they'd married far too young, and they'd made some bad choices that had haunting consequences. They'd met in Emma's freshman year at Washington University, where Jack was a junior. Both were smart enough to be chosen valedictorians of their high school graduating classes and to land college scholarships, but not smart enough to practice responsible birth control. Emma was pregnant with Elizabeth before her sophomore year; they married, and she dropped out. Katrina followed less than a year later, and Emma vowed to finish her degree once Jack had graduated.

Emma resumed writing dates in her calendar, and Ruth contemplated her approach. As a mother and grandmother, she was concerned, and rightfully so she thought, about the welfare of her family. If she asked Emma how she and Jack were doing, would she reply with an honest answer or avoid the subject? Ruth decided she had nothing to lose. "Not to pry, but how are things between you and Jack?"

Emma poked at the air with her pen, avoiding eye contact. "We're in counseling, trying to work through our problems, but the process is slow. And I'm not sure I like the therapist Jack found."

Ruth wasn't convinced Emma was telling the truth, even as she looked her mother in the eye.

"I'm not sure what else to say, Mom."

Ruth thought Emma's often volatile temper didn't help matters but wouldn't say another word. "I hate to see my family struggling," she said, distracted by the flickering television as *The Road to Calvary* was coming to an end. "Emma, would you turn that up? I like to recite the prayer of deliverance with the Reverend Ray."

Grabbing the remote, Emma increased the volume, the disgust in her voice obvious. "You understand this show is taped, right? I swear, Mom, I can't believe you waste your time on this crap."

4

The same day
Lincoln, Nebraska
Disciples of Christ Church

Darlene Jordan had left three messages on Captain Turner's voicemail by the time the women faced one another across a wooden table in a small church conference room. "My apologies for calling so many times, but I have information that can help you."

Captain Turner removed a notepad and pen from her purse and smiled at Darlene. "We appreciate that."

Across from her, Darlene sat up straight, penetrating eyes set in a round, expressive face. "The first thing you need to understand is that I never liked or trusted Nicole Hansen. I'll tell you right now she was embezzling from the church."

"That's a serious accusation, Mrs. Jordan. Let's start from the beginning, and take me through a timeline of events," Captain Turner coaxed, writing "embezzled" at the top of the page. "She came to the church?"

"Yes," Darlene said. "Walked in off the street in early 1996, saying she'd recently arrived in town and was looking for a church."

"That's not terribly unusual, is it?"

"Not at all. Shortly after she became a member, she started coming in during the week, asking to help as a volunteer. That's not uncommon either, and I had plenty of work I could use help with, so I took her up on it. Gregory was here most days during the week—pastors put in long hours—and pretty soon, if Gregory was here, Nicole was here, too."

"Is that out of the ordinary?" Captain Turner asked, tapping her pen against the pad.

"Not necessarily. But here she was, with no apparent job, which I thought was strange."

That's interesting, Linda mused. *Wife has mysterious past and possible motive.* Captain Turner wrote "Investigate wife's background" in a margin. "Did you ask her if she worked?"

Darlene's gaze was unwavering. "Oh, sure, but I never believed her answer. Something about getting laid off and being financially secure enough to make a fresh start. But, if you asked who she'd worked for or where she'd moved from, she'd change the subject."

"You mentioned she was volunteering a lot."

"Yes. Volunteers don't normally put in the kind of long hours she did, and her behavior was very flirtatious, which I didn't think was appropriate." Darlene's eyes narrowed in disapproval.

"Because of Gregory's position as pastor?"

From across the table, Darlene's brow arched slightly. "That was part of it. But Gregory was also newly widowed. His wife had died of breast cancer, and her illness and death were heartbreaking for Rev. Hansen and the congregation. Chris, his wife, was very active as the choir and music director. When she died, Gregory was devastated. He should've taken some time off to at least begin the healing process; instead, he threw himself into the work, sometimes staying here twelve and fourteen hours a day."

"When did Nicole show up?" Linda took notes at a fast clip.

"Not six months after Chris died."

Flipping a page, Linda asked, "What was Nicole's maiden name?"

"Allen, Nicole Allen."

"Did Nicole's flirting make Rev. Hansen uncomfortable?"

"No, and that's what bothered me. He was obviously attracted to her, and they started spending all their time together. The relationship formed quickly, and they were married only thirteen months after Chris passed away."

This is intriguing, Linda thought. *Pastor Hansen barely takes time to mourn his wife.* "You said you didn't trust Nicole. What makes you say that?"

"For someone just moving into town, she seemed to know a lot about Gregory. Nicole not only knew Chris had died of breast cancer, but also that they had tried to have a baby for several years and were considering fertility treatments. That's when her cancer was discovered. I remember asking Nicole how she knew so much, and she said parishioners had told her things."

"Talking is human nature, don't you think?"

"Yes, but it was as if Nicole was using Gregory's personal tragedy to manipulate him, and he was in a very fragile emotional state."

Linda ceased writing and eyed Darlene. "Why do you believe Nicole was manipulating Gregory?"

"It's hard to explain," Darlene responded, fleshy hands clasped in front of her. "She was very assertive, almost as if she'd come here with a plan to marry Gregory from the start."

"So, Rev. Hansen and Nicole fall in love and get married. Then what happened?"

"Nicole got pregnant right away, but she miscarried. They had a boy, Jacob, in 1998. Within two years, they had a daughter, Elizabeth. But the most disturbing thing, for me at least, was Nicole's attitude. Once she and Gregory were married, Nicole was often snippy with staff. She kept badgering Gregory about taking over as bookkeeper, even though the woman in the position had held it for twenty years and was very competent. Nicole was relentless, accusing Nancy of making mistakes and insisting she should be fired. That went on for over a year before Nancy finally quit." Darlene crossed her muscular arms and leaned into the table. "That's when I really suspected Nicole was embezzling money," she said in a near whisper.

Linda stretched her slim legs, sitting back in her chair. "What made you suspicious?"

"After Nicole became bookkeeper, those records were off limits to everyone but her. She was very secretive on financial matters; and if anyone pressed her, she became defensive."

"Can you prove any of this?"

"I can now. After Nicole and Gregory left, I had access to the books again and started reviewing expenses and income month by month. There were a lot of entries for 'miscellaneous expenses' of which we knew nothing. Nicole had the authority to write, cash, and deposit checks, and I believe she was taking collection money and donations for herself."

"Even Reverend Hansen couldn't sign checks?"

"He had the authority, but Nicole kept those books locked up."

"Which bank does the church have accounts with?"

"First Nebraska Bank, here in town. I've got a meeting scheduled next week to review these discrepancies. You're welcome to attend."

"That would be immensely helpful, and we wouldn't need a warrant." Linda tapped an index finger on the table. "Let's jump ahead to Gregory taking a different position as a Disciples of Christ missionary in Africa. When was that exactly?"

"He announced their plans to the congregation last November, and they left at the end of March. But Nicole absolutely did not want to be a missionary. She argued Africa was no place to raise Jacob and Elizabeth and insisted on staying behind. But Gregory was adamant that missionary work was his calling. They were fighting constantly, but Gregory wouldn't budge. Once the latest pastor was hired, they started packing. Reverend Martin accepted the position in early

March. Gregory gave his last sermon on March twenty-fourth, and we had a good-bye party that afternoon. Funny thing, though, no one knows when they left for missionary orientation in Cleveland. After the party, except for Nicole packing, no one saw Gregory or the children again."

There's motive, Linda thought. She moved ahead with her questions. "When did Reverend Martin move in?"

"The first of April," Darlene stated. "I didn't think anything of it then, but Bill mentioned more than once how clean the house was."

"My team is interviewing him now," Linda said. "When did the Disciples of Christ Church missionary office call to say the Hansens had never shown up?"

"The second week in April," Darlene said. "Gregory had mentioned they were taking a family vacation to Florida before reporting to Cleveland." She looked off into space, shaking her head sadly. "I took the call and forwarded it to Bill. When he came out of his office, he was ashen, not a drop of color. We called the police, and they did a preliminary search but found no trace of the Hansens."

"The Hansens were leaving the country. Was there any family that was contacted?"

"Nicole never spoke of having family. Gregory's parents are dead, but he had distant relatives in western Nebraska. They were as mystified as the rest of us."

Linda made notes to contact other law enforcement agencies. "Would you happen to have any photographs of Reverend Hansen, his wife, and children?"

Darlene considered this for a moment. "We have several of Reverend Hansen, so that's no problem, and some of Jacob and Elizabeth at church functions. But Nicole, I shouldn't be surprised she stayed out of photos."

Captain Turner rolled the pen between her long fingers. "We won't know for several days whether these remains are the Hansen family. You're suspicious of Mrs. Hansen, and I can understand that. But, Darlene, I need to ask you if there might be another individual capable of killing the reverend and his children—a neighbor or disgruntled parishioner?"

Darlene sat back in her chair, a pensive look in her eyes. She sat up abruptly, the palm of a hand slapping her forehead. "With all that's happened, I completely forgot this." She cleared her throat and continued, "Last year, when Nebraska played Notre Dame, Gregory was involved in an automobile accident. I'm not sure of the date, but it was soon after 9/11. You know how crazy this town gets during football season."

Linda leaned in closer. She understood rabid Husker fans, the entire state coming together in support of the football team. Ranked number one and two respectively, Nebraska and Notre Dame last year were playing each other for the first time in four decades. Bodies spilling from packed bars onto teeming streets had Linda and her department working extra hours on security detail. The accident only added to the controlled mayhem. Linda was intrigued by Darlene's fresh perspective on the tragedy and asked her to continue.

"I've tried to block out details, because Gregory could barely speak of it. He had an evening meeting the Thursday before the game, down by the university. Because this was Notre Dame, downtown had large crowds, especially in the bars. On his way home, a group of very drunk frat boys ran out into the middle of the street, and one of them lay down in a traffic lane. It was dark. Gregory didn't see him and ran over the kid, who died a few days later. Gregory was devastated."

Linda wanted knowledge on the state of Gregory and of the parents. "As I remember, the parents of the student tried to blame the reverend—"

"Yes," Darlene interrupted hoarsely. "The father showed up here shortly after the boy's funeral, accusing Gregory of deliberately running over his son. Threats were made, and Gregory was genuinely compassionate, trying to help. The guy screamed at Gregory that as a father himself, he would learn what it felt like to have a child taken from you. It was a terrible confrontation." Darlene stopped to brush aside a tear. "I'm sorry, this is more emotional now. The one thing that made us fearful was how he continued to intimidate Gregory on email. But Gregory said he was 'taking the high road' by not engaging this very angry individual and refused to call the police. The accident had a terrible effect on Gregory. I think it's the main reason he wanted to do missionary work, simply to get away from the constant harassment."

Linda glanced at her watch. "We'll need Reverend Martin's computer to access those emails. I'll call forensics right now to retrieve it." She returned the notepad and pen to her purse. "This interview has shed light on many of the questions we have, Darlene. I can retrieve the material, but if you remember even the smallest detail, here's my card." ·

5

Thursday, May 16, 2002
Lincoln, Nebraska
Outside Northeast
Police Headquarters

The results of the autopsy and forensic tests had taken several days. A throng of reporters threw questions at Linda in front of the Northeast Police Headquarters. In a quick succession, word of the gruesome triple murders tore across the flatlands, spawning unbridled rumors, conspiracy theories, and hearsay. Fielding questions in the bright spring sun, Linda spotted reporters from throughout Nebraska, Iowa, Kansas, South Dakota, and Colorado. It hadn't turned into a media circus, at least not yet, but CNN and FOX had both sent correspondents.

"The victims have been positively identified as the Reverend Gregory Hansen, age forty, and his children, Jacob, age three, and Elizabeth, eighteen months—"

"How long have they been dead?" a boyish and chiseled male reporter asked.

"Sir, if you'll just be patient, I'll get to that." Linda smiled and nodded. "The coroner believes the victims died approximately two months ago, estimating the time of death in late March."

"How did they die?" someone else shouted.

Linda kept her genial smile in place. Her first press conference, she needed to keep things on track.

"The coroner's report indicated Reverend Hansen died of blunt force trauma based on the skull fractures present, but we haven't gotten specifics. Most likely from a heavy object of some kind. The autopsy also revealed that all three victims had substantial amounts of the drug Ambien, a prescription sleep aid, in their systems. The children would definitely have died from a massive overdose."

"Fatal for the reverend?" the chiseled reporter inquired, his smile dazzling.

Linda didn't recognize him as a local reporter but identified his flirtatious behavior. She was well-versed in using her feminine charms to spur a suspect into talking. His enigmatic charisma, however, would not work in his favor. "Yes, we believe the amount was lethal for Reverend Hansen."

"How were the murders carried out?" an out-of-state reporter yelled.

Observing the red lights of recording cameras, Linda carefully phrased her response. "We are basing our assumptions on the autopsies, and we speculate the Ambien was mixed in with food or beverages to mask the taste. Let me be clear, we do not have proof that was the case, but it makes the most sense."

"Is Mrs. Hansen a suspect?" a brunette female reporter from one of the Omaha stations asked.

"Nicole Hansen's whereabouts are unknown, and she remains a person of interest we wish to talk to."

"Do you think Mrs. Hansen killed her family?" The same young brunette tilted her head, her lacquered hair unmovable in the brisk breeze.

"As I said, Nicole Hansen is a person of interest. We are asking for the public's help regarding Mrs. Hansen's whereabouts, and any pertinent knowledge related to this case—"

"Captain Turner—"

Another reporter started to interrupt, and Linda held up a slender hand and finished her sentence.

"We have set up the following telephone number," she said and repeated the number twice before continuing. "If anyone saw something or heard something, we want to talk to you. We believe there is information out in the community that may be helpful in solving the murders of the Hansen family."

The same reporter persisted. "Captain Turner—"

Linda held up both hands palms out. "No further questions. Chief Langston will provide you with additional details."

Reporters began shouting, "Chief Langston!" as Linda and her team moved back inside. Lyle and Amy Clair seated themselves in front of the captain's wooden desk in an office on the precinct's always busy floor.

Linda settled at her desk. "As you're aware, Darlene Jordan has provided some crucial data regarding Mr. William Dawson and the death of his son down at UNL during the Notre Dame football weekend. Dawson is convinced the Reverend Hansen was responsible for his son's death, making him our first real suspect. What have you uncovered?"

Amy spoke first, pulling a stack of emails from a file on her lap. "Dawson was obsessed with the idea Gregory was responsible. He frequently and graphically threatened the Hansens with bodily harm. It's not beyond the realm of possibility that he killed them all, burying Mrs. Hansen on a different piece of land to throw us off." She slid the folder to her boss.

Linda pulled her chair closer to the desk, thumbing through the emails. "Unis are picking Dawson up at the construction company he owns. I've sent two in case he's combative. I'll want you both observing the interview."

Lyle's frustration revealed itself in a long sigh. "This case keeps getting stranger."

6

LATER THE SAME DAY
LINCOLN, NEBRASKA
NORTHEAST POLICE HEADQUARTERS

illiam Dawson did make a scene, both at his office and Northeast Headquarters, screaming that his rights were being violated.

"What the hell is this all about? I've been sitting here over twenty minutes. You can't just bring me down here for no reason!" Dawson yelled into the two-way glass.

Linda waited for his tirade to end before entering the room. Carrying a legal pad and files, she faced an arrogant man used to having his way. "Mr. Dawson, I'm Captain Linda Turner, Northeast Team. Thank you for coming down today. You may possess knowledge that would be extremely helpful to us in a case we're investigating."

Sweet-talking him softened his angular features. "Well, it's not like I had a choice. Why am I here?"

Linda seated herself, closed manila folders on the table between them. "I have some questions regarding the Reverend Gregory Hansen."

"Finally!" Dawson declared, throwing his hands in the air. "I've been trying for months to get your attention; that man killed my son!"

Her face devoid of expression, she opened the folder to the accident report. "I have the accident report right here, which made clear that Brandon, whose blood alcohol content was 0.27 several hours after the accident, was extremely intoxicated and lay down on O Street—"

Dawson angrily pointed a rigid index finger at her. "I have witnesses that Gregory Hansen, a so-called man of God, deliberately ran over Brandon!"

She saw dual sides of this man—a bully and a father in the throes of grief and denial. "Who are these witnesses?"

"Brandon's fraternity brothers. They were there, and other witnesses who saw that accident!" he shouted.

She calmly returned to the folder. "Mr. Dawson, each of Brandon's fraternity brothers was interviewed, and none of them realized he was in the street. Witnesses corroborated the findings of officers at the scene that his fraternity brothers were also extremely intoxicated, and Gregory Hansen had no time to react. Here's the accident reconstruction. Brandon was lying in the middle of a busy street, dressed in black, after dark."

Dawson leaned his sinewy frame hard into the table. "I thought you said I had information that could help you. You cops are all alike. All right, so they had a few drinks. Hansen saw them; that area near the university is very well lit."

Linda leaned back, cornflower blue eyes gauging Dawson's twisted features as he twisted a hand through wavy salt-and-pepper hair. "This doesn't concern the accident, Mr. Dawson. What I'm interested in is your relationship with Reverend Hansen afterwards."

He laughed bitterly, a smirk across thin lips. "Did that ass file a harassment report against me?"

"No, but he should have." Linda removed the bottom folder from the pile, laying the most vicious emails in front of Dawson. Next to those, she placed the graphic photos depicting the Hansen crime scene, her voice firmly in control. "I should be charging you with stalking, harassment, and making terroristic threats. Don't pretend you don't have any knowledge of what I'm talking about. You made good on your promise to make Hansen pay by killing him, his wife, and two small children in late March. Then you buried their bodies in the flower garden behind the parsonage, except for Mrs. Hansen. Tell me where you buried her remains." She slammed her fist into the table.

Dawson's dark eyes widened in disbelief. "No, I . . . Gregory Hansen's dead?"

"The entire family. You've left quite the paper trail, Mr. Dawson. It leads straight to you."

William Dawson trembled, his face and voice full of agony. "This is terrible. But I didn't kill anyone. I never meant to hurt him or his family. I wanted Hansen to accept responsibility."

Linda knew the death of William Dawson's only son was devouring him. "I am deeply sorry for your loss, Mr. Dawson. But I find it hard to believe you didn't realize the Hansen family was murdered, since it's been the lead news story here, even on the national front."

He stuttered, "I've . . . I was in Kansas City at a contractor's convention."

"I'll need the name of the convention and any witnesses who can verify your whereabouts. The same goes for the period between March twenty-fourth and twenty-eighth. The Hansens were murdered on one of those days."

"I—I can give you the conference confirmation," he stammered.

Linda thrust a yellow legal pad and pencil toward him. "And the dates in March?"

He looked at Linda, his bravado replaced by fear. "I can't recall where I was on so many days two months ago."

"If you won't tell me, I will be charging you with murder in the first degree, in addition to making terrorist threats. You'll never see outside prison walls."

Dawson stopped writing, the pencil quivering in his grasp. He glanced toward the wall, then back at Linda. "You've got to promise me you won't tell my wife. I was in Cancun at a resort with my girlfriend. Things are very strained between my wife and me since Brandon died."

"I can't promise you anything," Linda replied evenly. "Give me your girlfriend's name, her contact information, the resort where you vacationed, and the dates of the trip. Otherwise, you are our prime suspect."

"Oh, God," Dawson exhaled and began hastily filling the legal pad.

7

FRIDAY, MAY 17, 2002

LINCOLN, NEBRASKA

NORTHEAST POLICE HEADQUARTERS

"William Dawson alibied out, but he's a deeply troubled man. He's one who'll never get over losing a child," Linda told Lyle and Amy the following morning.

"You sound concerned," Lyle asserted. "Do you feel Dawson is a danger to himself or others?"

"No, at least not right now. He genuinely believes it was no accident his son was killed. Let's keep casual tabs on him—the occasional welfare check. My fear is this will keep gnawing at Dawson, and he'll come completely undone in a violent manner."

"God," Amy said. "I hope you're wrong."

"Me, too. What other leads have we got?"

"We've looked at the missing persons reports filed by Reverend Martin, talked to Gregory Hansen's relatives in Scottsbluff, interviewed neighbors, and so far, we have nominal material," Amy said, slapping a light palm against the manila folder in her lap.

"Same goes for the family moving," Lyle explained, removing a linen handkerchief from his jacket pocket and wiping his nose. "Eyewitnesses' accounts vary. Some say they saw a moving van;

others tell us it was an unmarked truck. A third group insists it was a U-Haul. I'm working the local and U-Haul angle. Tuesday, March twenty-sixth was the last time Nicole Hansen was seen. Since then, there is no trace of her—no ATM or credit card activity, phone calls, or public sightings. My gut says Nicole Hansen no longer exists."

Amy sighed deeply. "I agree. Gone off the grid and into her next identity."

Linda cupped her chin in her hand. "Did we get any pictures of Mrs. Hansen? Darlene Jordan was going to check."

Amy Clair shifted the file on her lap, removing a photograph. She passed it to Linda. "It wasn't easy; but lucky for us, Darlene Jordan is tenacious. She found one picture from a church benefit, but part of Mrs. Hansen's face is obscured. The photo is from the late 1990s, so her appearance could have changed by now. Darlene remembered Gregory insisted Nicole be in the photo because she was on the planning committee."

Handling the picture, Linda studied it closely. A young woman sporting a multi-layered medium brown shag with blonde highlights smiled in profile. " I recognize her hairstyle. She's copying Rachel from the TV show *Friends*."

Amy peered over Linda's shoulder. "Millions of women got that haircut. Makes it easier for her to blend in as just another hip, suburban mom."

"Good point, Amy. Let's move on to the bank accounts," Linda said. "I met with the First Nebraska Bank president, and he's given us complete access to the church accounts. The 'miscellaneous' expenses Darlene discovered were drawn from those funds. However, one of the tellers who frequently waited on Mrs. Hansen remembered her mentioning another account at the National Bank of Commerce. We discovered an account under her maiden name, Nicole Allen. The savings account grew to over $150,000 before it was closed after withdrawing everything the last week in March." Effortlessly,

Linda changed topics, selecting another file. "Forensics pulled a partial handprint from the parsonage. I sent it to the National Crime Information Center, and there were several hits. The print matched Nicole Allen's, but also women named Susan Patterson, Pam Sayles, and Pamela Jane Watts. It was a lucky long shot. I'm investigating her aliases further."

Lyle chuckled. "Even with the house cleaned and occupied by somebody else, there's always the chance evidence will be left behind. Do we know anything about her identity as Susan Patterson?"

Linda stopped Lyle with a raised index finger. "We'll get to that. The medical examiner retrieved DNA from Jacob and Elizabeth's remains. I also entered the Hansen murder details into the FBI's Violent Criminal Apprehension Program. Mrs. Hansen is a fugitive. I can't get past the idea that she has probably killed before. This crime involved careful thought and preparation but I'm convinced she was interrupted. The CSI unit returned to the house and applied luminol. Large amounts of blood splattered in the entry way and on the walls were found. That would be consistent with Gregory Hansen's skull fracture. We need to spread the word on these murders to law enforcement agencies across the country, and ViCAP is our best option." Enlarged driver's license photos from Nebraska and Illinois were attached to a white board. In each photo, the woman's appearance was strikingly different. Names, hairstyles and color, physical markings, height, weight, and eye color varied.

Lyle leaned forward. "What do we know about her background so far?"

"Susan Patterson was married to a Reverend Darryl Patterson, now living outside Chicago. She also disappeared under mysterious circumstances. I've contacted Reverend Patterson, and he's agreed to talk to me. I'm flying to Chicago on the six thirty flight on Monday morning. In the meantime, I want you to continue trying to track the Toyota Corolla the Hansens owned."

8

Monday, May 20, 2002
Lincoln, Nebraska/Chicago, Illinois
Lake Michigan Disciples
of Christ Church

Living in a post 9/11 world meant Linda had to be at the Lincoln Municipal Airport at least ninety minutes before departure, just like any other air traveler. That also meant arriving at four-thirty, with the lights of the airport seemingly hovering in the inky darkness. It was too early for her taste, but terrorists had changed the rules. She would interview Rev. Patterson that morning in Chicago, then take a cab back to O'Hare and catch a three o'clock flight home to Lincoln.

On the flight, Linda assessed her questions and organized her thoughts. By eight o'clock, she was hailing a cab and speeding into Chicago rush hour traffic. In the backseat of a Yellow Cab weaving down Interstate 294, she decided she'd rather not know how high that speedometer was climbing. There were many horn blasts and more than one screech of tires as the cab braked hard to a halt, then shot off again, zipping between cars and trucks. When they arrived at the Lake Michigan church, Linda was certain the driver heard her great sigh of relief as the cab lurched to a stop.

Waiting to greet her in the parking lot was the Reverend Darryl Patterson. No hair remained on his head, but his face had the steel-wool gray of a neatly trimmed beard. His baldness made him appear older. Up close, Linda judged Patterson to be in his early to mid thirties. The rimless glasses he wore gave him a scholarly air. He'd insisted on paying the cab fare. "You've come a long way," he explained, "and this concerns Susan; it must be important."

Linda noted this comment as Rev. Patterson escorted her into an airy office filled with streaming bright sunshine. He offered good, strong coffee, which she gladly accepted.

"You said you have some questions about my ex-wife," he began. "I won't lie to you—that's a chapter of my life that's hard to revisit."

She made a notation to return to that comment and attempted to put the pastor at ease. "I'll try to make this as painless for you as possible. Can you tell me how you met Susan?"

Seated at his desk, Rev. Patterson drank his coffee. "She was a parishioner at my last church in Columbia, Missouri. We got acquainted through her involvement in church activities."

"So, Susan was a volunteer?"

"Yes. She approached me one Sunday after services saying she wanted to be more involved." Rev. Patterson paused for another sip of coffee, as if it were providing fortification. "I don't know if you're familiar with church work, Captain Turner, but we have more volunteers than paid staff. Without them, we literally couldn't function."

Linda saw a pattern emerging. "This is a hard question, but I must ask it. Were you married or involved with anyone else during this period?"

Rev. Patterson was resolute in his response. "Absolutely not. My first wife had died of breast cancer, and I was still grieving and trying to comprehend my loss. Susan came into my life offering comfort, and I enjoyed her company."

"When you met Susan, how long had your wife been deceased?"

"Less than six months." He fiddled with his glasses nervously as if he were pained by a distressing emotion.

"I recognize this is difficult for you," she soothed, "but honest answers will be very helpful. Was your wife's illness common knowledge?"

"Most definitely. Columbia isn't a large city—around eighty-five thousand. But it's also a college town, and my late wife, Laura, taught in the English department, where she was well-known and liked. When she became ill, there were several fundraisers and articles in both the school and local papers. When she died, the funeral was quite large."

"So, you met Susan six months after your wife died. How long was it before you married?"

His body twitched anxiously; the questions were clearly digging up uncomfortable memories. "Eight months."

Linda checked her notes. "And that was in 1992?"

"That's correct—May of 1992."

"Before you were married, what was Susan's last name?"

"Nichols," he replied flatly, deliberately saying each letter as he spelled it out.

She kept pursuing this line of questioning that might connect pieces of the puzzle. "Ms. Nichols's background—where was she from? Any family or friends?"

Still edgy, he was at least able to look her in the eyes as he spoke. "Susan never mentioned any family except once. Told me she'd grown up in Minneapolis, an orphan. I realized later Susan seemed to know a great deal about me when I knew almost nothing in relation to her."

Linda turned the page, sliding frontward in her chair. "You mentioned Susan seemed familiar with your background. Can you provide specifics?"

He looked toward the ceiling, as if he were deciphering the swirling patterns molded into the plaster. "She knew where I had gone to seminary and when I graduated, that the job in Columbia was my third as pastor, and my wife had died recently. Knowing details on Laura didn't seem odd at the time; but when I look back, I get the sickening feeling that Susan Nichols had researched my background."

A most definite pattern, Linda thought. "Let's go back to being married. You said you wed in May, 1992. I need you to tell me how long it lasted and your relationship."

Rev. Patterson again sighed. "We were married not quite two years. Once we married, Susan became the church bookkeeper. I suppose I was naïve, but this was my wife after all—and I trusted her implicitly to count the Sunday offering and make a deposit. And I loved her."

He stopped, his attention again diverted to the ceiling. Linda was sympathetic, but she needed the reverend to keep talking. As sore as the memory might be, he had no way of knowing the calculated plan he'd become a victim of. "Reverend Patterson, it's important you tell me every detail."

"I'm sorry," he said, shaking his head. Rev. Patterson eyed Linda, struggling to find the words to continue. "Talking about Susan is like watching a movie. And even though I know the ending, it still breaks my heart. But that's not why you're here." Patterson paused for a moment before exhaling loudly. "One day, our bank called a church trustee and said, 'You haven't got enough money to pay your bills.' We had no idea how extensive the damage was."

Rev. Patterson stopped again to collect his thoughts.

"Take your time," Linda said quietly.

He smiled his appreciation and continued his pace, slow and deliberate. "Funds were missing from all the church accounts at the bank. Susan had access, and suspicions on the board were high. I was very hesitant. I thought the board was being unnecessarily accusatory. But I was out-voted; a member followed her when she made the weekly deposit. She was observed taking money she skimmed from the offering to another bank across town and depositing it in an account under another name."

"When did you confront her?"

"This was in the spring of 1994. I was devastated. The finance committee wanted solid evidence to press charges and waited several weeks. I still couldn't believe this was happening and insisted the committee chair confront her. That was in early April. She denied it, and we had a terrible fight. Susan accused me of not trusting her. The next day, Susan told me I'd betrayed her. She refused to work. I had meetings until late in the evening, and by the time I came home, she was gone. Susan had emptied and closed her personal account."

"How much money was there?" Linda asked.

"Approximately $25,000, which isn't that much when you consider the risks she took."

"On the phone, you mentioned you divorced Susan—"

"That's correct," he interrupted. "In Illinois, I had grounds because Susan had willfully deserted the marriage, and I knew it would be uncontested. Once she was no longer here, I wanted to get the process over with."

"But you also left the church, and I have to ask why. You weren't the one taking money."

Rev. Patterson shifted his weight. "I was naïve in trusting Susan, but I still felt partly responsible. Sure, there were members who wanted me to stay, but as far as I was concerned, I had breached the trust of the congregation and the board. It was better for everyone if we made a fresh start." Patterson stroked his beard. "You may not know this, Captain, but embezzling in the church world is not that uncommon." She had been aware of that, realizing many people dismissed such a notion among communities of faith. Linda put fingers to her mouth, contemplating her next move. "Reverend, do you think Susan would be capable of darker crimes? Say, murder, for example?"

The pastor appeared shocked at the question. "Susan may be a con artist, but she is no murderer. This part of my life is extremely difficult to relive. I loved Susan, and I believe she loved me, too. We had a good marriage, Detective, and I was deeply saddened at how it ended."

Reaching into a leather briefcase, Linda selected a manila folder and pulled it free. She took the photograph from the church fundraiser Darlene Jordan had found and handed it to Rev. Patterson. Nicole Hansen was circled in permanent red ink.

"Rev. Patterson, is this your ex-wife?"

Accepting the photo, Darryl studied it hard, angling it in the light. "There's a resemblance, but I'm not sure, especially not being able to see all of her face. Another thing, this woman is a brunette, and Susan was most definitely a blonde. My ex-wife also had a prominent mole above her lip—you know, like the model Cindy Crawford. This woman doesn't possess any such marking. Another thing, Susan had a strangely shaped hole inside her right ear." He made a crude drawing on paper. "Almost like a half-moon. You didn't see it unless you were up close."

"Are you sure it wasn't an ear piercing? Many people have those," Linda said.

The reverend shook his head adamantly. "No, it was natural. Susan became self-conscious when people asked her about it."

Linda wrote these items in her notes as Rev. Patterson handed back the photograph and drawing. "Reverend, we're investigating a woman who may have deliberately sought out pastors, particularly those recently widowed. Very calculating and smart. What would help me is to identify the things that attracted you to Susan," she explained.

Reverend Patterson's elbows were propped up on the armrest, and he brought his hands together in a V-shape, silently contemplating Linda's request. When he spoke at last, his eyes glistened. "I could be philosophical and say that, due to my personal situation, the companionship Susan offered and what I perceived as love helped move me out of my grief." He hesitated, taking a long breath. "And she seemed so vulnerable, yet so willing to give of herself. I believed I could reciprocate in the role of protector. I convinced myself that we were each fixing something in the other that had been broken. That way, I didn't feel so guilty marrying her so soon after Laura's death."

Linda felt chills crawling up her back. She'd dealt with criminals keenly adept in the art of manipulation before, but this woman's charisma was so pervasive that her victims wound up feeling both guilty and responsible.

Linda finished writing the last sentence with a flourish, the ink skidding off the page. There was one last question she needed to ask. "Reverend, do you have any pictures of Susan I might have?"

The corners of his mouth curled into a sour smile, and she already knew the answer. "There aren't any photographs of Susan," he answered quietly. "She took every single picture with her the day she left."

9

The same day
St. Louis, Missouri
The cable TV station

Ray came to a decision on the ideas proposed by Susannah Baker, as he'd promised. He pulled her aside, explaining he'd reserved a conference room for the four of them to talk, which he hoped she'd be agreeable to.

His choice was more complicated than Ray had anticipated; the reality wasn't black or white, but a milky shade of gray somewhere between extremes. On the one side, he wasn't sure about operating electronic gadgets to eavesdrop on the needs of church members—it was quite possibly illegal and most likely unethical. But, as he engaged in a round of devil's advocate, he found himself wondering if real benefits might come out of hearing a prayer for help and being able to provide answers for his congregation and viewers.

Ray grappled with his dilemma for the week, the pros and cons of the argument constantly giving voice in his head. "Heavenly Father, help me make the right decision," he prayed often, bowing his handsome head and seeking God's blessing or some sign that this was the wrong path. But the reverend received no instructions from the Almighty, and he realized he alone would be answerable for his judgment.

Of one item, he was certain: if he chose not to accept Miss Baker's proposal, *The Road to Calvary* would be finished in a few short weeks. But if he agreed to it—or at least some of her ideas—might this be the jolt his ministry needed? And maybe he was defining the term *miracle* too narrowly. Perhaps that miracle had already manifested itself in the presence of Susannah Baker. If nothing else, her ideas were worth presenting to Buck and Jeff.

After they gathered at the small table, Ray explained the basic concept but decided to let Susannah do most of the talking. And talk she did, diving in without the slightest hesitation. He watched as Buck regarded Susannah cautiously, his reluctance etched across the crease of his brow.

"Let me get this straight," he said. "God came to you in a dream and said that the Reverend Ray, who has devoted his entire life to serving our Lord Jesus Christ, should work 'miracles' by duping our members through deception?" He clearly wasn't buying it, his stiff arms folded across his chest.

"Buck . . . it is Buck, right?" she asked with a smile.

"Yeah, Buck, like a deer."

"I'm sorry, Buck," she assured him. "Try to think of this as moving people toward their greatest potential. If members believe enough to overcome their problems and accept Jesus Christ into their lives, it shouldn't matter how they came to that decision. What does matter is they have a positive experience that gives them courage to go onward, changes their lives for the better, and tells others that Jesus Christ listens."

Sitting next to Buck, his muscular frame squeezed into a small chair, Jeff nodded his head toward Buck. "Buck's right, man. I mean, isn't this a crime like fraud or somethin'?"

Susannah's hands waved through the air as she spoke. "Look at this as transforming people's lives by helping them to discover Jesus Christ. It's not the methods that matter; it's the results."

Observing the discomfort on the part of his friends, Ray felt it was best to explain how he'd struggled with the same arguments. "Jeff, Buck, I'll be honest," he said, observing them. "When Miss Baker first approached me, I felt much the way you do now. But then I started thinking that my ministry has always revolved around serving others. And I asked myself, who am I serving right now? Maybe a few hundred folks, but that's probably overly optimistic." He paused, letting his words register. "I think we ought to give some of Miss Baker's ideas a chance, because unless you're willing to see five years of vigorous work and sacrifice go for nothing, which it will, we have nothing to lose."

"Weren't you willing to do exactly that a week ago?" Buck said, wagging his finger.

Ray studied his friend, concern in his voice. "Yes, but that doesn't mean I wanted to do it. Given my druthers, I want to keep this ministry going and see it become successful."

The cramped room was bursting with silence, and for a fleeting moment, Ray believed Buck, if not both men, might simply walk out. There was no emotion etched into Buck's features as his intense eyes stared back at him.

"You think this might help our viewers face their problems?" Buck asked.

"Yes, I believe hearing the problems of others will encourage people to try and solve their own difficulties with the help of God."

From the corner of his eye, Ray saw Susannah anxiously tapping her fingers and thought perhaps she had not predicted such resistance. But he understood where Buck was coming from—he'd been there himself. In fact, he hadn't completely vanquished his reservations, but he couldn't end *The Road to Calvary* without knowing he'd tried everything he could to save it.

Buck inhaled deeply. "Okay, I can't speak for Jeff, but I'm willing to try this on a temporary basis. But I emphasize the word 'temporary.'

If I think this approach is hurting us more than it's helping us, I'm out. No questions asked. I leave with proper notice."

"I can accept that," Ray replied, turning to Jeff. "What about you, Jeff?"

He ran a hand over the bristles of his short, cropped hair. "I'll do it; but like Buck said, if I'm not comfortable, I'm outta here. I can always find work installing floors."

"Fair enough," he said.

The mood shifted from apprehension to one of excitement. Buck started throwing out ideas, gates of a dam opening as the words gushed out. "We'll need equipment—surveillance cameras, microphones, earpieces, and monitors—and that's just to start. Where's the money going to come from—a loan? Since we rent our studio space, how will we monitor the audience? There will be equipment to set up and tear down on every show, and we can't let anyone catch on to what we're doing. And who among us has the technical expertise?"

Susannah enthusiastically returned to the conversation. "I knew you'd come around. We'll rent the necessary equipment to start. We won't be able to cover the entire audience, but monitors can be set up in one of these conference rooms. As far as money, taking out a loan is a possibility."

She considered the male faces around the table. "The thing we need to remember is *The Road to Calvary* won't save anybody unless you market it." She turned to Ray. "Reverend, start building relationships with the religion editors of area papers and make yourself available for interviews. Take out small ads in newspapers and on other cable stations to let people know that we—I mean, *you*—exist. You're also not taking advantage of your core audience. Give them more than a post office box during the offering and at the end of the broadcast; get a telephone number up there, 1-800-HE-SAVES, in the center of the screen, where people can see it during the entire show. You need to do something different from the other religious programs already getting air time here."

Ray was impressed. Marketing the show was a realm he had never felt comfortable with, simply because he didn't have the expertise. He knew other televangelists did it with flair and success. Brick and mortar churches often weren't shy about advertising either. For the first time, he recognized that saving souls was beyond the spiritual— it was a business. The key would be in doing both well. "You've given this quite a bit of thought," he told Susannah. "Do you have a marketing background?"

"I've had some marketing experience," she said. "I see the immense potential of your work—potential I was afraid you were going to throw away."

"It's a good thing God came to you in a dream," Jeff mused, but Susannah was already moving on to another idea.

"There are other ways to distinguish the service. A choir praising God in jubilant song, a welcoming space, and members witnessing to the power of salvation in their own lives." She paused. "As I mentioned to Reverend Ray, I've never seen a Christian makeover segment aimed at women. It would be another way of distinguishing the program."

Buck stared at Susannah incredulously. "I'm all for 1-800-HE-SAVES, but how do makeovers fit into the program? And what makes them Christian?"

"Why do you insist on making fun of me? There are plenty of other programs that would love the idea." Her voice had quickly turned defensive.

Taken aback by her sudden angry tone, all conversation ceased.

Her cheeks flushed. "Oh, my gosh, please forgive me. I've had a very recent family tragedy, and I've found survival itself challenging. I get frustrated, lashing out for no reason and saying things I shouldn't."

"I wasn't making fun of you. I fail to see how the concept of Christian makeovers fits into all this. Keep going," Buck said graciously.

Ray watched Buck smile at Susannah with encouragement; he remembered his friend knew a thing or two about the fairer sex.

"I believe a woman who looks good feels confident, happy, and empowered to spread the word of God. What makes them Christian is that you're bringing out that confidence by focusing on women who want to spread the Good News. Not 'extreme makeover' by any means, but showing any woman she can look good."

"That would distinguish us, all right," Buck replied dryly. "I'm simply trying to wrap my head around this. I know from firsthand experience, however, that all my wives loved their makeup."

Ray looked on in bemused silence as Susannah processed Buck's comment. Almost everyone was surprised by this revelation. Buck seemed too nondescript and mild-mannered to have had three marriages. But he knew from experience, stereotypes were meant to be broken.

"Wives?" Susannah said. "How many times were you—?"

Buck held up his fingers. "Three. My point is they all liked using makeup, so maybe this isn't such a crazy idea after all."

Susannah contemplated this. "I'm not saying we have to implement all these ideas. But here's one you need to seriously consider." She paused, eyeing each of the men. "Start broadcasting *The Road to Calvary* live."

Silence enveloped the room, the dead air thick. Ray spoke first. "That's something I've always wanted to do, but I'm not sure we have a large enough audience for a live show."

"And implementing all this technology—" Buck started in, but Susannah interrupted.

"Think about how much more effective HE SAVES will be as an 800-number on the screen if at least one broadcast is live. Start small; try one live episode you've heavily promoted as a test. Have the phones answered immediately and get viewers invested in watching *The Road to Calvary*."

"If ya ask me, it'd be a whole lotta work for maybe nothin'," Jeff said, shaking his head.

"Jeff's right," Buck agreed. "Scheduling could be a problem. What if nobody shows up?"

"You won't know unless you try," Susannah said.

"This is low-power cable; city meetings are broadcast live every month," Buck reasoned.

"Susannah has a point. Let's at least try one live broadcast and see what happens. If it fails miserably, we'll continue to rely on taping a weekly program. When I've considered broadcasting live, I've always thought it bestows a sense of urgency. Maybe I'm wrong, but as Susannah said, we won't know unless we try." Ray smiled at her.

"But who's going to be responsible for making all this technology work?" Buck asked.

Ray hadn't been this captivated by a woman or this excited about preaching in a very long time. He faced Buck with a ready answer. "You've got training in computer science and electronics, and Jeff here has a degree in broadcasting—"

"It's a certificate actually," Jeff interrupted sheepishly.

When Ray smiled, he radiated the warmth and charisma that hinted at a great preacher with the power to mesmerize. "You work as the camera operator and know more than you think. Both of you do. What Susannah is suggesting has merit. No, we can't do everything. I'll contact the cable station about presenting *The Road to Calvary* live on a Sunday morning in three or four weeks. I think this might have real potential, especially if it's promoted well."

Buck disagreed, shaking his head. "I'm with Jeff; this plan involves a huge amount of work."

"*The Road to Calvary* airs twice a week, on Wednesday evening and Sunday afternoon. It's taping the program where all the work is involved, and we're already doing that. Think of this as the same amount of effort with more benefits," Ray explained.

Buck seemed to relax a bit. Leaning back in his chair, he addressed Jeff. "I guess it can't hurt to try, Jeff. I mean, we don't have anything to lose. But, I do think we need to concentrate on doing a live broadcast before we start this eavesdropping on the congregation idea."

Jeff hesitated for a moment. "Might as well. I'm willin' to try goin' live."

"It's settled, then," Ray said, swiveling his chair. "Let's try going live first and see what kind of response we have. If the show's successful, then I'm willing to start putting the technology in place to anticipate the prayers and concerns of the congregation."

"Every one of you is right," Susannah acknowledged. "I realize I've kind of come in from out of nowhere with what may sound like some pretty crazy ideas. But I truly believe *The Road to Calvary* has a future."

Ray smiled. "I'll let the station know we're going live and see if a Sunday morning slot is available. It would be outstanding if they would help promote us. We have lots of work to do to get ready. Susannah, I hope I'm not being presumptuous, but I'm counting on you to help us with planning the first live *The Road to Calvary* broadcast."

"I'm more than happy to help in any way I can," she said with a smile, her long lashes fluttering.

10

Friday, May 24, 2002
Lincoln, Nebraska
Northeast Police Headquarters

Linda's trip to Chicago had proved enlightening, particularly since Patterson was still very much in love with his ex-wife. Even with a print match, this woman, who possessed a hard-to-see but unique mark inside an ear, had vanished. Nine excruciating days had passed since the Hansen bodies were discovered. In those fleeting days, the only good news was the discovery of the Hansens' beige 1995 Toyota Corolla in Cleveland. The police department was keenly aware that, rather than satisfying the public, finding the car would heighten the need of the residents of Lincoln to get answers to the murders. Linda would be flying to Cleveland soon in search of more clues.

The focus remained on finding Mrs. Hansen and determining her connection to the killings. Locating Nicole Hansen and easing people's fears were paramount. Otherwise, there was the bogeyman factor of the unknown, an invisible killer who slaughtered families and buried them in the backyard.

Linda, Lyle, and Amy stood in front of the shiny, white dry-erase board, adding details.

"The NCIC confirms the fingerprint matches the same woman,"

Linda said, "but she's been off their radar quite a while. We have DL photos of utterly different women with various names and a partial print. The shape Patterson drew was found on Nicole Hansen and Susan Patterson's pictures but was obscured by hair in Pamela Watts's booking photo. Let's start at the very beginning: 'Baby Pammy' as she was known by social workers, was born on or around June 25, 1964 and found abandoned at the door of St. Stephen's Catholic Church, an inner-city parish in Minneapolis." The marker squeaked as Linda began the timeline. "She was adopted at six months by Paul and Margaret Watts, who were originally her foster parents and named her Pamela Jane Watts. Her biological parents never came forward. In 1977, at the age of thirteen, Pamela lost both of her adopted parents in a house fire, which she survived. She spent the rest of her childhood in foster care."

Lyle's usually lively eyes were full of sadness. "This girl spent a third of her life in foster care. And that would be a helluva thing to find out—that you had been abandoned, thrown away like a piece of garbage. That's got to be a horrible realization that you were unwanted."

"The foster care aspect hasn't panned out into helpful intelligence thus far. Her criminal history as Pamela Jane Watts is short, but there's another suspicious incident. There's the house fire in which her parents died, orphaning her twice. The chances of that seem incredibly remote. I've submitted a request for the coroner's report, but that could take months. Amy, fill us in on her criminal history."

Amy coughed and pinched her nostrils. "Sorry, the smell of that ink gets to me. At age nineteen, Pamela was convicted of check forgery and sentenced to eighteen months at the Correctional Facility for Women in Shakopee, Minnesota. I've connected with Shakopee, and they're locating her prison records. Right after her release, she got married for the first time to the prison chaplain, Reverend Gordon Sayles, a much older man." Amy paused, scanning her notes. "This would make it 1985, when Pamela was twenty-one. They were married until 1990 when she filed for divorce. I've contacted the correctional facility to track down Gordon Sayles. He doesn't appear to have been a widower, but he might help us get a sense of her personality. In 1991, using the name Susan Nichols, she hooked up with Reverend Patterson, then living in Columbia, Missouri, also a widower."

Linda tapped the board. "The sooner we can talk to Sayles, the better. I'm thinking an older man, along father figure lines. When I interviewed Patterson, he said that after they were married, she was caught embezzling church funds. Again, she had wheedled her way into the position of bookkeeper."

Lyle propped his arms on the desk and rested his chin in his hands. "That brings us to 1993—"

"Right," Linda interrupted. "According to Patterson they were married barely two years, and he filed for divorce in April 1994."

"Thirty years old with two marriages behind her," Amy said. "She works fast."

Linda eyed the lieutenants. "Then she meets Gregory Hansen. Let me back up. Lyle, how large was his parish?"

"Reverend Martin told me the University Place congregation serves around five hundred families, which meant a bigger budget."

Amy picked up the conversation, her pink nail polish bright on her hands. "Now going by Nicole Allen, she meets Gregory Hansen early in 1995. I confirmed with Ms. Jordan they were married thirteen months later, in February of 1996. Their son, Jacob, was born in December 1998, and their daughter, Elizabeth, in July 2000." She paused again to read over her notes. "Then she campaigned for the job of bookkeeper by harassing the current one into quitting."

"It put her in contact with the money—always the money." Linda stretched out manicured hands on her desk. "The people of Lincoln, Nebraska, want to know if and why Mrs. Hansen killed her husband

and children. This will be a time-consuming investigation; but if we don't have a suspect soon, we may run into budget and manpower issues."

Lyle cupped a large hand under his chin. "Understood. Did Darlene say anything about the Hansens' possessions? They were leaving the country; surely, they had to have some."

"Good point, Lyle. I'll see if I can reach Darlene today," Linda said, rising and glancing at her watch. "I may be able to still catch her."

✝

Linda parked in the lot next to the church, but her gaze instantly found the parsonage. She was drawn to the site of the garden at the back of the house. The crime tape was gone, but the mounds of dirt unearthed by forensics were still in piles near the gaping holes where the bodies had been found. These were a father and little children. *Those children were mere babies.* Linda stared in mournful silence. She found it impossible to erase the memory of those little bodies dressed in their innocent Disney pajamas. *I promise you I will do everything in my power to find your killer.*

A gust of wind blew her hair across her face, and she hurried to the church. A chill crawled up Linda's back as she opened the church office door. She didn't blame Rev. Martin for moving out of the house; it was simply too sickening to live there.

"Shit!" Around the corner, Darlene cursed the copy machine.

Embarrassed by catching Darlene in an uncomfortable moment, Linda announced her presence. "Hi, Darlene. I hope I'm not coming at an inconvenient time."

"No. I shouldn't swear in the church, but this damned copier jammed again."

"That's quite all right." Linda chuckled. "I've heard it before. Even in church."

"Good." Darlene slammed the front of the copier shut.

Linda slipped her bag off her shoulder, removing her notepad. "Thanks for agreeing to see me. I have a few additional questions."

"Sure. Anything to help get this solved," she said, starting the copier again.

"My colleagues and I keep coming back to the fact the Hansens were going to Africa and what they were bringing with them. Were their possessions and clothing being shipped? Or were they being held in a storage locker?"

"Neither," Darlene said, taking a seat at her desk, while keeping a watchful eye on the copy machine. "Most of their furnishings were sold at three huge moving sales. That was another thing Gregory and Nicole argued over. She was unhappy with the prospect of doing missionary work, and she wanted their things held in storage. But Gregory thought they might be gone for ages and decided to sell most everything."

Linda wrote furiously. "Did Gregory give any indication of how long they might be gone?"

"No, but the Disciples of Christ Global Ministries office in Cleveland, likes for people to come home every five years, so they won't get burned out."

"Five years in a foreign country is a long stretch," Linda said. "Did they get paid for their work?"

"They were to get a stipend while working as missionaries, but you can't get rich on that. Gregory thought they could use the money from the sales to start over whenever they moved back to the States."

"These garage sales—the Hansens sold their clothes, too?"

"All the winter ones anyway. Gregory wanted to travel as light as possible. And the children were small and would have outgrown most of their things. They sold nearly everything they had." Darlene paused and walked to the copier, which was making a rhythmic *thwack, thwack* as pages stacked in the sorter. She grabbed a pile, bringing them to her desk.

Linda stopped writing and watched Darlene sort pages. "The Hansens' car was located in Cleveland, where I'll be heading shortly. We have some idea of the path Nicole took. But we have no witnesses recalling a moving truck."

"It wasn't a moving truck," Darlene said emphatically. "The main thing of value the Hansens were keeping was their car. They rented a small U-Haul to pull behind the Toyota."

Damn! She probably switched the license plates. Pulling a U-Haul behind the vehicle made it harder to identify, Linda thought as Darlene kept talking.

"I'm so sorry I didn't think to mention the trailer sooner," Darlene said, stacking pages of the bulletin on her desk. "This whole ordeal has been a terrible shock. But I can help explain the confusion of witnesses. It was the end of the month, and there are apartments up the street. Around the same time the Hansens were moving, one of our members was also leaving, and they hired professional movers. They told me when they changed their address."

This was starting to make sense. "So, eyewitnesses did see a U-Haul and a moving van, but for two separate events. Can I get the name and address of the parishioner who hired the moving company? I'll want to verify those sightings."

"Sure," Darlene said.

Linda was angry at herself for missing the crucial details of the Hansens' car and trailer. Even more troubling was the time lost, giving their suspect the chance to become another nondescript face in the crowd.

II

Saturday, May 25, 2002
Lincoln, Nebraska
U-Haul Rental Office

As soon as the Hansens' Toyota was located, Linda and the team had gone to work, trying to find the local dealer they had used. There were over a dozen U-Haul rental outlets in the city, and halfway into her search, Linda took a call from a U-Haul manager. He was positive the Hansens had rented a trailer from him and insisted they meet.

Linda joined Bill Smith, the owner, that afternoon. He was tall, and his white hair had her gauging his age to be early sixties.

He produced the Hansens' paperwork from a file and handed it to Linda. "I read the story in the *Journal*," Smith explained. "Here's the contract both Mr. and Mrs. Hansen signed."

She pulled on latex gloves and opened a transparent plastic evidence bag. "I'll need this—if we're lucky forensics might be able to lift prints." Linda bagged the contract. "They each came in to sign?"

"They had to, since they were both drivers. I needed to make sure their driver's licenses were current. Here are the license copies and the credit card they used."

Linda saw that the picture of Nicole Hansen was clear, but figured her appearance had been altered. She was drawn to her signature, attached to the contract. If forensics pulled a usable print or even a partial, a match with Pamela Jane Watts would be additional evidence, although they were compiling it inch by inch.

Smith gazed at Linda sadly. "Those poor little kids, it makes me sick thinking about it. Who would do such a thing?"

✝

Tuesday, May 28, 2002
Cleveland, Ohio
U-Haul Rental Office

Following Memorial Day, Linda maneuvered her rental car into the U-Haul parking lot located in an industrial area of storage facilities and low-slung office complexes. She caught the odor of gas, oil, and tar on the breeze as she reached the front glass door. It buzzed an alert as she entered.

A heavyset, middle-aged man with twinkling blue eyes smiled at her. "May I help you, ma'am?"

"I'm Captain Linda Turner here to see Dave Ahlstrom."

"That's me. You've come a long way to discuss a previous customer," he said, motioning for her to come around the front counter. "I've gotten all the materials together on the woman you mentioned. There's a table and chairs in back here where we can talk privately."

"Thank you," she said, following him behind the counter.

Dave pulled a dog-eared folder off a metal filing cabinet, situating his girth in a plastic chair. "I have the original of the contract Mrs. Hansen signed when she returned the trailer. I do remember her, this Nicole Hansen."

"Why is that?" said Linda, opening the folder.

"Most folks just turn in the vehicle they've rented, sign off, and leave. But Mrs. Hansen? She asked me right away if I knew of any car dealerships where she could sell her Toyota."

"A Corolla, right?"

"Yep. Beige, four-door sedan. A 1995, I think. Looked to be a nice car."

"Did you give her the names of any dealerships?"

"Yeah. The first one was a Toyota dealer, but she said something about being in a hurry, so I gave her Cars A Dealin' up the road a bit," Dave said, pointing northward.

Linda placed the document in another evidence bag. "All of this is evidence. You also mentioned on the phone you had surveillance video of Mrs. Hansen," Linda said, thumbing through the remainder of folder contents.

"Yep, that's on this cassette. You were lucky you came in when you did because we only keep these six months at most. It's ready to view."

"Let's do that." Linda put down her pen while Dave inserted a tape into the VCR, moving the TV on a metal-wheeled stand in front of her.

"There's no sound, just the tape." As an afterthought, Dave added, "And it's date-stamped, if that'll help."

The tape was queued up to April 1, 2002. Linda watched intently as a woman wearing sunglasses entered the frame. *Damn*, Linda thought, *those sunglasses are no good.*

"Watch when I give her the papers to sign on return of the trailer," Dave said, as if he knew what she was thinking. "She'll remove her sunglasses. That should give you a better look."

The picture was a bit fuzzy, and Linda peered closely. In black and white, she couldn't tell if Nicole had changed her hair color, but she imagined that she had. She watched as she removed her glasses and accepted a pen. As she signed off on the contract, Nicole firmly planted her open right palm on the contract to steady it as she applied her signature with her left hand. *Breathe*, Linda told herself. Unless Nicole Hansen was ambidextrous, the pool of potential suspects had narrowed to ten percent of the total population.

"Can you rewind that and replay it?" Linda asked, her heart beating faster. *If we could get a useable print off that contract . . .*

"Sure," Dave said. "I'll play it forward, this time in slow motion."

Linda moved nearer to the television screen and watched as Nicole Hansen held the contract with her right hand for a solid three to four seconds and signed with her left. Linda tried not to get overly excited, but this could be a big lead. Looking through the translucent plastic bag, Linda studied Gregory and Nicole Hansen's signatures. *We can compare handwriting samples, too.*

"I hope this helps you, Captain." He smiled and handed her the materials.

Linda rose to leave and shook Dave's beefy hand before handing him her card. "I appreciate your cooperation. If you think of anything else, here's my contact information. Then, if you will point out the car dealership you think Nicole went to, that would be great."

✝

Cars A Dealin' wasn't a dealership, but the kind of small used-car lot that specialized in getting cars sold quickly. Linda didn't expect to find the Corolla still on the lot and wasn't disappointed. The manager on duty, no older than twenty-one judging from his acne, confirmed her suspicions.

"I remember her because the Toyota was in good condition and very clean. It even smelled clean. That's not normally the case with the cars we get."

Linda queried him. "What do you mean by that statement?" she said, glancing at his nametag, which said Patrick. "I mean, can you be more specific, Patrick?"

His smile was sheepish, as though he wasn't sure how much he should tell her, particularly since he now knew he was dealing with the police.

"I need you to recall your interaction with Mrs. Hansen that day," she cajoled.

Patrick's shoulders heaved, resigned to having to tell what he knew and hoping he wouldn't be in any trouble. "You being with the police and all, you probably know places like this deal strictly in cash. We try to get a title, but if there's none, we don't ask a lot of questions."

Linda wasn't interested in Cars A Dealin' and its business practices. She could tell she surprised Patrick with her next question. "Do you remember if inside the car there was a particular odor? Bleach, for example?"

He rubbed the back of his neck, as if it were stiff. "No, not bleach, but the interior had that 'new car' smell, which you can achieve with automotive cleaning products. Totally vacuumed out, washed, and waxed. We don't see that very often."

"What about a vehicle title—did Mrs. Hansen have that?"

"Yeah, she did. She signed it, and I paid her."

"How much did you disburse to her?" she asked.

"I think $4,000," Patrick said, the pitch in his nervous voice a notch higher.

"No need to be anxious, Patrick." Linda smiled, placing a comforting hand on his forearm. "I'm not here because you've done anything wrong. But I assume even Cars A Dealin' keeps some type of financial records. Can you confirm how much you paid her?"

Patrick's body relaxed. "I'll find the receipt for you."

She smiled reassuringly. "I'd appreciate that. And Patrick, if you're worried what your boss will think of you talking to a cop, you won't have to tell anyone I was ever here."

Patrick's relief came in a loud sigh. He went in back, and Linda heard a file cabinet open and papers being shuffled. He came out carrying a file folder. "She brought the car here on a Monday. Monday, April first—April Fool's Day."

That's ironic. She'll be the one that's the fool. Linda pulled her notes from her bag to confirm some dates. *The last day anyone saw the Hansen family was Sunday, March twenty-fourth. Eight days later, she sells the Toyota and disappears.*

Linda looked at Patrick, posing a question. "Selling her car leaves her with no vehicle. Or did she buy another from you?"

"No, that was the weird thing. She asked me where the Greyhound bus depot was and called a cab to pick her up."

Linda's notepad was halfway into her bag. "Do you remember the name of the cab company?"

Patrick shook his head. "No, another customer came in; and by the time I was finished helping them, she was gone. But I can tell you we sold the car three days later to a couple from Oklahoma. Do you want their names?"

"Sure," Linda answered but doubted it would do much good. Any forensic evidence was long gone. Patrick wrote down the buyers' names, and she thanked him for his cooperation. She wasn't surprised Nicole Hansen had resorted to the bus. It was the perfect way to slip off the grid into anonymity, as Linda had expected.

12

June 29, 2002, Sunday morning
St. Louis, Missouri
The Road to Calvary set

Five weeks earlier, Ray Williams had been resigned to failure, preparing to shut down *The Road to Calvary* and any attempts to find another way to spread the Word of Salvation. But as the result of meeting Susannah Baker, he had become willing to take unconventional risks, and the pieces were falling into place. They took advantage of any free advertising to raise their profile. Ray gave interviews on religious radio stations in the area and submitted articles to local suburban papers. The publicity paid off. The studio was nearly full, and Ray knew a good first impression increased positive word-of-mouth. The phone number "1-800-HE-SAVES" lit up the bottom of the TV screens.

Live on the air, Rev. Ray was a man renewed, as if he'd been sparked by the touch of God himself. Mid-sermon, he prowled the stage, delivering his revitalized message with fervor he hadn't felt since Lorraine died. Scanning his audience, he saw more attentive faces than in the past, but the crowd needed a jolt to bring them home.

"Remember that the Lord makes His face shine upon *you!*" he proclaimed, the slight southern drawl slowly building toward a crescendo. "Jesus in your heart is the radiance of the Lord God shining upon your face in a dark room."

The pastor paused, making deliberate eye contact with his audience, searching expectant faces. "I recognize that many of you are going through troubled times, but I tell you here and now that if you seek the loving face of the Son of God, you can walk through the most treacherous valley and not fear. You can face the greatest storm, and the water will not drown you, because when God is with you, the Light of Our Lord Jesus Christ will help you fend off the forces of darkness!"

In the brief recess, a voice rose from out of the audience. "I know that the Reverend Ray speaks the truth!" In the front row, Susannah had stood and announced to the audience, "My name is Susannah Baker, and without the reverend I would not be here today!"

Mesmerized, Ray watched her from his position on stage. Dressed in a modest navy suit, she clenched her fists, pulling her arms tight into her chest as she faced them. "I have walked deep into the valley of darkness—alone, broke, an alcoholic. I was clinging to life by a thread, ready to wash down a handful of sleeping pills with a bottle of Jack Daniels and end my troubles."

Even though she faced away from him, Ray could see the rolling of Susannah's shoulders as she began to cry. He stepped off the stage and walked alongside her, holding the microphone without being intrusive, so the audience could witness her story. From his breast pocket, he handed her a handkerchief.

Susannah accepted the gesture and dabbed at her moist eyes before resuming her story. "But for some reason, I turned on the TV in my dingy hotel room." She laughed a bit self-consciously, wiping away a tear. "I guess I wanted company in my final hour. I came across this program and Reverend Ray, and you know what? I started to listen. He didn't tell me I was a sinner or that I was a drunk; he told me that God was there with me! That Jesus Christ would help me—me, Susannah Baker! All I had to do was ask."

She held their rapt attention, keen faces living every word of her story. "I'd poured myself a tall glass of Jack Daniels, and the bottle of Valium was on the bedside table. But instead of drinking or swallowing a handful of pills, I kept listening to Reverend Ray and his message that I could be saved if I turned my life over to Jesus Christ. And that dark, dank hotel room rapidly filled with the brightest light, and I realized the saving power of Our Lord Jesus Christ was right there. It was a miracle!"

There was fleeting silence before an audience member called out, "Amen!"

Another rose to his feet, shouting, "Praise Jesus!"

Surveying the crowd, Ray realized he had never seen his congregation this engaged.

"I got up off the bed, took the bottles of Jack Daniels and Valium, and flushed them all. The program ended, and I immediately found an AA meeting. I'm proud to stand here and say I have kept sober for the last year." Applause erupted throughout the studio, and the audience was on its feet, cheering. To get them to pause, Susannah held up her open palm. "But, without this program and Reverend Ray's wonderful message, I would not be here telling you this story. And I promise you I am not the first person whose life *The Road to Calvary* has changed for the better."

The applause kept coming, growing louder with each round. He wasn't sure where the tale would end but was confident that God would provide. Gripping the microphone, Susannah implored the crowd, "So I am asking all of you here to get out your pocketbooks and help keep this ministry alive! And for those of you at home—" She turned directly into the camera. "Just call 1-800-HE-SAVES, the number right there at the bottom of your screen. I am living proof of the miracles taking place on this program, but they cannot continue without your support!"

Congregation members were still on their feet, clapping and shouting, "Amen!" Susannah handed Ray the microphone and returned to her seat. Ray noticed many tear-streaked faces among the audience. Susannah had touched a vital nerve, promoting *The Road to Calvary* in a completely new way, and Ray grabbed on. "Thank you to Miss Susannah Baker for the courage to share her story. She is living proof of the wonders Our Lord Jesus Christ offers us if we give ourselves over to Him and believe."

Examining the crowd, the reverend saw checkbooks and wallets being opened with a passion he hadn't witnessed before, and he was moved to speak in a way he never had. "Before we recite our prayer of deliverance, won't you take a moment to call 1-800-HE-SAVES and help us to change the lives of many more? Brothers and sisters, let us pray . . ."

✝

THE SAME DAY DURING THE LIVE BROADCAST
St. CHARLES, MISSOURI
RUTH PERKINS'S HOME

Ruth Perkins watched the broadcast with anticipation, excited to see the program live. She found herself caught up in Susannah Baker's tale of near death and redemption. She was a loyal viewer of *The Road to Calvary*, and Ruth had never experienced this kind of connection. If this young woman could vanquish the demons of alcoholism, destitution, and loneliness with guidance from the Reverend Ray, these good works were truly worth preserving.

The epiphany Ruth Perkins underwent at that moment was akin to the bright light flooding Susannah's shabby hotel room. Clearly, she had not accepted Jesus Christ completely. If she had, her life would most assuredly be different. There would be less strife and turmoil with her only child and granddaughters, and the familial bond Emma seemed too willing to sever would be unbreakable. Ruth knew what she must do to transform their lives.

As the reverend began the prayer of deliverance, Ruth took a pad and pen from a desk drawer. Repeating the phone number aloud as she wrote it down, "1-800-HE-SAVES," Ruth moved to the kitchen wall phone where she punched in the number. From her wallet, Ruth removed a credit card.

"Thank you for calling *The Road to Calvary*. How may I help you?" asked the male voice politely at the other end of the line.

"Good morning! I want to donate. What an amazing story. The Reverend Ray truly works miracles."

"Thank you, ma'am, glad for the feedback. How much do you wish to give?"

"Do you accept credit cards?"

"Yes ma'am," the voice asserted. "MasterCard, Visa, and Discover."

"Good," Ruth said. "I want to give $1,000 using my Visa card." Ruth rattled off her name and the card number.

After confirming the number, the male voice continued with enthusiasm, "Thank you for such a generous donation, Mrs. Perkins. May you continue your support and God bless!"

13

Later the same day
St. Louis, Missouri
The Road to Calvary set

Immediately following the broadcast, the mood was euphoric. Too often, the offering basket funds barely covered the costs of operation; but with the fresh phone number in place and Susannah's compelling story, Ray was hearing numbers he'd merely dreamed of.

"There's over $3,000 in here," Jeff enthused, pointing to the studio offering. "And we had at least fifty newcomers in the audience."

"And the phone calls," Buck added. "I took at least 30 and who knows if I got them all? That's another $3,000, and one lady made a $1,000 donation on her credit card." Just as quickly, Buck stopped smiling; his face etched in seriousness. "But we're going to need to get extra help. I can't answer the phones, take up the offering, and monitor the audience all at once."

Ray chuckled. "Remember, one step at a time." The group of four huddled around a distressed table in the empty studio. "But this is an excellent start."

From across the small table, Susannah radiated elation. "This is a good thing, but I have to apologize." Her gaze connected with Ray, her fine-boned face luminous. "I didn't mean to take over the show, but the Spirit came upon me saying, 'Tell your story!' And I had to because without you and this program, Reverend, I truly would not be sitting here today."

Ray smiled, taken with her honesty and humility. "No apology necessary," he replied. "It was a beautiful story, and I'm thankful you've come into our lives. This is the first real assurance I've had that everything we've done hasn't been in vain." Ray, Buck, and Jeff stood, the offertory piled between them. "Today is confirmation that *The Road to Calvary* does indeed have a future and will continue!"

"Hallelujah!" Jeff hollered, pumping balled fists over his head. Observing Jeff's reaction, Buck's response was tempered.

"That's great news, Ray, but we gotta discuss getting those phones answered if we're going to do live broadcasts permanently. I can't split myself into multiple people."

Ray's eyes twinkled as he stood and came around to pat Buck's tense shoulder. "I know, Buck. We will get you the help you need." But he wanted to savor this moment of renewed energy and faith. "The Lord was truly present here today. As Susannah was telling her story, a voice said to me, 'Ray! Use the resources you have available to you!' That means we involve the very community we serve, giving them ownership of this program—"

"And a sense of empowerment," Susannah interjected. Just as quickly, she stopped herself. "Excuse me, I didn't mean to interrupt."

Ray faced her. "You're exactly right. We empower our congregation to use their gifts and talents, and remarkable things can happen."

"Please, no women empowered by makeup,'" Jeff said, his squeamish expression impossible to hide.

The three chortled, and Ray patted Jeff's shoulder. "You might have to get used to that, Jeff. A five-minute segment may be a real selling point."

Jeff looked at everyone, stuttering slightly. "Uh, w-well, that's okay,

I guess. I just need to get used to the idea. I never thought 'bout religion and makeup at the same time."

The reverend laughed. "As I said, let's take it one step at a time." He stopped for a moment. "Can you all meet Thursday evening?"

All three nodded their heads. "All right, then, come at six o'clock prepared with a list of members you think would be interested in volunteering. I think we can safely say our live experiment was a triumph, and it needs to continue." Ray felt the thrill racing through his body. He turned to Susannah. "I'm starved. Would you be interested in getting a bite to eat after locking up?"

Her smile was warm and inviting. "I'd love to."

Buck waved the couple onward. "You go get something to eat. Jeff and I will lock up."

The lines in Ray's face softened when he smiled. "I'd appreciate that. I'll see you gentlemen on Thursday," he said with a nod in Buck and Jeff's direction before offering Susannah his arm. He never saw the quick, slightly curious glance between the two men.

After the couple departed, Buck turned to Jeff. "I've never seen Ray react to a woman like that." He sighed. "He's been a widower so long; it never occurred to me that he might find someone."

"Me either," Jeff acknowledged. "But, there's a first time for everything, bro," he said.

As Jeff headed out the door, Buck remained sitting deep in thought. He had no problem with Ray falling in love; it was the fact that he hadn't ever considered it that gnawed at him. After several minutes, Buck rose from the table with the thought that more than *The Road to Calvary* was changing.

✝

Later the Same Day
St. Louis, Missouri
Kay's Diner

The summer breeze caught Susannah's skirt as Ray held the diner's glass door. He couldn't help but notice her shapely legs underneath.

"It's nothing fancy—good home cooking that fills the hungry emptiness in a single man's stomach." He gestured toward the hostess who seated them in a corner booth.

Menus before them, Susannah scanned her options for dinner. "It all looks wonderful."

"I've never had a bad meal here. In fact, I think I've eaten almost everything on the menu. On Sundays, the roast beef dinner special is particularly good."

"Hey, Reverend," said the waitress in the crisp yellow uniform, her name, Mavis, stitched across the pocket. With a familiar smile, she was already pouring Ray coffee. "Coffee for the lady as well?"

"Yes, please. With cream. What are you having, Ray?"

"I'll do the special. It reminds me of Sunday dinners growing up."

Mavis returned with Susannah's coffee, and they ordered the special. Ray genuinely wanted to learn more about Miss Susannah Baker who, like an answer to a desperate prayer, had appeared in their lives at exactly the right moment. "Tell me about yourself," he said. "Are you from St. Louis?"

Her coffee turned light brown as she stirred in cream. "I've been living here slightly over a year—since I watched you on *The Road to Calvary* and got sober."

"What brought you to our fine community? Family? A job?"

She tilted her chin upwards. "Neither. I needed a fresh start after a contentious divorce and family tragedy. I thought a bigger city in the Midwest might have potential."

Ray paused, watching her bring the cup to her full lips, her eyes never leaving his face. "You certainly discovered your potential on *The Road to Calvary*, Susannah. I genuinely appreciate what you did today. I haven't seen that level of enthusiasm among the congregation since we started."

"Give yourself due credit, Ray. Your idea to reach out to the congregation and ask them to contribute their gifts is wonderful. They'll respond."

Mavis arrived with steaming plates of roast beef dinner. "Anything else I can get you two?"

"I'd have more coffee, Mavis," Ray said, his eyes never leaving Susannah's luminous face. "I'm not trying to pry," he continued to her, "but you said you suffered a family tragedy. Can I be of help in any way?"

Susannah smiled. "The food smells delicious, and I don't know about you, Reverend, but I'm starved."

When she changed the subject, Ray felt as though he may have overstepped his bounds; after all, he barely knew this woman. "I'm sorry, Susannah, this is a personal matter, and I have no right asking you to share it."

She finished her first bite, wiping her mouth with a napkin. "You have the right to know, as that tragedy is what sent me spiraling into the depths of alcoholism and despair, from which you, Ray, saved me. This roast beef is wonderful, by the way."

"Good, I'm glad." He reached over the table, patting her hand.

"I learned in AA that life-altering situations are very often the catalyst that lead people to drugs or alcohol to cope with a trauma they can't begin to know how to handle or survive. In my case, the divorce was a result of circumstances that neither my husband, Perry, nor I could comprehend. We lost our two young children in a car accident." She paused, gazing darkly at the water in her glass, as if seeing the terrible events unfurl again before her eyes.

Ray had heard plenty of stories detailing sorrow and misfortune in his business, but this was particularly wrenching. He said nothing and let her finish.

"Perry's sister, Carla, was babysitting our kids. On her way home from a birthday party, a drunk driver ran a red light, killing all three instantly. The autopsy later revealed Carla was pregnant, and the driver was charged in the deaths of four, including her fetus. Everything you've heard about the immeasurable grief a parent feels in burying her children is true. Our marriage collapsed within a year, each of us blaming the other." Susannah took a breath, rubbing away tears. "I had already started drinking to ease the pain of losing my children. I thought if I moved away, the past wouldn't follow me, but it did. I kept drinking and falling closer and closer to the bottom. Then I found you and *The Road to Calvary.*"

"I am so deeply sorry for your loss—both of your children and your marriage. But you seem to be a very strong woman, Susannah, and I'm glad you found us."

Over the remainder of dinner, their conversation returned to how taking *The Road to Calvary* live had made the possibility of success a sudden reality. Ray was struck by Susannah's determination to move on from unendurable heartbreak. Lorraine's death had ripped at Ray's heart, but he had known they might lose that battle. Despite their different circumstances, Ray believed this woman understood the meaning of profound loss and redemption. Perhaps they were destined to meet, he thought.

"Any dessert tonight, Reverend? We've got your favorite, home-made apple pie."

He looked toward Susannah who waved that she'd had her fill. "I think that'll do it, Mavis," he replied. "We'll take the check."

Turning toward her, he met Susannah's gaze, trying to show appreciation without sounding overly forward. "This is going to sound corny, but you came into my life at precisely the right moment.

If I hadn't made your acquaintance, *The Road to Calvary* would be through. I can't thank you enough—"

Susannah held her palm open, interrupting him. "If anybody should be giving thanks, it's me—because if I hadn't turned that television on and heard you, I'd be dead." She paused, her scrutiny intense. "But for someone who does so much for others, what about you, Reverend?"

Ray wasn't sure what she meant. He tried to keep his face expressionless, but he knew he furrowed his brow.

She held the coffee cup in her slender hands, elbows perched on the table. "I was curious to learn more about the man who'd saved my life, so I did some research. Reminiscent of your father, the Reverend David Williams, you've devoted your life to serving God in small congregations throughout the Midwest—Bellville, Illinois; Greencastle, Indiana; Louisville, Kentucky. But I'll bet your faith in God was sorely tested, wasn't it, when you did everything you were supposed to do, but your wife, Lorraine, still died from ovarian cancer? After your wife passed, you could have turned away from God, but you didn't. Instead, you put your message on television and forged ahead, risking everything to save even a few."

As he listened to her, Ray wasn't angry or bothered that Susannah Baker had inquired into his life story. Instead, it made perfect sense that this amazingly perceptive stranger would seek answers and put someone else's hardships above her own. He said nothing, preferring to let her continue.

"Our paths crossed, and through you, I've gotten a second chance at life. If a few of my ideas can help *The Road to Calvary* achieve success and see you happy, that's a bargain in my eyes."

It seemed like decades since anyone had been concerned about his happiness. "You are one incredible woman. But I'm not unhappy," he lied.

"If my prying is uninvited, I apologize," she said. "But it seems to me that a man who devotes his life to helping others should have someone who's willing to show that same kind of devotion in his life. And I think God wants you to be happy, too."

Ray couldn't take his eyes off her beautiful smile and was about to reply when Mavis's cheery voice brought him back to earth. "Here you go, Reverend," she said, placing the check on the table. "You both have a nice evening."

"You, too, Mavis," he replied. "Tell Bernie the food was delicious as always."

"I sure will." Mavis winked.

"Let me get this," he said, removing a leather wallet smoothed by use and time from his jacket pocket, the check and wallet in his strong grip. "I should be getting home, but can I drop you somewhere?"

She had risen from the chair, ironing the crease in her skirt with her hands. "If you could drop me off at the bus stop, that would be fine." She fidgeted nervously, snatching her purse off the table and clutching it tightly.

Ray stood, watching her; she had started rummaging through the bag, refusing eye contact, and his curiosity was piqued. "Drop you at the bus stop? This isn't the best of neighborhoods. I'd be more than happy to drive you home."

Susannah stared into the void of her open bag and shuffled her feet. She still didn't look at Ray, and after a few long seconds, she spoke, "You know, that is so sweet of you, Reverend; and I do appreciate the offer, but I can't let you take me home."

The woman who had so confidently told him of her dream and relayed her story of salvation in front of the congregation now seemed to be retreating into her body. His mind buzzing with questions, Ray wanted to understand her dilemma.

"Why not?" he asked, trying hard not to be crushed at the possibility there might be someone else. "Is there a jealous boyfriend at home who doesn't know you're here? I'd be happy to explain everything."

She dropped back down into the chair, one arm through the strap of her purse as she searched for words. "This is embarrassing, but . . . there is no home."

He squeezed her arm with a comforting hand. "You don't have anything to be ashamed of. Tell me, so I can at least try to help you."

Her voice grew anxious, and as she relayed details of her situation, the words tumbled out faster and faster. "You've heard my story and that you helped me find sobriety. But what you wouldn't know is that financially things haven't gone so great. I work temporary jobs when I can get them, and when I can't, which is right now because I haven't worked in almost three months, then I . . . I have to live in my car or stay at a shelter."

This was not where he had expected this conversation to lead, but Ray was moved by both the desperation of Susannah's plight and her determination to maintain her dignity. His fingers slid softly along her arm, lightly grasping her trembling hand. "I can find you a place to stay. We can go to your car and get your things—"

"No," she interrupted, the quiver in her voice evident. She wouldn't look at him, but still clutched his hand.

"All right," he said, trying to soothe her. "If you'd rather I didn't see how you've been forced to live, that's fine. But I won't allow you to spend another night sleeping in your car. We'll go to Target and get you a toothbrush and some pajamas. There's a motel I know of where you can stay and be safe."

Her whole body shivered as tears rolled down her flushed cheeks. Squeezing his hand tighter, she spoke in a hoarse whisper, barely audible, "Okay, we can go to Target, if it's no trouble."

Ray patted the top of her hand, feeling she was holding onto him as if he were a lifeline. "It's no trouble. No trouble at all."

✝

Once finished at Target, he drove to a hotel specializing in extended stays. He knew the manager, a former drug addict whom he had helped get a fresh start after rehab. Ray had called ahead and arranged for Susannah to stay there.

Doug Snyder, the owner, met them at the motel. "Any friend of Reverend Ray's is a friend of mine." He smiled, extending a muscular hand. "You're welcome here as long as you need."

Susannah shook Doug's hand as Ray registered her. Ray said, "I'm not sure how long Miss Baker will be staying, but I'll keep you informed."

"No problem. There's a bedroom, kitchenette, bathroom, and sitting area," Doug said, directing his comments to Susannah. "If I can be of any further assistance, please let me know."

Ray carried in the red-and-white plastic bags, and they made their way to her room. He opened the door and guided her in. "As Doug said, you're welcome to stay here. A week, a month, however long until you're back on your feet, understand?"

"But how will you pay for this? I can't accept—"

He touched his fingertips together. "Susannah, you have helped me see the potential for *The Road to Calvary* and not give up. This is my way of saying thank you. As for money, God will provide. Tomorrow, we'll get you some groceries, so you won't starve." The reverend stretched out his right hand. "Good night, Susannah." Ray reached into his pocket, removing a business card and pen. "I almost forgot—here's my home number if you need anything. If you're an early riser, I'd be happy to pick you up for breakfast."

She gratefully clasped his hand, eyes wet and glistening. "Breakfast sounds wonderful. Thank you, Reverend. I'm very, very grateful."

14

Wednesday, July 10, 2002
St. Louis, Missouri
The Road to Calvary set

Two weeks after the first live broadcast, the Reverend Ray stepped from behind the podium, skimming the congregation from the stage. He estimated the audience had grown to over three hundred, a perfect occasion to offer every one of them an opportunity to live the word of God.

"Friends, today we heard about using our many and varied gifts in answering God's call. But I leave you with a challenge." Ray, in a contemporary navy suit, looked across the many faces. "*The Road to Calvary* requests your gifts and talents—singers, songwriters, musicians, carpenters, electricians, seamstresses, and many others—to keep this ministry alive. In the fellowship line today, we will be asking those of you we are acquainted with to heed God's call and put your talents to use." He smiled warmly at his flock. "How many of you will accept the challenge and answer God's call?"

Several audience members raised their hands in response, waving them around like kindergarteners eager to pass out a snack. For the next hour, the reverend and Susannah asked enthusiastic members to take on various duties.

An elderly woman with fleshy forearms grasped Ray's hand, shaking it firmly. "I'm Mildred Watson, and I'm a seamstress. I've been sewing since I was a young girl. I'll make new choir robes."

"As soon as we have a choir," he began, and before he finished the sentence, hands raised down the line, voices clamoring to be heard.

"I'll be in the choir."

"Me, too!"

"I have experience directing a choir," another voice added.

"Well, this is answering God's call." Ray grinned.

"All you had to do was ask, Reverend," said Mildred. "I'll start a sign-up sheet for members, and I can start measuring folks today," she said, pulling a tape measure out of her purse.

Susannah slipped from the receiving line and helped Mildred take names and measurements as excited parishioners queued up for the choir.

The man who'd expressed interest in directing the choir made his way to Ray. "Reverend Williams, my name's Ryan McCarthy, and I have a degree in music from the Boston Conservatory. I believe I can assist with directing the choir."

Ray marveled at what he was hearing, privately chastising himself for not thinking to approach the congregation sooner. Amid the bustling crowd, he caught Susannah's eye. She beamed with contentment, and Ray wondered if she had any awareness of how much she had changed his life. Much had happened in a brief period, and he was a better pastor and a happier man for having realized that simply listening to Susannah Baker was just the beginning. Believing her seemed natural.

15

August 7, 2002
St. Louis, Missouri
The cable station

In four weeks, the hard-working congregation had completely transformed the studio space. Carpenters built a moveable background of stained-glass windows and a raised stage. Mildred Watson delivered custom-made blue choir robes.

"Aren't these robes beautiful?" Susannah clasped her hands together. "Mildred assembled a team of seamstresses to make these. And wait until you hear the choir sing!"

The choir gathered on the stage for a last run-through as Ray and Susannah looked on. "I understand Ryan directs both our singers and musicians and has written a song for today's live broadcast," he said.

The musicians finished tuning up, and Ryan began directing the choir, strains of a familiar melody filling the space.

Yesterday's past and gone
And tomorrow's coming into sight
Yes, it gladdens me in song, singing,
Help me make it to the Light.

Yes, it gladdens me in song, singing,
Help me make it to the Light.

"Well done, my friends, well done!" Ray was ecstatic.

"I'm glad you enjoyed it, Reverend," Ryan said. "I think we'll be even better live. We're eager to share our gifts."

Susannah put her hand on Ray's forearm. "What did I tell you—God is bringing out the best in us."

The cable station had a Wednesday evening slot open, and *The Road to Calvary* was happy to fill it. Ray had hoped for a permanent time slot on Sunday mornings since most people thought about church then, but right now, the costs were prohibitive. When the cable station offered Wednesday evenings, he had taken it. Even if this wasn't their ideal hour, he trusted *The Road to Calvary* could use it to their advantage.

Glancing around the studio and seeing the handiwork of the congregation filled Ray with pride. Fresh flowers on stage bloomed in colors complementing the backdrop. Musicians and choir members were finishing Ryan's song. This was all good, yet he felt vaguely apprehensive. Tonight would be the program's first foray into technology. If they pulled this off, as Susannah was sure they would, *The Road to Calvary* would move in an entirely new direction.

†

A few moments later, Ray studied his audience from the stage. He was trying not to get distracted by thoughts of how the technology would work.

"How many of you are in the pit and want to come out?" The reverend paused as a few tentative hands went up. "How many of you are bogged down in the pit of addiction—drugs, sex, debt—and want to come out?" A few additional hands rose haltingly, and Ray kept talking, his voice growing louder with each question. "How many of you are trapped in the pit of adultery? In the pit of denial? In the pit of dishonesty? In the pit of abuse?" Ray deliberately scanned his audience as more and more hands rose into the air.

Into his earpiece, Buck's voice crackled, "Okay, Ray, let's see if this works. The overweight gentleman in the red short-sleeved shirt, sixth row from the front—he's seated on the end and starting to cry. Name is Jim, and we're lucky enough to have us a last name, Jameson. We've got ourselves a drinking problem."

Ray sought out Susannah's face. She smiled and nodded, as if to say, "Go ahead." Encouraged by her presence, he marched with purpose up the aisle and took a deep breath. "You sir, Mr. Jim Jameson! You are trapped in the pit of alcoholism, but you are desperate to be free!"

Stunned as to how exactly the Reverend Ray knew his name, the quivering mass of a man stood up as Ray motioned for him to rise. Jeff tightly focused the camera on Jim's tear-streaked face, words stammering out of his mouth. "Yes, sir. My name is Jim Jameson. How did you know? I've lost everything—my job, my house, savings. My wife said that if I didn't come with her today, I'd lose her, too."

"The Lord works in mysterious ways," the reverend affirmed, and Jim Jameson began to sob uncontrollably. Susannah slipped up behind Ray and took the microphone so that his hands were unencumbered. "Jim Jameson, you can be *free* and take back your life, if only you ask *Him*. Do you want to leave the pit of alcoholism, Jim?"

The pained wailing from Jim grew louder. "Yes! Yes, I want to come out of the pit!"

The Reverend Ray stood before Jim and placed a large hand on each of the man's heaving shoulders. "Rise, my brothers and sisters," he commanded. Sensing something amazing was about to happen, the congregation dutifully rose to their feet. "Extend your hands over your brother James, that we may help him be *free*."

To Rev. Ray's amazement, the audience did as they were told, rising with arms outstretched toward the sobbing man.

"Repeat after me, James," he said, "'Lord Jesus, I ask you to help me climb out of the pit of alcoholism!'"

"Lord Jesus, I ask *you* to help me climb out of the pit of *alcoholism!*" Jim closed his eyes and stretched open arms toward the ceiling.

It had taken a few simple words, but Ray hadn't felt this influential since he was newly ordained. Susannah was right; he truly believed he was helping this man overcome temptation and create a better life for himself and his family. Ray closed his eyes tightly, his voice rising, shifting into that smooth, southern drawl. "You are leaving the pit, Jim, unlocking the shackles of alcoholism and setting yourself free!"

Jim Jameson's body convulsed with sobs as he looked heavenward again and proclaimed, "Thank you, Jesus!"

Susannah handed the microphone back to Ray, who gently turned the still teary Jim toward the camera. "James, what you do from this day forward will reflect on your Lord Jesus Christ. He has saved you from the depths of the pit. Find a good AA meeting, get yourself sober, and help others rise up out of the pit of alcoholism."

The big bear of a man responded with great enthusiasm. "Yes, sir, Reverend! I will turn my life over to *Him* and help others to be free of alcohol!"

Wild applause emanated from the audience as the pastor walked up the aisle. Ray had never experienced a service such as this, and he called out to the audience, "The pit is vast and deep, but you can be *free!*"

In his earpiece, he heard Buck's words. "Well, that went darn well, so let's try another one. Lady on your right, third row from the front this time. Fourth seat from the end and wearing a print blouse and has gray hair. Thelma wants to mend the rift among family members."

Immediately, Rev. Ray began scanning the rows for Thelma, without being obvious. When he spotted her, he proclaimed, "Thelma! With the help of Jesus Christ, this family rift can be *healed*, and your loved ones will rise from the pit of estrangement!"

16

Later the same day
St. Louis, Missouri
The cable station

Afterwards, Ray and Susannah stood together in the receiving line, shaking all the attendees' hands. For Ray, it had been as exhilarating as preaching his first sermon. Members complimented him on his words and truly seemed to be listening. An hour later, the four of them were packing up the monitoring equipment while they critiqued this first experiment.

Jeff was giddy with enthusiasm, and for him, that was something to take note of. "That was amazing! Did ya feel the energy between Ray and the audience?"

"Did you see the look on that guy's face when I called out his entire name?" Ray asked with a mild chuckle. "How did you know his last name?"

Buck was occupied with packing up a computer monitor. "Luck. He's sitting there, and his wife is raggin' on him, you know, 'I'm telling you, Jim Jameson, either you listen to this man or it's *over*,'" he said. His laugh was nervous, almost jittery. "It was funny in a pathetic sort of way."

Ray had moved onto loading the next box. "Now, it would be nice if some of this took hold, and these folks did improve their lives."

Buck laughed. "Yeah, everybody got pretty swept up. Now, if it keeps Mr. Jameson out of the bars for a few weeks, it can't hurt."

On the opposite side of the room, Susannah stopped packing and addressed the men. "This is exactly what I mean by giving people a little push toward their greatest potential! They *will* change for the better, and they'll be *back*."

"Yeah, and hopefully, they'll have friends! From what I can tell, the crowd seems to be gettin' bigger every week."

Ray nodded at Jeff's observation. "Well, we've got a choir now. Mrs. Watson did a fantastic job on the robes, and what a song Ryan wrote! The set is colorful and inviting."

Susannah beamed at him. It would have been obvious to anyone else in the room that she and Ray had entered a comfortable familiarity in the next stage of their relationship. But neither Buck nor Jeff knew that Susannah was living with Ray, a fact he planned to keep secret indefinitely. "And once Buck gets the website up, word will spread even wider."

Buck's shoulders arched when he answered her. "It's comin', okay? I'll have it up by early next week. I'm still working two jobs, remember?"

Susannah looked hurt, as though she felt Buck was taking unnecessary offense.

"I realize you are, Buck. You're working hard, and I didn't mean to suggest otherwise." She stopped and surveyed the men. "I'm glad the site isn't up yet because I have another idea."

At her pronouncement, everyone ceased packing. Ray wanted to hear additional details but realized Buck was getting annoyed with Susannah's constant questions about his progress. While he understood that she meant well, he sensed his friend was feeling enormous pressure to turn her ideas into reality. On the other hand, this was the woman Ray realized he loved, so he smoothly intervened.

"I think Buck has his hands full. Let him get the site up and running, and then we can talk about your latest proposal."

But Susannah wouldn't be denied. "One last proposal and I promise that it doesn't have anything to do with makeovers, though I still think that one has merit. I was thinking that if we added a tag line it would give the show more punch, something easy to remember. For example, *The Road to Calvary,* Your Salvation Station!" She paused, watching them mill over this latest idea.

Ray was the first to break the silence. "*The Road to Calvary,* Your Salvation Station," he repeated slowly. "We're not actually a station, but I like it." He looked at Jeff, then over to Buck. "Susannah has a point—something catchy to remember us by."

Standing directly across from the reverend, Jeff signaled his agreement.

Buck's tone was sarcastic. "I'll be sure the slogan is prominently displayed on the website's home page. I'll make sure it's big and bold, where our audience can't miss it."

Susannah's reaction was bursting with sweetness as thick as honey. "You won't regret this; the tag line is simply another aspect to set us apart."

From his vantage point, Ray swore Susannah's eyes narrowed to a cool, almost ruthless gaze. But then he blinked, and there was the woman he loved right before him, as charming as could be. He figured the excitement of the day had worn Buck out. He prudently hoped Buck would feel better after a good night's sleep.

17

TUESDAY, OCTOBER 1, 2002
RICHMOND HEIGHTS, MISSOURI
RAY'S HOME

R ay looked out the window at burnished orange, red, and mustard leaves wafting gently to the ground under an azure blue sky. He didn't want to share this letter, but he had to. Buck, Jeff, and Susannah sat around his kitchen table, glum looks across their faces. He had received the notice lying at the center of the table in yesterday's mail and called the group together at once. The letterhead displayed the name of the property management company that owned the cable station building.

"Effective November 1, 2002, Management Properties is increasing television studio rent from five hundred dollars each week to one thousand dollars to contain rising expenses." Seeing the dour faces, Ray knew no one had anticipated the news.

Jeff picked up the message, started to read it again, but threw it down in disgust. "We've finally got a little bit of success, and the building's owners want to increase their cut by doubling the rent? Shit."

Ray didn't have an answer. Slowly grasping the document, he again read aloud, "Notice to terminate your lease must be given in writing by October 15, 2002. If we have not received written notice of cancellation, Management Properties will assume the tenant has agreed to these terms." He couldn't hide the exasperation. "We aren't bringing in that kind of money."

The diamond in Buck's single pierced ear glinted in the fall sunlight. "This doesn't have anything to do with our success," he reasoned. "The area is undergoing gentrification, and the property management company sees this as an opportunity to increase revenue. Other programs will smart from an increase, too."

"I want to have faith that we can overcome this and that the Lord will show us the way to two thousand dollars more a month, but I'm a realist," Ray stated, scowling at the uninvited missive.

Susannah lifted the page off the table. She read it deliberately, before throwing it back into the center. "This doesn't make sense. If there's no program, there's no rent."

"True," Buck acknowledged. "But they are banking on us not cancelling and renewing our lease at the higher price. The building's owners think they have us between a rock and a hard place."

"Well, don't they?" Jeff asked.

On the verge of responding, Ray was interrupted before he could speak. Her fists clenched, Susannah proposed a plan Ray initially believed too far-fetched to broach with the others. "Fine. Let's find another building."

Buck's weight shifted in his seat, the doubt rising in his eyes. "How? Susannah, we still have a ways to go financially and little time to find something, even if we did have the money."

Susannah's features softened, and her fists opened as if their problem had been solved. "We've had to ask members for support before, and they've come through in spades. Now we have real urgency; we need a building, or we shut down."

Jeff and Buck's words overlapped, heads shaking in unison. "No way!" and "That's impossible!" but Ray stopped the chorus of naysayers. "She's right," he said, slowly meeting the doubters' gaze. "Have we come this far only to give up? The worst that can happen is that nobody has a building or space to rent, but we won't get an answer unless we ask."

Buck folded his arms across his chest, and Jeff remained quiet. Ray forged ahead before they could open their mouths and start arguing. "We've walked this path before and with quite positive results. There's no guarantee we'll find a building. The spot we're trapped in has little wiggle room for other options. This is the best we've got." When Ray looked toward Susannah, goose bumps prickled his skin. He'd last felt this kind of courage with his wife—a complete willingness to go against convention as a team and trust in the unexpected. "Susannah is right," he said again, softly brushing her hand. "I know exactly what to do."

†

Prior to the broadcast's conclusion the following Wednesday, Ray placed Susannah's proposal before his congregation. The stage was nearly bare, so the audience could focus their attention on Ray's urgent message. Standing at the center of the unadorned space, he spoke to his flock.

"Before we go forth to serve the Lord, I come before you today with the greatest challenge *The Road to Calvary* has ever faced. I have asked you to heed God's call, and you have risen to the occasion and given of yourselves fully. But what I am about to reveal will affect each one of us." He waited, looking deep into the faces before him. "We are confronted with a fiscal crisis of great magnitude—the inability to continue renting this space."

Ray paused again as the murmurings of surprise and concern rolled among the audience.

"Unless we can find another location from which to broadcast *The*

Road to Calvary, the program will shut down at the end of this month, four short weeks from today. I realize that what I am asking is no small thing, but I ask each of you to search your heart with humility and prayer for a solution. It doesn't matter whether it's another building we can rent for a reasonable amount or even negotiate to purchase. But we must find a new home, or we will not be able to continue." Ray paused again and judged by the creased brows that he'd made his point. "Let us stand together and pray our prayer of deliverance."

The congregation rose, repeating the prayer in strong, clear voices. Ray's eyes met Susannah's, and the reverend thought how distressing it would be if this beautiful woman's presence, dreams, and ideas did not fulfill their potential. He had never met anyone like Susannah. Though he initially had been skeptical, he had come to trust that God had indeed spoken to her. In a few short months, she had bared her soul by coming forward and bravely telling her story of how *The Road to Calvary* kept her from the brink of death, handing her a second chance. Everything she had done was a completely selfless act; Susannah seemed simply interested in spreading the message of the Good News to a greater audience.

Ray listened as the congregation repeated the final stanza. This was the toughest obstacle they had ever faced. But he truly believed the Lord would see them through.

✝

Less than three days passed before Ray received the phone call that was a remedy to his and many others' prayers. Jim Jameson, whose miraculous "healing" from the ravages of alcoholism had changed *The Road to Calvary* from just another religious cable show to one delivering life-altering miracles, had a friend he wanted Ray to meet. Sober since Ray had called him forth, Jameson was working again, salvaging his marriage, and spreading the word about Ray's gift.

And now, Ray, Susannah, Buck, and Jeff stood on the cement floor of a vast warehouse in an industrial section of St. Louis near the Gateway Arch and Riverfront. Jim stood alongside his friend and boss, Karl Wilcox, who expounded on ways the space could be developed to fit the needs of their program.

"The building is sixty-five thousand square feet and air conditioned. Jim's told me that it's important to keep all the television equipment cool," he explained, waving muscular arms around the space the way a wizard might wield a magical scepter. "There's room to erect a stage, seating can be expanded or contracted as needed, and you can add walls where you want offices, conference rooms, whatever. You can utilize the space any way you need."

Ray's eyes traveled across the open space. It was impressive and had endless potential, but a sticky subject needed to be addressed—price. The reverend cleared his throat. "Mr. Wilcox, this is all very remarkable, and I'd be a liar if I said we couldn't make use of every single inch. But you're a businessman, and I need to ask your price."

Karl Wilcox gave a jovial laugh, unexpected for the situation. He grinned broadly at the assembled group. "Reverend, Jim Jameson and I have been best friends since we were kids. We've gone to school together, raised families together, and been there for one another in the good times and the not-so-good." Karl regarded his friend. "Jim, I hope you don't mind me telling this story—"

Jim casually interrupted Karl. "Not at all."

"As you know," Karl said and smiled at the faces before him. "Jim had a drinking problem that was destroying his life. With the help of your program, Jim released himself from his addiction and reclaimed his life. He did what you asked, Reverend; he found an AA meeting and has gone faithfully ever since. I can't tell you how often I dreaded getting the phone call that Jim had been found dead after a bender. But thanks to you and the miracle of faith in Jesus Christ, Jim is on the road to recovery." The big man paused for emphasis. "How much is this building going to cost you? Not a cent, Reverend, because I'm giving it to you."

Ray heard Karl Wilcox clearly, but he found the words eluding him.

"You don't believe me, do you? I'll say it again. I'm donating this building to your fine program, *The Road to Calvary*. It won't cost you a dime." Wilcox stopped talking and removed an envelope from his shirt pocket, handing it to Ray. "I also understand there will be numerous expenses as you start up. Consider this check for $50,000 another crucial donation to continue your good works."

Ray could not believe his ears or his eyes. This was a miracle indeed. He inhaled deeply and let the news sink in. "I'm overwhelmed—we all are. This is incredible." Karl Wilcox's astonishing words repeated themselves in his head: *"I'm donating this building to your fine program,* The Road to Calvary. *It won't cost you a dime."* Ray chastised himself for ever doubting Susannah. As he looked to her, tears of joy trickled down her cheeks. There were so many emotions—both Buck and Jeff were sniffling—and so much Ray wanted to say. "Mr. Wilcox, sometimes even a pastor's faith in God is shaken, but you, sir, have given us a miracle. God bless you, this is truly a momentous day."

Karl Wilcox grasped Ray's hand in a hearty grip. "My pleasure, Reverend. I'll have my lawyer draw up the necessary paperwork for donating the building, but in the meantime—" Karl removed a cluster of keys from his pocket and placed them in Ray's outstretched palm. "I imagine you folks need to get to work and keep this show on the air."

Regaining their composure, Buck and Jeff were already exploring the huge warehouse, tossing around ideas on how best to utilize it.

Alone for a moment, Susannah slipped her hand into Ray's and whispered softly, "What did I tell you? Ask for the stars and know at least that we tried."

Buck and Jeff were still jabbering as Ray gently squeezed her hand, too emotional to say another word.

18

October 11, 2002
Lincoln, Nebraska
Northeast Police Headquarters

Friday marked just over five months since the Reverend Martin's dog had unearthed the gruesome discoveries in the parsonage flower garden. Linda sat at her desk sorting through paperwork from other cases, but the murders of Gregory Hansen and his children were never far from her mind.

She had asked Darlene Jordan for a picture of the family and taped it to her desk. She requested photos with most murder cases. Linda believed it was important to put a face to the victims who, regardless of the circumstances, had lived as someone's children, spouses, siblings, and friends. Cops often had a macabre sense of humor, a protection mechanism that kept the horror of situations at a safe distance. But Gregory, Jacob, and Elizabeth Hansen were unusual.

It wasn't simply that children were involved; in her fifteen-year career, Linda had investigated enough cases concerning children to understand that the shock value eventually tapered and the sheer revulsion no longer made her fight the urge to retch in disgust. The factor that made this case so horrifying was a mother killing her family with no hesitation, vanishing, and slipping into another identity. Discovering who Nicole Hansen had become was verging on an obsession.

Linda stared hard at the picture, a sweet shot of Gregory and the children from autumn 2001 taken at the entrance to Disneyland. Nicole was absent; she was undoubtedly the photographer. What struck Linda was the children and Gregory enjoying "the happiest place on Earth." She tried to stop her mind from wondering if this was the trip where the children had gotten their Disney pajamas. In a few short months, these children would die in those joyful pajamas. The twisted turning of her stomach would not ease.

There was something else crowding her mind—unfortunate news regarding the status of the investigation. Lyle and Amy would be as devastated as she was.

"None of this will come as unexpected," she told them, "but I've been told to cut back on the Hansen investigation. After five months conducting dozens of interviews and following countless tips, we still don't have one solid lead." She read the disappointment in their eyes. They had quietly gathered in Linda's office, the door closed to the hum of the precinct.

Lyle was the first to speak. "I can't say I'm surprised, but not to have one viable lead borders on failure."

"You know better than that, Lyle." Linda tried to keep her tone of voice even. These murders were hard on everyone. "I'm under orders to concentrate on fresher cases that require our attention and resources."

"I figured as much," Amy said, folding her arms. "I suspect that most people can't stomach the idea of Nicole Hansen killing her husband and children. The stereotype that women rarely commit murder is a hard one to break."

Lyle stretched his lanky frame against the chair, a knowing smirk turning up his mouth. "But they do, and far more often than people think."

Their foe was a formidable one, but Linda wanted to be certain Lyle and Amy understood that no one had failed. "This one's exceptionally good—exceedingly smart, a master manipulator with an amazing ability to find people's weaknesses and exploit them to her advantage. After all the interviews, I'm convinced that's her gift—finding the weak spot and twisting it to her advantage."

The corners of Lyle's mouth again turned up in a smirk. "I agree."

"It doesn't spell the end, but the investigation will slow down," Linda continued. "The toughest part of police work is patience. Let's go over the evidence we've collected again and see if there isn't an angle we've overlooked."

†

MONDAY, OctobER 14, 2002
RichmonD HEights, MissouRi
RAy's home

Ray wanted to be up and running in the new space by November sixth. The donated building brought a different set of challenges. The $50,000 from Karl Wilcox would help immensely, but equipment, air-time options, and improvements were costly. Digital technology was making filming affordable, and with Buck and Jeff scouring the internet for good buys on new or used cameras, lights, and editing consoles, they agreed to take out a $25,000 loan to cover further expenses.

The need to reach a larger audience was now paramount, and Susannah offered an innovative option. Sipping coffee, she made her pitch. "Paid programming—but before you say anything hear me out.

Most religious programming is distributed this way. Yes, we pay for the program, but we have control and a portion of donations we raise pay for airtime."

From his seat at the table, Ray smiled at Susannah. "When I think of paid programming, I tend to think of cheesy infomercials selling some product you don't need."

Susannah stretched out her hand, clasping Ray's. "There are some of those, yes. Let's research this, and I think you'll see the advantages. The program gets distribution from infomercial brokers, which can go beyond local. You know the saying, 'Sometimes you have to spend money to make money.'"

He continued stroking her knuckles yet was conflicted. "Paid advertising costs thousands of dollars, and we haven't access to that kind of money. It's interesting but expensive."

"I thought the loan you took out was for expenses like this."

She gazed into his eyes, and Ray could feel himself starting to waver.

"Let's perform our due diligence," she continued. "There are infomercial brokers, and we should start with them and see what the process is. And of course, I'm sure both Buck and Jeff will have suggestions on how to proceed."

Ray kissed her hand, mesmerized by Susannah's warm, brown eyes. "Speaking of Buck and Jeff, we can't go on hiding our relationship from them."

"Aren't you worried about the congregation's reaction to us living in sin?"

He smiled, his lips caressing each of her slender fingers, drinking in the scent of lavender. "I'm not ready to openly explain our arrangement to worshippers, but I'd feel better if our staff knew the truth. Then we could at least have our meetings here." Ray continued kissing the tips of her soft fingers.

"Well, I, for one, can think of better things to do." She rose from the table and came to him, her full, moist mouth covering his, and Ray felt the passion spark between them.

Susannah tugged at his button-down shirt, and a button flew off, bouncing across the hardwood floor.

Susannah giggled. "Sorry, I'll sew it on tomorrow." They barely made it upstairs.

19

TUESDAY, NOVEMBER 5, 2002
St. Louis, Missouri
THE ROAD TO CALVARY SET

When the final live broadcast of *The Road to Calvary* aired the last week in October, Ray addressed the congregation on trying the paid programming format in their new space. Much to Buck's surprise, people had shown both support and enthusiasm for becoming part of a community. Willing to donate money for a paid broadcast, the worshippers proved that their faith in their leader was passionate.

For all the good news, one item gnawed at Buck. Ray and Susannah were very close to giving their relationship away. They looked at one another too long, hung on each other's every word, and clasped hands when they didn't think anyone was looking. Who was Susannah Baker, really? Where had she come from? Ray was in love, something Buck had never thought he'd see, but there were so many questions. In less than six months, this woman, who seemed to have dropped out of the sky, had ingrained herself into the pastor's life and the program. Sure, Buck reasoned, she had attended services faithfully for several months. But she had stayed to speak with Ray at the moment he had become convinced that shutting down *The Road to Calvary* was their only choice. It was almost as if she had known. Had she eavesdropped on their conversations, planning to swoop in at the last moment?

Buck analyzed that question from every angle, and he couldn't quite put his finger on her motives. To be sure, Susannah wanted to make money, and her approach was questionable. Initially, Ray was so strongly resistant to the idea of blatant fraud that Buck had never expected him to agree to her plans. But Ray was clearly smitten by this dark-haired stranger, another fact that left Buck trying his damnedest to understand her power over his friend.

It was common knowledge Ray had left his church after Lorraine died of cancer, his faith sorely tested. Buck and Jeff had been members of that congregation, and Ray had told them he needed to step away from religion. Buck remembered him taking a contract position with a large company as an ethics consultant, earning a six-figure salary. He'd stayed in corporate America over five years. Having money convinced him to launch *The Road to Calvary* on cable and return to his calling full time. He'd asked Buck and Jeff to come along on the journey.

Buck entered the warehouse, contemplating one of Susannah's stories that he'd never quite believed—her claim of spiraling into the depths of alcoholism, ready to commit suicide with booze and pills just before she came upon Ray preaching on television. That wasn't the part that bothered him. From experience, Buck had maintained years of sobriety, after enduring an unpleasant stint in rehab, by attending so many AA meetings that he'd lost count. Susannah never spoke of any kind of recovery or of fighting the urge to drink again. Buck thought about drinking every single day, and it was truly one day at a time for him. He knew every alcoholic was different, but the fact that she said nothing was another red flag that only he and Jeff appeared to notice.

Glancing at a wall clock, Buck realized Ray and Susannah would be there any minute. They wanted his input on some paid programming options. Buck was glad to assist, but after a full day at his IT job with an area bank, he was tired.

"Hello? Anybody here?" Buck's voice boomed into the vast space.

From the depths of the warehouse, Ray called, "In the conference room."

The moment Buck entered, Susannah announced, "We've come up with a multi-pronged plan that takes into consideration all our broadcast options. We've made a brief PowerPoint presentation."

Buck forced a smile. "I'm excited to hear about it."

Ray opened PowerPoint, and the first slide appeared on the screen. Susannah began speaking while Ray took a seat. "We've heard back from the infomercial broker, and they loved the demo—Ray's rapport with the audience, commitment, and sincerity." She clicked to the next slide. "We'll get right to business. We commit to the thirty-minute weekly infomercial for a thousand dollars." The slide faded into the next. "We also started researching area television stations. There's an independent St. Louis station that bills itself as 'family friendly' and offers other religious programming." The station's call letters and ad rates came up on the screen. "For another couple hundred dollars a week, we can broadcast there as well."

Ray interrupted, tilting forward in his chair. "Our goal is a decent time slot and expansion of our market and revenue, so we can get back to broadcasting live."

Buck found himself impressed with the amount of research they'd done.

Susannah looked him straight in the eye. "We can't guarantee the perfect hour or anything else," she acknowledged. "But what we can do is take advantage of as many options as we can afford when broadcasting live."

She punched the remote and the next colored slide displayed Christian beauty tips. "Both of you have pooh-poohed the idea of

Christian makeovers, but this is exactly the way we can set ourselves apart by offering more than just religion."

Makeup and religion do not mix, Buck thought, stifling a groan. He tried to be civil. "These are different programs; how will viewers know they're related?"

Susannah's curls bobbed as she shook her head. "I'm talking short sequences offering quick beauty tips for the Christian woman prior to the service. The rest of the broadcast focuses on Scripture, Ray, and his message."

Buck rested his chin in his hands. He found himself considering a new perspective. *This might work to distinguish us from the crowd.* "What are we looking at in terms of costs?"

With a click of the mouse, Susannah brought their website up on the screen. "Buck, you've been overly modest. You've completed the website, and we are up and running." Looking squarely at him, she chose her words carefully. "I realize working a full-time job definitely slowed the progress, but this is a fantastic site. Tell me if I'm missing anything. I love the history of the show, but especially a listing of all the times and outlets broadcasting the show, a link where individuals can send prayer requests, and a button to click for PayPal donations."

Buck felt appreciated and quickly added, "Technology's changing so fast that very soon we'll also be able to have Ray's past sermons for people to view as video clips."

"You've done an amazing job on this," Ray added. "This website looks great."

Susannah was ecstatic, too, barely able to contain her excitement. "With all the different avenues, paid programming will pay for itself! And the beauty tips give women something else useful to take away from the broadcast."

Ray followed up her comment. "Our goal is returning to at least one live broadcast a week, which I thought suited us very well. We're hoping to get a decent time slot with either option, preferably Sunday mornings."

"People record programs now, so the hour or day we're broadcast may not be that big a deal," Buck said. "I want us to get back to broadcasting live, too. New options with the internet are emerging at a fast pace, and I think we should re-launch the ministry. I can post broadcast dates, times, and stations on the website. We want others to discover us through word of mouth. And if one option doesn't pan out, we still have alternatives. Excellent job, you two."

Susannah spoke up. "I'll contact the religious station in town regarding time slots and research further bids for paid programming." She crinkled her small nose. "I'm so glad you approve, Buck. It means a lot. The focus will always be on Ray, but the beauty tips make us unique. If we see they're not paying off, we end them."

She kissed Ray full on the mouth, and Buck felt his brow arch. *At some point soon, you're going to have to tell Jeff and me that you're a couple.*

Ray broke into Buck's thoughts. "I want to review the website."

"No problem," Buck answered. "Circle your chairs around the computer, and I'll take you through it." The sound of the metal chairs screeched against the cement floor. Buck watched the interaction between Ray and Susannah and for a fleeting second, wondered if he should say something. He didn't trust her and made a mental note to start asking her specific questions, particularly about her past.

20

WEDNESDAY, NOVEMBER 6, 2002
Iowa/Minnesota

It took some cajoling, but Chief Langston came around to the importance of Linda going up to Minnesota and meeting with those most knowledgeable about Pamela Watts's foster care.

At the picturesque Iowa-Minnesota border, Linda stopped at a rest area, her melancholy thoughts wandering to her husband, Tom. He would have loved this trip. Drives like this were especially tough because such sojourns had been theirs alone. When they reached this point, Tom would have found a picturesque landscape to admire and indulge his passion for photography. The limestone bluffs, rolling green hills, and placid waters of Minnesota would have made for stunning pictures to be turned into calendars or enlarged custom panoramas.

That was the deal. As soon as they reached retirement age, Tom wanted to pursue photography on a larger scale, and Linda's passion was to compete in target shooting competitions across the country. When she graduated from the police academy, Linda had been noted as the best marksman, not just in the women's division or the department, but in the state. She'd competed early in her police career, but eventually, she put those plans on hold until retirement. They would travel the country pursuing their interests while, most importantly, sharing their lives together.

After five years, she'd grown accustomed to living alone, but that didn't mean she liked it. Every year in June, on the anniversary of Tom's passing, she would be reminded how arbitrary death was. Here was a thirty-six-year-old EMT, in top physical condition, who had dropped dead in the kitchen while cooking them breakfast.

She had frantically dialed 911, performing CPR until the paramedics arrived, but Tom's best friends and coworkers could do nothing to bring him back. The autopsy showed an embolism had slammed into his heart, meaning he was dead even before crashing to the hardwood floor.

Still, Linda had spent guilt-wrecked months wondering why she hadn't done more, hadn't called 911 quicker, hadn't pumped more chest compressions, breathed more air into Tom's lungs. Finally, her grief counselor arranged a meeting with the coroner who explained step by step how the embolism had formed and how, without knowledge of its existence, Tom had become a human time bomb exploding that Saturday morning. She couldn't have diffused it, and she needed to cut herself free from the brutal guilt strangling her existence.

Eventually, coworkers and her three older brothers had tried setting up introductions and dates with acquaintances, but it always felt too soon. Her oldest brother, Paul, an EMT in Tom's squad, had originally introduced them. Linda sensed Paul felt responsibility in looking out for his little sister. She had been thirty-two when Tom died, and Paul worried incessantly, saying over and again, "You're too young to be a widow, Linda. Play the field. Go out and have fun!"

The guys she met were nice enough, but there was never a spark to light a romantic fire. Instead, she made her career the top priority. Being promoted to captain proved her sacrifice had paid off.

Pushing thoughts of Tom aside, her mind returned to the open questions in the Hansen case. Her team had known of Pamela Watts's time in foster care but needed money to pursue the possible lead. And then Sister Monica had called, asking her to come to Minnesota.

Catholic Charities was the social justice network for the Archdiocese of St. Paul/Minneapolis, and a large part of its mission was placing children in foster care. Sister Monica was a no-nonsense nun who had worked with the organization since the late 1960s and knew its history. Even after inviting Linda to meet with her, the nun had asked to see a warrant before she would divulge any information. On this frosty morning, Linda and Sister Monica were meeting in the nun's meticulously organized office.

From behind a neat stack of files, the broad-shouldered nun peered over her glasses. "It took some digging, but I think we've found at least some of what you're looking for." Brisk and to the point, the sister selected the top file. "Pamela Watts came into the Catholic Charities foster care system for the second time after her adoptive parents died in a house fire. There were no other living relatives, and that's how Pamela ended up here. When I was going back over these files, I started remembering details of her case because it was so tragic."

"I've been waiting for the coroner's report on her parents for months," Linda acknowledged with slight irritation.

"You no doubt already know she was abandoned at birth. Mr. and Mrs. Watts were heavy smokers, and the fire investigation determined the blaze started in a wastebasket. The search also concluded the wastebasket was full of paper, accelerating the fire. It spread quickly, and the panicked barking of the family dog is what woke Pamela. I know it's speculation, but I have always believed that this was a double suicide."

Linda stared at the old nun. "Why do you say that, Sister?"

"For several reasons. First, there's the fact the Wattses were in financial trouble. They were filing for bankruptcy because their antique store was failing. Second, there was a reason a fiercely barking dog didn't wake her parents. Not only was their bedroom door locked, but during the autopsies, toxicology screens found significant quantities of Valium and Librium in both their systems. The parents had prescriptions. Mr. and Mrs. Watts were already dead when the house caught fire. And third, they had a large life insurance policy with Pamela as the beneficiary. I've witnessed how extreme stress can lead people to do something horrible because they believe it's the right thing to end their problems. By killing themselves, they would at least leave their daughter well off." Monica folded thick arms across her desk. "You should also know that Pamela tried to save her parents."

Linda was incredulous but put on her best poker face. "That would be an entirely different story. How do you know this?"

"She had burns on both her hands from trying to open the bedroom door, which had a metal knob. The fire was getting too hot, leaving her no choice but to flee. By the time Pamela was thirteen, she had endured unimaginable trauma. No one deserves that."

Linda struggled to keep her composure. As a nun, Sister Monica clearly wanted to see the best in everyone. Linda kept returning to the presence of substantial amounts of prescription drugs in the victims' systems in both the Hansen and Watts cases. That meant the fire might not have been an accident. "Can I see the coroner's report?" she asked, her voice growing hoarse.

Sister Monica handed the file over, and as Linda fumbled through the pages, she realized her throat was very parched. "Could I have some water, please?"

"Certainly." Sister Monica rose and went to fetch a cup and water.

This woman murdered her children, her husband, and her parents. Rev. Patterson would have become a victim, too.

"Here you are, dear." Sister set the Styrofoam cup on her desk.

Drinking the cool water in one gulp, Linda fixated on Sister Monica's deeply lined face. "You're right. What happened to Pamela must have been unbearable. What other details can you tell me?"

Sister Monica shuffled folders across her desk before she found what she was looking for. "I read over Pamela's file to refresh my memory. Catholic Charities is here to aid children in need, and Pamela was clearly that, but we had a challenging time placing her, which only made her feel more unwanted. She frequently acted out, usually fighting with the biological children. When she was brought back to Catholic Charities, Pamela was devastated and became withdrawn and inhibited. The rejections were extremely hard on her. Pamela loved to read, and I think those fantasy worlds made her feel safe."

"Do you recall specific examples that would make multiple families choose not to adopt her?"

Monica searched for another file. "There was a horrific incident with the Anderson family."

Linda jotted the name "Anderson" on the page. "That's a pretty common name—"

"But their story involving Pamela isn't," she said, sliding the open folder across the desk. "In most cases, the foster family contacts us and says, 'This isn't working out,' and the agency sends a social worker to pick up the child and so forth. In this case, Mr. and Mrs. Anderson brought Pamela to Catholic Charities with her bags packed. They dropped her off, saying they had reached their limit and didn't want this child in their home any longer."

Even with all of her police experience, the idea that a child so terrified her foster family that they brought her back was chilling. "The Andersons were afraid of Pamela?"

Monica followed the text with her index finger. "'Fearful for their safety,' the parents said. It's all here—the Andersons' Labrador had recently given birth to a litter of puppies. The parents claimed Pamela didn't appreciate the competition for attention from the pups and drowned them. I remember how upset Pamela was, and frankly, I never believed the story. It makes no sense that Pamela's life was saved by her pet dog, and then she drowns puppies? No. She kept saying that the Anderson children were lying and blaming her for an act perpetrated by the sister, Louise."

Sister has a point, Linda thought. *Still . . .* She nodded at Monica. "How old was she?"

"Fifteen."

Linda made additional notes on her pad. "Pamela had to receive some type of mental health counseling."

"That's in her medical records—here." Sister Monica flipped open another file. "She saw one of our psychiatrists, Dr. Bennett, who was worried about Pamela's mental state. It says that when Dr. Bennett asked Pamela if she drowned the puppies, she replied, 'Louise did it because she didn't like me.'" The nun glanced over her desk at Linda. "Catholic Charities didn't provide the kind of in-depth therapy for children that we do today, so Pamela obviously didn't get the care she needed. That girl never had a chance."

"Catholic Charities seems to have let Pamela fall through the cracks," Linda remarked.

Sister Monica peered at Linda over the top of her glasses. "I disagree. Instead of continuing to place Pamela and risking further rejection, the board voted to keep her here with other foster children until she turned eighteen. She did make friends with some of the kids, and we enrolled her in one of our schools. Pamela was very bright and graduated from high school near the top of her class."

Linda paged through her own file. "Pamela has a criminal history, unfortunately. She was convicted of check forgery and sent to the Shakopee Corrections Facility. However, she volunteered as a tutor to help other inmates obtain their GED."

Sister Monica overturned another pile of folders. "I am sorry to hear that. But I'm not surprised she tried to help fellow women obtain their degrees. As I said, she was a voracious reader and loved learning. She tutored other kids during high school." Sister abruptly changed topics. "You mentioned photos. You may have something more recent, but here's a picture."

The detective sat up straight in her chair and accepted the dull photo of a plump teenage girl with pale alabaster skin, ginger hair, and a mole above her right upper lip. Linda could barely detect the dark spot on Pamela's right ear. Unlike the stark mug shot showing a sullen young woman, with a prominent nose, platinum hair streaked with black, dark roots visible, this girl was smiling into the camera. "Along with duplicates of the files, I need a copy of this picture, too."

"Sure." Sister Monica scribbled a note on a Post-it. "You've got the subpoena, and I thought you'd need one."

Linda decided to test her theory that Pamela Watts was extremely adept at changing her appearance. She removed the unmarked driver's license photos and mug shot from the folder, placing them side-by-side in front of Sister. "I know it's been years, but which photo is Pamela's?"

The old nun pursed faded lips, pointing to the newer images. "None of these are her. Two of the women have smaller, pert noses while their faces are thinner."

Linda wrote a note on the file. "Thank you, Sister. All of these pictures are of Pamela."

Sister Monica scowled, closely inspecting various pictures. "As you said, many years have gone by since I last saw Pamela."

Linda deliberated on how to proceed. "I'm in contact with the correctional facility, and I'm awaiting her files. I think it would be most helpful to talk with the Andersons, if they still live in the area."

Sister Monica scanned one of the folders. "I can see if the Andersons' contact information is still current; but even if it is, they may not want to talk to you."

"I understand. But innocent lives have been taken here, and I need you to do everything possible to get in touch with them." Linda continued tapping her pen absentmindedly, questions of Pamela's motivations and circumstances thrashing around in her head.

†

Tuesday, November 11, 2002
Minneapolis, Minnesota
Catholic Charities Office

Linda had been in touch with the correctional facility in Shakopee from the beginning, and while they had been cooperative, the warden pointed out Pamela Jane Watts had been imprisoned back in the '70s and didn't qualify as a cold case. Spring and summer faded into autumn before corrections located her files. In early November, while Linda was still in Minnesota, her prison records arrived in Lincoln. Shakopee had more news; they did not know the whereabouts of Gordon Sayles, which Linda thought strange. While Lyle combed Pamela's incarceration history for any useful nuggets, Amy was busy trying to locate Sayles, hitting plenty of dead ends.

As she awaited the arrival of one of the Anderson children in Sister Monica's office, Linda was relieved he had agreed to speak with her. The rest of the Andersons had flatly refused Monica's request for a meeting. She worried that she might not be able to get firsthand accounts. But the brother had changed his mind and agreed to talk with her. The office door opened, and a tall, slender man in his early forties followed Sister Monica into the room.

"Mr. David Anderson, this is Captain Linda Turner from Lincoln, Nebraska. She is working a case you may be able to assist her with. I'll leave you to chat."

Sister Monica closed the door behind her, and Linda rose to shake David's extended hand.

"I appreciate you agreeing to speak with me. You may be able to shed some light on the kind of person we're dealing with." She took a seat and motioned for David to sit. "I'm not sure how much the sister told you, but we're investigating a triple homicide, and Pamela Watts is a person of interest."

"Anything I can do to help, although many years have passed. But there are some things you never forget."

"Having your puppies drowned is a terrible ordeal. But let me start from the beginning. How long did Pamela stay with you?"

"I think it was slightly over three months, but it seemed much longer."

"Do you remember how you and your siblings got along with her?"

David settled into his chair. "There are just me and my sister, Louise. Neither my sister nor I could stand Pamela. Mom and Dad referred to it as 'only child syndrome,' and because she was an only child, they were patient. We had several foster kids, some of whom Louise and I became very close to. But Pamela always had this attitude that she was somehow better than us, even though we were providing a loving home and family."

"Three months isn't a terribly long period. Was it the puppy incident alone, or were there other things leading up to removing her from your home?"

"Pamela was such a brat that it had gotten to the point where my sister and I wouldn't be in the same room with her. Our parents were aware of the tension and had caught Pamela in lies about where she had gone or who she'd been with. Typical teenage stuff, except that she totally disrespected the rules my folks had. She frequently missed curfew and wore lots of makeup and smelled of pot." He coughed and looked Linda in the eye. "They knew it wasn't working out and were going to contact the social worker. But when she drowned Maggie's puppies, that was the last straw. We realized there was something seriously harmful with her mentally. Rather than risk something more serious, they packed her bags and took her back to Catholic Charities."

"Anything else that you can remember?"

David shook a fist in recollection. "I don't know if this will help, but Pamela had an odd mark on her body besides that mole. Her right earlobe had a small hole, like a partial moon almost. I remember because it was so unusual. Besides that, she insisted that it was Louise who had killed our puppies. It wasn't true; Louise was heartbroken when they died. By then, my parents had reached their limit. They never took in any foster kids after that, which is a shame. As devout Catholics, it was kind of their mission to help children who didn't have families, but Pamela Watts destroyed their faith."

Linda scribbled a note regarding another confirmation of the oddly shaped hole. "I'm sorry your parents' faith was tarnished. They were only trying to provide a loving home."

"It still makes me angry, as it does my sister. We provided kids with a good, stable family environment, and it took only one bad apple for our parents to question whether what they were doing was worthwhile."

21

Friday, November 15, 2002
Richmond Heights, Missouri
Galleria Mall

It was going to be difficult keeping his intentions from Susannah, but on this sunny autumn afternoon, Ray told her he was going to visit a former church member who was ill, which was true to some extent. After his pastoral visit, he drove out to the Galleria in Richmond Heights in search of an item he never expected to purchase again. Moving with purpose past upscale stores, he reflected on how much one's life could change in less than a year. He thought that perhaps that was naiveté on his part. In his line of work, he saw more often than most how their lives could change overnight. Usually, it was the tragic circumstances of an accident or untimely death, but if he thought over the last several months, his feelings shouldn't come as a surprise at all. And it was time he made an honest woman of Susannah Baker.

At the curve in the mall corridor, he spied Helzberg Diamonds, and his step quickened. He went directly to the case of diamond engagement rings, his air of purpose catching the attention of a young, blonde sales clerk.

From behind the glass counter, she smiled. "May I help you, sir?"

To Ray's surprise, he was genuinely nervous, his first words more of a stammer than a statement. "Yes, I want to see some . . . I'd like to see what you have in engagement rings."

"We have a wide selection in all price ranges. How much were you thinking of spending?"

He smiled at the clerk. "You know, it's been a long while since I've done this, so I'll take all the help I can get. What would be the average price a gentleman would spend?"

The blonde clerk grinned. There seemed to be a flash of recognition as she directed Ray's attention to a line of exquisite rings. "That depends on the carat weight of the diamond, its shape, color, and clarity. I can show you rings covering a price range from a thousand dollars on up. The average amount a man spends ranges from two to five thousand dollars. The rule of thumb is a month's salary." Unlocking the case, the sales clerk removed a tray of sparkling diamond rings set against black velvet. Placing the tray on the glass, she posed another question. "How would you describe your fiancée's tastes?"

"Fiancée," he nearly whispered the word to himself. Ray's face glowed. "That sounds lovely."

"Second marriage, I take it?"

Ray nodded. "Yes. My first wife died of cancer in 1992."

She brought her hand instinctively up to her mouth. "Oh, I'm so sorry."

"Thank you. But in the last few months, I've met someone special, the reason for my visit here today."

"That's wonderful," the blonde enthused. Recall unexpectedly brightened her face. "You're Reverend Ray from TV—*The Road to Calvary*!"

Caught off guard by the woman's enthusiastic response, Ray fumbled for a reply. "Why yes, that's our show, *The Road to Calvary*."

"My aunt watches your show, and one day a couple of months ago,

I was visiting, and we watched it together. And, Reverend—may I call you that?"

"Sure—"

"Reverend, we watched you call a man, Jim, you knew him by name, out from the pit of alcoholism that was destroying his life. It was the most moving thing I'd ever seen. And I never thought I'd say this, but I started watching regularly with my aunt. The work you do is truly amazing."

"Well, thank you, Miss—"

The bubbly clerk extended her small hand across the glass countertop. "Sally. Sally Sullivan. It is a pleasure to meet you, Reverend. My aunt Julia won't believe it! You said you're getting engaged; that's wonderful!" Stopping only long enough to catch a breath, Sally made a sweeping motion over the cases. "What kind of jewelry is your fiancée fond of?"

"Hmmm. Something simple, but elegant. Susannah—"

"Susannah Baker, the woman who helps on your show?"

"Yes, that's her."

"This is good news. Pick out whatever ring you wish, Reverend, and I'll make sure you get the best price."

The sufficient money Ray had made as a consultant would pay for a lovely engagement ring. "Show me that one," he said, smiling and pointing to a pillow-cut diamond for nearly $6,000.

"You have wonderful taste!"

Ever the preacher looking to spread the good news, Ray examined the ring. He pointed to another. "Let me see the solitaire diamond in yellow gold." Ray stopped looking at the rings for a brief moment and glanced at Sally. "You know, we have a website and are looking at some new broadcast opportunities. Here's my business card—one for you and one for Aunt Julia. We're not broadcasting live right now, but here are the days and times we do prerecorded broadcasts. We'd love to have you in our studio audience!"

"She will be thrilled to have a personal invitation. My aunt has lots of friends, too; she'll get the word out to all of them about the new programming time."

"That would be much appreciated." Ray took the solitaire diamond from Sally, slowly turning the gleaming jewel in his large hands. "Let me ask you something. Am I being old-fashioned in wanting this ring to be a surprise? Do most couples pick them out together nowadays? I want to do this right."

"It's about a fifty-fifty split in terms of what couples do. Trust me, Reverend, there is no wrong way to give a woman an engagement ring."

22

On her return, Lyle presented Linda with organized stacks of Pamela Watts's correctional files, which they hoped would offer insights into her personality. Mounds of yellowed brittle paper and forms, including transcripts from the trial convicting her of forgery, lay in neatly arranged piles.

The timeline displayed on the white dry erase murder board was different than most. It didn't span a few hours or days but crossed into the territory of years and the unsolved. Some pivotal event had made Pamela angry enough to blame and then possibly kill her families.

Linda paced before the board discussing Pamela's check forgery conviction with Lyle and Amy. "The files provide the case number for Pamela's crime. By Minnesota law, if a check forgery is over five hundred dollars, the crime is a felony, and the forger faces up to five years in prison."

"Didn't you say Pamela Watts was convicted of forging ten thousand dollars in checks?" Amy asked, pointing a pencil toward the board.

"Yes, and it involved a single check." Linda directed her finger at the name William Gunderson. "Court documents indicate Pamela befriended a Mr. Gunderson, an elderly gentleman in his eighties, who was her neighbor. She gained his confidence and trust by doing grocery shopping and cleaning for him. He gave her a key, and she was able to obtain a blank check from his home, which she made payable to herself for ten thousand dollars."

"She would've had to forge his name," Lyle said, clasping hands behind his head.

"Which she did, and quite well." Linda handed out copies of Gunderson's real signature and Pamela's forged check. "The forgery of Gunderson's signature was nearly identical. She forged Gregory Hansen's signature on the final bank withdrawal she made of $150,000, and that of every other pastor she embezzled from."

Amy examined the documents and returned to her notes. "Pamela Watts didn't serve anywhere near the maximum sentence."

"No, she got three years. She was nineteen, and the jury felt she was young enough to redeem herself. She only served eighteen months in Shakopee, getting time off for good behavior. In fact, Pamela Watts was listed as a model prisoner."

"Did the court records ever indicate why she forged Mr. Gunderson's check? Was there an accomplice?" Lyle asked.

Linda pulled the court file. "Her attorney claimed Pamela got involved with the wrong crowd. But counsel had difficulty finding these friends, and they may never have existed." The air reeked of sulfur, an odor Linda disliked as it gave her a headache. *Detective Morris must be dieting again and having hard boiled eggs for lunch.*

Lyle leaned on a desk, arms crossed. "Her crime wasn't well conceived. She forged one check, and Gunderson caught her."

"But Pamela bided her time, helping her neighbor for months before she stole anything. She had the patience to commit a serious crime. However, she completely misjudged that Gunderson would not press charges and back down just because she was a teenager.

And she insisted that Gunderson had wanted her to have the money." Linda clasped her hands behind her head. "She said on the stand it was all a misunderstanding. Mr. Gunderson might have been old, but he was no dummy. The money Pamela took was a substantial amount for him, and his attorney asked for the maximum sentence."

The phone on Amy's desk jangled; and after a moment's hesitation, she answered the call.

Linda continued to speak. "It's fortunate for us that Pamela got caught because, as a convicted felon, she and her aliases were in the NCIC database. So she turned to embezzling, which takes longer to detect, especially if you're good at it. She always left town whenever congregations began to suspect her."

"Literally absconding with the church funds." Lyle stretched his arms above his head. "Any possibility of interviewing Mr. Gunderson?"

"Long gone. Died in 1986 at the age of ninety-two."

"We have a good idea of her MO—preying on the vulnerable." Lyle waved an open hand toward the murder board. "I can't help but believe her anger at being abandoned as an infant is the real motive here."

Linda crinkled her nose, still smelling the intense odor of hard boiled eggs. "I'm torn about that theory. She had a loving family— parents who adopted her, and later two beautiful children and a handsome husband. Yet she threw it all away in an inconceivable manner."

"I have always believed—and I think you do, too—that money truly is at the root of all evil. We've both seen murder committed for far less."

Linda acknowledged Lyle's statement with a shake of her head and glanced toward Amy, who was rapidly scribbling on a legal pad. "I keep returning to the reason she became this amoral being. I can't dismiss the idea that discovering you were left by your mother or father, to die for all we know, evolved into a relentless rage. Sister Monica disagrees, but I'm not convinced."

Amy dropped the receiver into the cradle of her phone. "Sorry to interrupt, but that was the Minnesota Bureau of Criminal Investigations. I have disturbing news."

23

The same day
Minutes later

Linda grabbed a chair from an unoccupied desk. "Let's have it."

"We thought Reverend Gordon Sayles was a father figure to Pamela, but the good pastor had some nasty skeletons in his closet." Amy ran an index finger along the page. "While they were married, Sayles was caught having sexual intercourse with an inmate and fired by the prison. This inmate claimed Sayles raped her when he was providing spiritual guidance in his office. Sayles denied the allegations, calling the woman a 'mentally disturbed liar.' But other inmates came forward with similar tales of Sayles forcing himself on them."

Linda's shoulders hunched, her dejected face in her hands. "Was Sayles convicted?"

"Yes. He was sentenced to twenty years at the Minnesota Sexual Offenders facility in Moose Lake, Minnesota."

"Wow," Lyle said. "Do we know his current whereabouts?"

"He died of pancreatic cancer in 1995."

"Can you blame Pamela?" Linda said sympathetically. "I'm not justifying her crimes, but this woman cannot catch a break. Interesting that her prey of choice were all widowed pastors."

Lyle stretched his long legs. "What if Pamela knew these men earlier in life and they, like Sayles, did something that scarred her, and it became her goal to extract punishment?"

Linda's lips drew into a tight smile. "Nice work, Amy. As to your theory, Lyle, it would require meticulous planning to reenter their lives as someone they wouldn't recognize. It's worth investigating that angle, but we'll have to push much deeper into her past. These were recently widowed men, sucked in by her charm. They lived all over the Midwest, so she'd have had to track their movements and lifestyles. It's a long shot at best. Plus, the pastors' wives all succumbed to cancer."

"What if they didn't, but were murdered instead?" Lyle stated.

Linda felt jitters up her spine. "You mean Pamela killed them to get close to these men?" She shook her head. "That's farfetched at best. She'd have to be a criminal genius." She thought a moment. "If you want to pursue this approach, start with Sayles. It will take tenacious investigators willing to go over the same territory multiple times. If you hit a dead end, let it go. We need to get these murders solved."

"Agreed. But I'm willing to delve in if the road takes us there," Lyle said. "I have a gut feeling widowed pastors aren't the only common denominator that connects everyone."

Linda cocked her head. "I'll contact former LPD officers who have moved onto other departments. A lot have stayed in the Midwest. It can't hurt. They may have stumbled across a link we've overlooked."

Lyle and Amy nodded their heads in unison.

"I'll request that list," Linda said, rising from the chair. *Maybe Lyle is onto something,* Linda thought, returning to her office. *Only time will answer that.*

24

DECEMBER 6, 2002
St. Louis, Missouri
BUCK'S HOME

From the moment the website launched, the response was remarkable. It had allowed them to broadcast live on KNSL, which served the St. Louis Metropolitan area and beyond. With the combination of live and taped broadcast formats, *The Road to Calvary* was bringing in plenty of money to pay for programming.

Sitting in Buck's home office, Ray peered over his shoulder at dozens of prayer requests, completely in awe.

"This is a lot of folks asking me to pray for them, which is great. I never imagined we'd get this kind of response so quickly."

Buck turned his chair toward Ray. "That's why I wanted you to see for yourself and decide how to proceed. Are you serious about answering each individual prayer request?"

"Absolutely."

"Do you want me to create a form letter for you to sign? We can type in the specific issue they've asked you to pray over, so it doesn't appear to be a form letter."

Ray's voice was firm. "No form letters. Personal responses to people's needs are important. They remember that."

"There must be over a hundred requests here." Buck pointed to the computer screen. "This will be time-consuming."

"I'm aware of that. But these folks are seeking guidance, and a personal response to their situation shows that *The Road to Calvary* isn't some canned program asking for money. Most of these requests came in via email. You may not know this, but I used to type a hundred words a minute. I'm up to the challenge, and it will serve us well in the long run."

"Are you comfortable reading emails off a computer screen?"

Ray considered Buck's question. "Forward them to me as emails every Wednesday, and we'll see how it works out."

"Once a week it is." Buck sat back in his chair, smiling. "I never knew you typed a hundred words a minute."

"Probably closer to a hundred and ten. My father believed typing was an important skill for a pastor to have because a lot of the time, there was no church secretary. Lorraine, God bless her, spent many hours typing correspondence for me, usually during Easter and Christmas." Ray was silent, misty-eyed at the memory of his dead wife. "Then she got sick, and it was up to me again . . ." His voice trailed off. Rousing himself, Ray turned to Buck, his voice strong and enthusiastic once more. "Let's get started."

The second week in December, Ray sat at his desk reviewing prayer requests—everything including family squabbles, illnesses, chemical dependency, financial problems, and work-related issues. One stood out—written in elegant script by someone who understood good penmanship. It concerned a family matter. Ray held the letter in his hands and began reading.

Dear Rev. Ray,

My name is Ruth Perkins, and I have watched your wonderful program, The Road to Calvary, *since it went on the air. I have seen the many miracles you've performed, and, while it is difficult for me to ask, I request your assistance in a family matter.*

My daughter, Emma, and her husband, Jack, have had a troubled marriage for some time and are considering divorce. Quite frankly, they married far too young with a baby on the way, which put their union under stress from the start. Both were in college at the time, and my son-in-law finished his degree and works as an engineer in the medical field. Emma wasn't so lucky. It's not that Jack held her back, but another baby convinced her she should stay home raising the girls.

As the years have gone by and the girls have grown, Emma's bitterness regarding her lack of education and career opportunities has steadily increased. It's not as if Jack hasn't encouraged her to complete her schooling and find work that interests her—that she finds "fulfilling" is how the young people phrase it.

I want to see them attempt marriage counseling again, but Emma has a stubborn streak which often turns to anger. Reverend, I can't bear to see my granddaughters suffer because their parents divorce or see my family torn apart. Is there anyone you could suggest to help mend this situation without my coming across as meddling? I would especially appreciate your prayers.

God bless you and your fine work.

Sincerely,
Mrs. Ruth Perkins

Ray propped his elbows on his desk, re-reading the letter. Mrs. Perkins was clearly worried her family was collapsing, and he understood her fear of being perceived as nosy. These domestic situations were never just about the couple but the entire family, and he wondered if Mrs. Perkins's daughter might be more receptive to family counseling than marriage counseling.

He positioned the letter next to the computer, contemplating the blank screen. While he admired Mrs. Perkins's penmanship, Ray would never be able to answer all the incoming prayer requests personally if he used that approach.

Dear Mrs. Perkins,

Thank you for your letter. It is always a pleasure to hear from our viewers, especially those who have been with us from the beginning.

You mentioned your daughter, Emma, being a bit stubborn when approached regarding further counseling, and I can certainly understand your frustration at what you may perceive as her unwillingness to continue. Some people view having to get counseling as failure, and nothing could be further from the truth. It takes courage to try and fix something that is broken. It takes courage to accept that you need support, and perhaps that's where Emma's hesitancy is coming from.

With that in mind, I am enclosing information regarding Dr. Jane Moore, whose family counseling work is in the St. Louis area. Dr. Moore's therapy focuses on helping the entire family anticipate triggers that are cause for disharmony. I can't guarantee success or even that Emma will agree to it. Perhaps, she would be more open to family counseling than therapy focusing on their marriage.

I would also recommend that a person besides you (Emma's husband, Jack, for example) be the one to suggest the family meet with Dr. Moore. This approach should also help concentrate counseling on the entire family.

I will keep your family in my prayers, and please write me again on your family's progress.

In the love of Jesus Christ,
Rev. Ray Williams

The printer hummed, and he retrieved the page for his signature. He made a notation he'd responded to Ruth Perkins on this date. He was glad she had trusted in him and very much hoped she'd stay in touch.

†

December 9, 2002
St. Charles, Missouri
Ruth Perkins's home

Ruth's mail came every morning by 11:15; and she liked to complete her daily walk by then so she might greet the postal carrier, Mr. Wilson (nicknamed "Fuzz"), who'd had this route since Emma was a child. At precisely 11:10, the front bell rang.

"Good morning, Fuzz," Ruth said. "Any mail of interest today, besides bills?"

"Morning, Ruth." Fuzz handed her a stack of catalogues, flyers, and envelopes. "No bills at all, which makes it an extra good day," he said. "There's a letter from a Reverend Williams that looks to be interesting."

Ruth shuffled the mail to bring the reverend's letter to the top. "Only a mail carrier with your experience would recognize this as very important." Not bothering with a letter opener, she tore the envelope by the corner, unfolded the letter, and gave it a cursory look.

"Good news, I hope," Fuzz said.

"Wonderful. I consulted the reverend for advice on Emma and Jack's marital difficulties, and he's provided a therapist for them to contact for family counseling. It's a small step, but one I think worth taking. If Emma has her way, the marriage will wither and die. Jack, on the other hand, has expressed interest in seeing another marriage counselor."

"I'll say a prayer for them at Mass."

Ruth Perkins was beaming, full of newfound energy. "I'm much obliged, Fuzz. I'll take all the prayers I can get."

✝

Ruth phoned Jack at his office and asked him to stop by on his way home. The doorbell chimed at five thirty, and she opened it to find her son-in-law looking quite dapper in a camel overcoat.

"My, but you cut a sharp figure," she said. "Let me take your coat."

"Thanks, Mom," Jack said, giving her a peck on the cheek.

Guiding Jack into her cozy living room, Ruth settled into a Queen Anne chair. "I won't keep you long. I know Emma likes dinner at six o'clock, but I want to run something by you."

Clad in a suit and tie, Jack took a seat on the couch across from her. "Nothing's wrong, I hope?"

"Not quite." Ruth cleared her throat, gathering up her courage. "I hope you won't think me a meddling mother-in-law, but since you and I have had numerous conversations about you and Emma going to marriage counseling again, I contacted someone who provided the name of a therapist who does family counseling."

Jack moved to the edge of the sofa cushion. "That's great. Is it a referral?"

"Yes. Please don't tell Emma, but I got it from Reverend Ray, the preacher on television she absolutely hates." Ruth reached for the therapist's card and handed it to Jack. "This is a therapist specializing in family counseling." Jack listened as Ruth explained what Rev. Ray had suggested. When she finished reading him the letter, Ruth said, "I think part of Emma's pigheadedness comes from my suggesting she do something. She didn't care for the therapist you were working with, so that gave her an excuse to stop going. If you suggest making another attempt, I think she'd be more apt to listen."

Jack brushed the card against the open palm of his hand. "I think you're right. I like the idea of the entire family involved in counseling. Our issues go deeper than our marriage. I'll coordinate schedules and make the appointment. It's a start at least."

Ruth clapped her hands together. "I was hoping you wouldn't be upset with me, Jack. But it isn't fair to you, the girls, and even Emma to hide problems amongst the dust. I know you still love one another, and it breaks my heart to see so much tension and conflict in your relationship."

"Mine, too." Jack stood up. "I appreciate your help, Mom. And I promise, your secret is safe with me."

25

Monday, December 23, 2002
St. Louis, Missouri
The Road to Calvary set

R ay stood before the choir, having completed rehearsal for the Christmas Eve service. "You were all marvelous, simply marvelous," he said, enthusiastically, as he admired the choir members dressed in Christmas red robes. He nodded toward the seamstress, whose sewing magic had produced numerous robes and vestments. "Mildred, you have outdone yourself."

The choir members broke into appreciative applause. "My pleasure." Mildred Watson beamed at Ray. "It's a labor of love."

"I have a special announcement." Ray smiled at the group, their faces attentive with expectation. "KNSL will be filming our Christmas Eve service. Buck will provide the instructions." Ray waved his long arm toward his friend, who he swore was blushing at all the attention.

Buck blinked rapidly. "Hello, everyone. All choir members, altar servers, and anyone else on stage needs to be here by four o'clock. The film crew from KNSL is bringing equipment. Everyone needs to be dressed by then, so the TV station's technicians can get the lights set up. Anyone have questions?" He looked over the assembled group.

Ryan raised his hand. "I don't know about the rest of you, but since it's Christmas Eve, I'd like to run through the service again, particularly the music."

Ray looked over at the excited faces. "I'm not opposed to rehearsing again, if you all are available."

To his amazement, voices responded in unison, "Yes!"

†

Once rehearsal was completed, Ray corralled Buck for a private conversation.

"I want to review this one last time. Immediately following the prayer of deliverance, and while they're still filming, I'll tell the congregation I have a special message. I'll step off the stage and ask Susannah for her hand."

Buck had tried not to show his hesitancy when Ray informed him of his plans to ask Susannah to marry him on live TV. He refrained from asking Ray about his haste to marry a woman both he and Jeff had mounting doubts about. Buck figured their concerns would fall on deaf ears. However, he was startled by Ray's decision that the KNSL staff wouldn't know about the proposal until it happened.

Buck held up an arm. "Can I ask you something?" He had an inkling of what was motivating his friend to take such a permanent step so soon.

"Sure."

"Why now, at Christmas?" Buck asked, giving Ray a cheerful grin.

Ray hesitated, looking around the room to be certain they were alone. "The message of the Gospel, and you are familiar with this, is that the birth of Jesus Christ brought light into a world consumed by darkness. Susannah is not a Christ figure; however, she has brought a shining light into my life, and I wish to share it with her. I love her with all my being."

"Well, Ray, I do see the positive effect she has on you," he said, not altogether truthfully. Buck took a deep breath; it wasn't often that he challenged Ray, but if he wasn't going to present his concerns, he at least felt he needed to make a decisive point about the broadcast itself. "You're sure KNSL won't think you're using the broadcast for personal gain?"

"The proposal will be its own entity, after the service is complete. If they balk after the fact, I will take full responsibility with KNSL. You have my word."

Contemplating Ray's words for a moment, Buck looked Ray square in the eye. "You're the boss. Maybe this kind of personal moment shared with viewers is exactly what we need."

26

December 24, 2002
St. Louis, Missouri
The Road to Calvary set

Ray and Susannah greeted members of the congregation as they filed in, and he was pleasantly surprised to see Sally Sullivan, the young woman who had helped select Susannah's engagement ring. An older woman with her was using a walker, and Ray surmised she must be Aunt Julia.

Stepping forward to greet them, he gave a charismatic smile and extended his hand. "Miss Sally Sullivan, how wonderful to see you! And this lovely lady must be Aunt Julia."

Genuinely surprised, the elderly woman balanced herself on her walker as she shook Ray's hand. "Why, it's a pleasure to meet you, Reverend! And to call me by name on a first visit—I feel right at home."

Sally almost blew Ray's carefully kept secret. "Well, the reverend and I, we—" Glancing at Susannah's unadorned ring finger, she caught herself. "We know each other from my writing a request to pray for your health, Aunt Julia," she fibbed.

Susannah was at Ray's shoulder in an instant, her gaze coolly sizing Sally up. She stiffly extended her hand. "That's funny, Ray wouldn't recognize you on sight; prayer requests aren't usually handled in person."

The meeting was verging on the disastrous. Ray remembered Sally telling him her aunt was recovering from a major heart attack and surgery and asking him to pray for her. "Julia was recovering from a life-or-death situation, and I felt it appropriate to meet with her niece in person. We discussed visiting at the hospital but met at the mall where Sally works instead. We had coffee at Starbucks in the Galleria Mall."

"Yes, we did," Sally added, still grasping Susannah's tightening hand. "I very much appreciate the reverend taking time from his busy schedule to meet with me. And as you can see, my aunt Julia is on the mend."

"Oh, for heaven's sake, it was just a little heart attack," the old woman said, waving her hand dismissively.

Sally rolled her eyes. "A heart attack that almost killed you."

Susannah finally released her grip, and the young woman said to her aunt, "We need to find a seat. We're looking forward to the service, Reverend."

Seeming to realize her suspicions were unfounded, Susannah smiled warmly at the women. "I'm so glad you're better, Julia. And welcome to *The Road to Calvary*."

Ray breathed a sigh of relief and checked his jacket pocket, making sure he hadn't forgotten the ring.

Ray searched through the crowd, seeing many additional faces. He felt a surging pride at the show's growing membership and improving the aesthetics of the set. The stage was covered in red and white poinsettias donated by parishioners. Christmas candles burned, and a solitary gold star glowed above the stage.

The live broadcast was flawless. Ray felt slight tremors in his hands, realizing he was more anxious than he expected.

"We have seen God shining His presence in His gift to us of His only son. This infant will change the world, ministering to people through divine miracles and healing. Every one of us has the opportunity to experience God's miracles if we open ourselves to His divine plan and love."

Ray paused, casting an eye over the attentive faces. "But before we go forth to celebrate the miracle of Christ's birth, I have a declaration I wish to share with all of you. Many of you know that I've been a widower many years, having lost my wife to cancer. When I started *The Road to Calvary* back in 1997, I did my best to serve God and you, my congregation, unconcerned about my own needs. Until recently, I thought perhaps my being alone was God's will, part of His perfect plan for me. Then I realized He had another plan."

He paused again, surveying his audience, curious faces waiting for their pastor to continue. "That plan was the realization I could accomplish more with a partner."

The reverend left the stage, walked to the front row where Susannah was seated, and stood before her. Dressed in a red sheath, her auburn hair framing her face, Ray thought for a brief moment he spied the aura radiating from her being. "After an existence of being alone, I've met someone who has changed my life." Ray stretched his long arm toward Susannah, his smile that of a man deeply content. "Susannah, would you please join me?"

Susannah rose, accepting Ray's beckoning hand and facing him. He sensed the cameras were still rolling. "Susannah Baker, you have enriched my life beyond my greatest dreams. And I am asking you, here, before God and these Christian witnesses, if you will join me in the covenant of Christian marriage and partnership?"

Her fingers slipped from his grasp, covering her mouth in stunned silence, joyful tears glistening against her cheeks. He used his free hand to retrieve the black velvet box from his coat pocket, displaying the solitaire diamond ring. The expectant crowd gasped in excitement, anxiously waiting for Susannah's response. Regaining her composure, she proclaimed loud enough for all present to hear, "Yes, Ray, I would be honored to join you in the bond of Christian marriage."

Ray passed the microphone off to Ryan and taking her slender left hand, slipped the sparkling solitaire on her finger. Susannah inhaled at the beauty of the ring as tears streamed down her flushed cheeks. On their feet now, audience members clapped and cheered. From the back of the back of the congregation a voice shouted, "Kiss her, Reverend!"

Ray smiled at Susannah, and they kissed tenderly. Ryan returned the microphone to the beaming Rev. Ray, who tried unsuccessfully to quiet the audience. "Thank you, thank you." The crowd gave the couple a standing ovation.

At last, the audience settled down, and Ray spoke into the microphone, "My brothers and sisters, on this blessed day of Christmas Eve, let us go forth to love one another and celebrate the birth of our Savior, Jesus Christ. Amen."

The KNSL crew was still filming as the crowd circled around them, with congratulations and shouts of "Merry Christmas!" For far too long, Ray had sacrificed any type of relationship, always maintaining that his duty as a pastor serving his congregation was his primary calling. Yet, as he stood here, surrounded by worshippers ecstatic with the news of his impending marriage, he realized that Susannah was the perfect helpmate, and that, as partners, they could accomplish far greater good than he could alone.

A heavy woman grasped Ray's forearm to shake it. "Thank you, Reverend Ray, for helping heal the rift in my family. Jesus brought my children back together. My kids were skeptical at first; but when I told them you called me by name and knew about our problems, they became convinced. After many years of being angry with one another, we're going to celebrate Christmas as a family."

Ray smiled. "If we truly believe, the Lord is there for us, Thelma."

Still clutching his arm, Thelma clasped Susannah by the wrist. "And congratulations to the both of you! This is wonderful news."

✝

Ruth would be attending Christmas Eve services later with Emma, Jack, and the girls, but she was delighted *The Road to Calvary* was carrying a live broadcast. It had been a lovely service; but the moment the Reverend Ray presented Susannah Baker with the glittering diamond solitaire, Ruth had found herself reaching for tissues to dry cascading tears. The romance of the reverend asking the woman he loved to marry him after being so long alone had gotten to her, but so had memories of her own happy marriage. And, now, perhaps her daughter and son-in-law were on their way to mending their troubled union.

Clutching a tissue, Ruth dialed 1-800-HE-SAVES, which scrolled at the bottom of the TV. Next to it also scrolled the tag line: *The Road to Calvary—Your Salvation Station.*

"Merry Christmas, and thank you for calling *The Road to Calvary.* How may I help you?" a man's voice asked Ruth over the phone.

"Excuse me, the Reverend Ray's proposal to Miss Baker brought tears to my eyes," Ruth sniffled. "What a beautiful service. I want to make a Christmas donation in the amount of five thousand dollars."

On the other end of the line, Buck thought he recognized the elderly woman's voice.

Large donations were increasing in frequency and he was certain this was her, but he wanted to choose his words carefully. "This wouldn't by chance be Mrs. Ruth Perkins of St. Charles, would it?" As three ex-wives could attest, he was a charmer, but never phony.

"Why, yes, it is. How did you know it was me, Mr.—"

"Call me Buck, Mrs. Perkins. We've spoken in the past, and I recognized your voice and a prayer request. I remember you so well because we don't receive many handwritten letters."

"A dying art, I'm afraid. I'll be using the same credit card as before."

†

On set, groups were still congratulating Ray and Susannah twenty minutes later.

"Now, you understand how I know Reverend Ray." Sally Sullivan came up to Susannah. "I almost spilled the beans, but the reverend has offered guidance regarding my aunt's health issues, too."

Putting her left hand, where her engagement ring shone under the studio lights, prominently on Sally's shoulder, Susannah was all apologies. "I apologize for being short with you. It never occurred to me that Ray would meet someone making a prayer request in person. And a marriage proposal certainly wasn't on my mind!"

"Apology accepted. And that ring looks great on your finger."

"It fits perfectly!"

"Well, I told Ray to make asking you for your ring size part of an ordinary conversation, so you wouldn't catch on."

Susannah pretended to look sternly at Ray. "That's where the 'You have such delicate hands' conversation came from."

Ray smiled. "I had to find out somehow without giving my true intentions away!"

Balancing on her walker, Aunt Julia smiled at the happy couple. "Well, this truly is a memorable visit. Congratulations and Merry Christmas!"

Across the soundstage, unnoticed by almost anyone, Jeff Jones sat alone, observing the celebration. Since KNSL had brought camera equipment and operators, he hadn't filled his usual role. *I might not be very smart,* Jeff thought, *but I'm smart enough to realize* The Road to Calvary *is changing.* He was glad Ray hadn't shut down production, but this was no longer the pastor he had once felt so close to. He felt less and less useful, and Ray's agreeing to look for larger markets surprised him.

His and Buck's mounting concerns about Susannah and her increasing influence over Ray and the show's direction seemed to be a point not worth arguing over. Ray was going to marry her. Jeff had a sickening feeling in his stomach that he and Buck were going to have to be extra cautious in their dealings with the reverend's fiancée.

27

Saturday, January 25, 2003
St. Louis, Missouri
Buck's home

Success seemed to be raining down on *The Road to Calvary* in sheets of good news. To Buck's astonishment, Susannah's two-minute Christian beauty tip segments were an instant hit. Women sent in their stories of makeup triumphs right along with the prayer requests. Susannah was often insufferable, forever reminding Buck and Jeff that makeup was the component that made them different from every other religious broadcast.

The segments did separate the program from other religious fare. As Buck suspected, Susannah relished the attention parishioners lavished on her makeup tips. He assumed being noticed was the real reason she had been so insistent on producing them.

Soon after Ray's proposal, Jeff called Buck to discuss the happy couple. Susannah was already making plans for a spring wedding, and the men agreed to meet after New Year's.

Freshly brewed coffee infused the air of the small kitchen where Jeff and Buck sat at a wooden table in the early morning. Buck found himself taken aback at how quickly Jeff dispensed with the pleasantries. They normally tried to catch up with each other's lives, but this conversation would solely revolve around Susannah Baker.

"It's a weird coincidence that Susannah appeared right as Ray was calling it quits. First Ray listens to everything she says, then he falls in love, and now he wants to marry her. And we don't know a damn thing about this woman." Jeff took a swallow of black coffee from his ceramic mug.

"Agreed," Buck replied, stirring cream into his mug of steaming liquid. "While part of me is glad there's still *The Road to Calvary*, I've never gotten comfortable with this idea of eavesdropping to pull off 'miracles,' no matter what Susannah's rationale."

"Me neither. Honestly, I don't like her or the direction we're headed, and I'm disappointed in Ray. Like I said from the start, this is fraud, ain't it?"

"Yeah, it is. We're using trickery to deceive people into thinking Ray has a direct line to God, and he's healing them. Remember at the beginning how hesitant he was? You can't tell me he doesn't honestly realize this is wrong."

Jeff put down his coffee mug and chuckled. "Direct line to God— wouldn't that be sweet?" He took a deep, heavy breath. "You and I both said that if we were ever uncomfortable with this, we were outta there. At the Christmas Eve show while you worked the phones, I sat and watched all the excitement over their engagement. It made me think I shouldn't be a part of this anymore."

"I hope you're not serious, Jeff." Buck broached the subject of the two of them undertaking research on Ray's bride-to-be. "If we're serious about investigating Susannah's background, we need to act now. We have five months until the wedding, not a lot of time."

Jeff picked up his coffee again. "I'm thinkin' with Susannah soon to be Mrs. Williams, anything we discovered wouldn't change Ray's mind. I'm keepin' my nose outta this." Buck's shoulders drooped. "We've been doing this since the beginning, buddy. We're a team—"

"Used to be a team," Jeff said. "Now, it's whatever Susannah wants, and she almost always gets her way. You think you don't like the current changes? Wait until they get married. She's after somethin'—money for sure, fame, power—I dunno. But it all goes against everything Ray has ever stood for as a preacher."

A spoon tinkled in Buck's mug as he stirred his coffee absentmindedly. "If you leave, what would you tell Ray? He'd be devastated."

"He ain't gonna be devastated, especially now that he has a fiancée," Jeff said, emphasizing the word *fiancée* sarcastically. "Besides, Bush is talkin' about invading Iraq soon. I'm thinkin' seriously of reenlisting in the army."

Buck's posture went from slouched to ramrod straight. "Jesus, Jeff, you were awarded a fucking Silver Star in Desert Storm! Why risk going back?"

"Thanks for the appreciation, dude, but I was doin' my job." Jeff paused, running his open palm over his short-cropped hair. "Right now, I'm more afraid of Susannah Baker than any Iraqi enemy. Maybe if we could uncover her story before Ray marries her, I'd feel differently."

"I don't believe for a minute that our broadcast stopped her from committing suicide before she came here. If the program was that powerful, it wouldn't require trickery now." Buck clasped his hands behind his head. "And Ray, a guy who's been a widower for a long time, fell for her hard and fast."

"That's what I'm talkin' about, bro. Not so much as a mention of another woman, then boom! Wouldn't even admit that he and Susannah were livin' together; it was this big secret. They honestly thought we didn't know."

Buck's arms were outstretched. "I've had my share of experience with picking the wrong woman. After enough bad choices, you become a good judge of character. There's something not right about her tale of suffering. I tell you what. Let's get on the internet in my office—there's a new search engine called Google that's pretty popular." Buck stood up. "And maybe I can keep you from reenlisting and getting yourself killed."

Jeff laughed. "We haven't even gone to war yet. Just somethin' I'm considerin'. But I'm game for your internet search idea."

In his office, Buck motioned for Jeff to pull up a chair. "I recently got a broadband connection, sure as hell a lot faster than dial-up." In the blank box above the colorful letters spelling out G-O-O-G-L-E, Buck typed in "Susannah Baker, St. Louis, MO" and hit search. There were pages of Baker family genealogy, and a few listed Susannah Bakers, but they had died decades ago.

"Maybe Baker isn't her real name," Jeff suggested.

"My gut instinct says it isn't, but I haven't got any proof of it."

"Yet." Jeff moved his chair closer. "She must have a driver's license because she had that old Buick she sold."

Buck sat back from the computer screen and looked at his friend. "You obviously have a strategy."

"Yeah, we get a copy of her driver's license."

"How are you planning to do that?" Buck asked with a nervous twitch.

"We get a copy of her license and take it to the St. Louis PD. A buddy of mine, Malachi Johnson, joined the force after we returned from Iraq. He's a detective now. I'll send him the information we've collected and explain the situation. He has access to other databases, and we'll see if that's even her real name." Jeff's arms opened expansively. "Even though we work in the building, we've got to get the layout down cold, specifically where she leaves her purse and the distance to the copier."

As edgy as their plan made him, Buck couldn't believe what he said next. "Maybe we should go over there now and start memorizing the layout."

"Sounds like a plan, bro," Jeff said with a hearty slap to Buck's back. "Man, I haven't felt this jazzed since I was a ranger!"

28

Wednesday, February 19, 2003
St. Louis, Missouri
The Road to Calvary set

B uck and Jeff channeled all energy into their covert operation. They set a deadline to come up with her license. Over three weeks, they monitored Susannah's regular placement of her handbag in Ray's office, always on a chair in the corner out of view. They memorized the building's layout in case they required an escape route or hiding place. Ray's office was almost never locked, but to be sure, Jeff and Buck checked and rechecked the door. Neither knew how to pick a lock, so if somebody decided a locked door was warranted, they were screwed.

And then the plan unfolded. As Jeff filmed Ray ending the show in prayer, he realized tonight was going to be tricky, and everything had to fall exactly as it had over the previous few weeks. Through the camera's lens, Ray finished the prayer of deliverance, and after a fifteen-second pause, Jeff yelled, "That's a wrap!"

Now that Buck had phone duty, Jeff had taken on the added responsibilities of stage director. Immediately, Ray and Susannah headed toward the entrance, shaking hands and chatting with parishioners.

Buck would come up front and make sure Ray and Susannah kept their attention on the members. If everyone said their good-byes sooner than expected, Buck was charged with distracting them a bit longer. Buck was a talker, and he could gab endlessly about the merits of getting more employees answering donation requests.

Nearly twenty minutes passed with no sign of Buck. Jeff saw the visitors' line getting shorter; there were perhaps a dozen remaining. He suspected Buck was still taking donations. Adrenaline pumping, Jeff realized he would need to copy Susannah's license himself. After he passed by the stage, he would no longer have visual contact and would be flying blind.

He walked purposefully toward the office, glancing over his shoulder and assessing Ray and Susannah's involvement in conversation. Maybe five minutes tops, he thought. At the office door, he turned the knob, pushing to open it. The door didn't budge, and for a moment, panic crept up his spine. Was it locked? *Shit.*

Jeff could still hear Ray and Susannah talking with members of the congregation as he gave the door a hard shove with his broad shoulders. The stuck door loosened, and he quickly entered Ray's darkened office. He debated turning the lights on—how much time could he afford to waste looking for her bag in the inky blackness? He switched the fluorescent lights on and found her leather shoulder bag in the corner. He stopped to listen—chatter was still coming from near the exit.

Opening her purse, he retrieved Susannah's wallet and immediately found what he was looking for. Removing the Missouri driver's license from behind the translucent plastic, Jeff sprinted to the copy room next door. The copier was warmed up, turned on beforehand. He placed her license on the glass and pushed start, the mechanism photocopying the document flashing beneath the cover.

The copy complete, he folded the paper neatly and placed it in his back pocket. Rushing back to the office, Jeff could hear two or three distant voices. He didn't recall his nerves being this shaky in Iraq.

His fingers seemed fat and oversized as he struggled to return the license to its proper place and replace Susannah's wallet.

He never heard the footsteps. "Jeff, what are you doing in here? And with Susannah's bag?" Ray's voice was stern, edging toward accusatory.

Jeff spun around, making up the lie as he spoke. "I thought I left my keys in here and came to look for them. I found them on the floor—they must've fell outta my pocket—and I knocked Susannah's purse off the chair when I knelt to grab 'em. I spilled her stuff all over and just finished putting it all back. Totally my fault, Ray. I apologize."

From around the corner, Buck appeared slightly out of breath. "We need more staff answering the phone. We had over a hundred fifty calls tonight, and those are the ones I managed to get answered. There were probably others, but there's no way I can continue to be the only person on the phone and monitoring conversations. I need help."

Buck's plea diverted Ray's attention from Jeff to the matter of money and staff.

"Over a hundred fifty calls? That's great, Buck! Any idea how much money we brought in?"

It was a risk, but Jeff would have to take it. Buck and Ray stood in the doorway blocking his exit, and the only way out was to brush past them as if nothing had happened. *Like bein' in enemy territory*, he thought to himself and slipped past the men engrossed in deep conversation.

Ray's attention was captivated by the numbers. "The good Lord blesses us indeed."

"Here's another thing. We need phones answered during the rebroadcasts, and not by an answering service. Staff needs to be working the phones, the same as during the live broadcasts."

Buck had positioned his body between Ray and Jeff, giving his friend the opportunity to slip into the shadows, away from further questions.

Jeff was safely in the hallway, their conversation fading. As he walked away, he heaved a huge sigh of relief at his quick thinking and went on as if nothing had happened.

✝

Minutes later, Jeff was completing his shutdown of all studio equipment when Susannah stopped him. "Have you seen Ray?"

He was calm and polite. "He and Buck were discussin' gettin' extra help with the phones in Ray's office, where I left 'em. There were lots of calls, which is good, but Buck can't handle 'em all." He grinned at her. "I've turned everything off and need to get goin'. Would you tell Ray I had to go, and I'll see you all next week?"

"I'll tell him, Jeff," she said, clearly excited. "Can't wait to hear about all these phone calls. Have a good week."

"You too," Jeff said, not meaning it at all.

He grabbed his coat, and as he left the building, he patted his back pocket to make sure the paper was still there. He didn't dare take it out to look at it; he would do that at home. *I gotta call Malachi. We need the help of police to figure this out,* he thought and drove off into the winter's night.

29

Saturday, February 22, 2003
St. Louis, Missouri
The Road to Calvary set

Buck was regretting his appeal for assistance with callers. Ray had found Seth Benson and Cole Leon through his friend Doug Snyder, who helped recovering drug addicts turn their lives around, and Buck just hoped they could be trusted with money. His own recovery had taught him to be wary of tempting addicts with money that wasn't theirs. However, he had proven to Ray and his full-time employer that he could handle it. *Don't be so damned judgmental,* he berated himself. *Give these guys a fair chance.*

It was taking Jeff's detective friend forever to come back with answers, but Buck realized this probably wasn't a priority. He needed to focus his attention on training Cole and Seth. He hated that Ray was allowing Susannah to help. He couldn't let her corrupt them by insisting they push would-be donors for larger amounts.

Susannah smiled brightly as she instructed their newest employees. "It's imperative we treat our donors as family so they'll feel good contributing again. Double-check the amount they want to contribute, but don't be afraid to ask if they can't give just a little more, to help us do God's work. After you write out the receipt, move onto the next call as quickly as possible."

Damn it, Susannah! I knew you should never be involved in training these guys. Buck figured he would have to quietly tell them not to be aggressive and ignore what Susannah said.

"How many calls are we talking about?" Seth asked, tattoo sleeves of symbols and colors covering his arms.

She answered before Buck could even open his mouth. "Two hundred calls at least. That's the current number, correct?"

Buck turned toward Susannah, his quizzical face questioning her statement. "No, that number is too high. For the live broadcast, the numbers are closer to one fifty. With the pre-recorded broadcasts, numbers tend to be lower."

Susannah shrugged Buck off. "That will change when we launch the live Sunday service next week. It's only a matter of time before we get three hundred calls per broadcast. And they'll keep climbing. Soon we'll have a whole team in place, answering phones to meet the demand!"

Buck was thoroughly annoyed with her but tried hard to stem his increasing irritation. "While considering the future is nice, we need to focus on the present. It's important that all the calls get answered with courtesy and in a professional manner. We don't pressure individuals into giving—"

"Of course, we don't want to *pressure* anyone," Susannah interrupted Buck, emphasizing the word pressure. She honed her gaze on Seth. "But if they are willing to increase their donation, that's wonderful. Remember, it's all for the great cause of doing God's work!"

Cole frowned. "You're each saying different things. Are we, or are we not, to pressure people for additional money?"

Buck made his point quicker. "Accept their contribution, thank them for their generosity, and move to the next call. We want this to be meaningful, so they'll give again."

Susannah's nostrils flared, and Buck recognized that if her eyes had been daggers, they would have cut right into him. "There is absolutely nothing wrong with asking for a little bit more!" she snarled.

Buck observed the tense expressions on Cole and Seth's wide-eyed faces and tried to smooth things over. "When you're comfortable in the job, you'll get a sense of who you might be able to ask for larger donations. But for now, let's concentrate on answering the phones well." Buck sensed from Susannah's narrowing eyes that she wasn't happy. This conversation would get back to Ray, and Buck had to be strong.

She looked over at Cole and Seth. "As soon as you are comfortable, however, getting donations above the amount pledged will be a priority."

Buck fought the urge to sigh or roll his eyes. *You won't quit, will you?*

As he expected, Buck heard from Ray that Susannah had voiced her irritation about his training methods.

"Susannah's concerned you're not training Seth and Cole to be assertive enough. My lovely fiancée can be quite forceful in her opinions, but I want to hear your side." They were alone in Ray's office.

Buck straightened up to his full height, knowing he would need to state his case decisively. "Let me finish this, Ray. I've worked on the phones since the beginning. With all due respect, Susannah has done it a few times, but it's about more than getting donations. Building relationships is what makes for repeat donors."

Ray sided with him, but Buck was reminded of the disagreement every time he encountered Susannah's stinging gaze in the ensuing weeks. Still, somebody had to start telling this woman no.

Cole and Seth both proved to be exceptionally fast studies, and Buck grew confident in their work and trustworthiness. All he needed to worry about was Susannah.

30

MARCH 7, 2003
St. Charles, Missouri
Emma's home

Ruth Perkins didn't much care for birthdays, at least not her own. From her common-sense perspective, every passing year was simply a number, and reaching eighty in good health was no more significant than turning fifty. But Emma had other ideas.

Emma insisted this was a milestone to be celebrated. Her original idea had involved the planning of a party that Ruth determined too closely resembled a wake and politely declined. In addition, Ruth's birthday fell in early March, and you could never be sure winter storms wouldn't blow in and make for risky travel. Ruth would have rather have gotten cards from her family and been done with it.

But the forecast remained clear with no sign of a winter storm in any part of Missouri. Emma had honed her stubborn streak for her entire life and would not be denied giving her mother a party. After much argument, Ruth eventually relented, agreeing to a small family celebration. Appeased, Emma presented her mother with her favorite meal of beef stroganoff, which Ruth noted she hadn't cooked for herself since Orville had died.

The dinner dishes had been cleared, and the small group of Emma,

Jack, the girls, Jack's sister Andrea, her spouse, Bob, and their sons, Nick and Jake, all wore "Happy Birthday" polka-dot paper hats.

Katrina snapped pictures. "Smile, Grandma!" she said as the flash popped, temporarily blinding Ruth while the group hit the final notes of "Happy Birthday."

Emma carried what looked to be an enormous chocolate cake—it had to be to accommodate all those candles—and Katrina commanded, "Make a wish, Grandma," as Ruth sucked air into her lungs and blew it back out as hard as she could, extinguishing every candle. The family clapped and cheered at Grandma's lung capacity.

"Jack, go ahead and get Mom started opening her presents. Katrina and Elizabeth, you come into the kitchen and help me cut the cake."

His own party hat slightly askew, Jack asked his wife, "What's the rush, Emma? Let's eat some cake and ice cream; then Mom can open her presents. Nobody's going anywhere."

"The girls have school tomorrow—"

"Mom," Katrina interrupted, clearly annoyed, "we're in college. We don't even live at home anymore."

As if she couldn't stand Katrina getting in the final word, Emma said abruptly, "You're not living at home *right* now." Her feet stamped loudly into the kitchen.

"Mom, quit treating us like little kids," Elizabeth chided.

This comment elicited a short and surly, "Forget I said anything."

"Let's go help your mom," Andrea said to the girls to ease the tension.

"Dad?" Nick asked, avoiding looking at his grandma. "Can we go play some video games? This is kinda boring."

"Sure, but only until Grandma opens her presents. Is that all right, Jack?" Bob asked.

"Fine," Nick replied and gave Ruth a sheepish grin before he sprinted into the living room.

"I'll come, too," Bob called after them.

"That Emma, always so bossy. The girls are right. They're young women now." Ruth paused, and Jack smiled wistfully. She eyed the kitchen, making sure Emma was out of hearing range. "How's the family counseling going? I can't ask Emma."

"It's going very well. We're making progress and meeting every week with Dr. Moore, but Emma still has trouble hearing she's too controlling from anybody, whether it's you, me, or the girls. But especially from me."

"Well, it sounds as though you're making some progress."

"Yeah, we have good sessions and bad. But this Dr. Moore that the Reverend Ray recommended has years of counseling experience. She gives us exercises to do as a family, and those are very helpful."

Their conversation ceased as Katrina appeared carrying a tray of coffee cups.

"Here you go, Grandma. And Dad, we put cream in yours."

"Thanks, honey," Jack said, smiling at his lovely daughter.

"Thank you, sweetheart."

They could hear the boys shouting over the video game as they sipped their coffee.

Ruth replaced the cup in the saucer before she spoke. "The Reverend Ray asked me to let him know how you're doing. I hope you won't mind if I write him back. This is a very positive sign."

Jack didn't reply, and Ruth realized his gaze was focused over her shoulder and into the kitchen.

Then, she heard Emma's angry voice rising steadily. She turned in her chair; Emma was wielding a cake knife in her clenched fist, her face flushed. "You mean to tell me that both of you are in on this, and you asked that shyster evangelist for a referral? Mother, how dare you do this behind my back—?"

"Emma, that's enough!" Jack retorted. "Dr. Moore's insights are good for all of us."

"Enough? Excuse me, Jack, but you're discussing our marital and family problems in front of God and everybody, and you expect me not to make a scene?"

"We were only talking among family, Em. You're making way too much out of this."

Ruth spoke up. "Jack's right, dear. You're making a scene." She thought to herself that Emma's temper was getting the best of her again.

It was a mistake to side with her son-in-law because now Emma was shouting at everyone, waving the knife wildly and sending bits of cake and icing flying across the dining room. "That's right. It's always Emma's fault. No one else is to blame. No one." She gulped a breath of air, her fury rising. "I cannot believe you asked that goddamned preacher for advice. Advice and a referral! You lied to me, Jack. You said *you* found Dr. Moore!"

Emma was cut off by an artificially cheerful Andrea, who breezed past her with plates of cake and ice cream.

"Here we go—cake and ice cream for the birthday girl. And you, little brother." She set plates before Ruth and Jack. "Who besides me needs a fork?"

Katrina was on her heels with napkins and silverware, and Elizabeth came carrying more plates of cake and ice cream.

Rigid in the open archway of the kitchen, Emma stood fuming. The rest of her family was returning to the dining room and ignoring her, which made her even more furious. "This family is unbelievable." Tugging at the ties of her apron, Emma pulled it off and let it fall to the floor. "The hell with all of you!" she yelled, her shoes clacking across the wood of the kitchen floor. A door slammed, then the roar of a car engine and a garage door rising.

"Good thing we parked on the street," Bob said from the living room, watching Emma peel out of the driveway, the screeching tires leaving streaks of black rubber. "She's pissed."

"That she is," Jack responded.

"She needs to calm down. Just because Emma doesn't approve of who the referral came from is no reason to act like a child." Ruth shook her head in dismay, silver curls of hair bouncing.

"You know I can slip her some drugs—Xanax, Valium, Prozac— I've got them all," Andrea said, smiling at her brother.

Jack laughed weakly. "Thanks for the offer, but isn't that a felony?"

"Only if I sell them to you."

"Mom didn't have to ruin Grandma's birthday party," Elizabeth said.

Ruth looked at the distraught faces of her family. *At least I talked Emma out of a big celebration.* She told them a white lie in hopes of calming everyone. "She didn't ruin my party, dear. I'm still having a lovely time."

"And that's what we want," Jack said. "As soon as we finish eating, Grandma has presents to open."

31

MONDAY, MARCH 17, 2003
St. Louis, Missouri
THE ROAD TO CALVARY BUILDING

Increased phone calls, revenue, viewers, and a larger audience told Buck that word of Ray's "healing powers" had spread swiftly. People with chronic illnesses, severe pain, and other health issues began attending the show on a regular basis.

Buck also noted that, once again, Susannah saw these healings as an occasion for making money. Susannah was already using these "miraculous events" to cast Ray as a redeemer.

"Don't you see?" she cooed. "These people have put their faith in you, Ray, that they have found a place for healing. We'll want to start promoting your gift." The four of them surrounded the small conference table.

Ray's voice arched up a notch, showing his unhappiness at Susannah's word choice. "This whole healing thing makes me a bit uneasy. It's one thing to help our members face things they have the power to change, like drug addiction or a divided family, but it's another thing to give them false hope around an illness they have no control over."

She stroked his arm softly. "Forgive me if it sounded flip. Think of yourself as the instrument through which God works. I think of the Prayer of St. Francis when he says, 'Make me an instrument of your peace.' I believe God is telling you to be an instrument of healing."

After a long day in IT, Buck's tired body ached, and his voice oozed with sarcasm. "What, we're Catholic now?"

Susannah's anger flashed in her eyes. "Why are you always so rude about nearly every suggestion I make?" she asked, voice cutting. "Plenty of my ideas have worked out quite nicely. But I would appreciate it if you weren't so condescending."

An uncomfortable silence fell over the group; Susannah and Buck were at odds again.

Looking at the men's weary faces, Susannah reddened. "I'm human, too. But it's maddening to get shot down all the time."

Buck shifted uneasily in his chair. They played nice on an artificial level, but neither one cared for the other. He tried another approach. "I apologize for being rude; it's been a tough day. But I'm trying to be realistic. Ray's right, Susannah. We're taking risks the way it is, but promising miraculous healing is something we absolutely cannot provide."

"Yeah, what you're suggestin' is a whole new ballgame," Jeff said, shifting in his seat. "Buck and I told y'all we're both gone if this made us uncomfortable, and right now, I'm feelin' pretty damn uncomfortable."

As quickly as her anger had appeared, it was replaced with a bright smile. "But we didn't ask people looking for healing to search us out. They're here, seeking help and comfort. What's wrong with that?"

"It's giving them false hope. What happens when someone who thinks they were 'cured' by Ray dies? What then, Susannah?" Buck's voice grew louder as he felt the anger simmering inside him. "Don't you think their families will call us out for the frauds we are?"

"We are not *frauds*." Offended, Susannah's eyes grew steely. "My goodness, Buck, what do you take me for? We don't have to promise them anything, just pray with them and be in the moment, as they ask for God's help. This is what I mean, Buck. You're always doubting me—"

Buck threw his hands up. "Because I don't see how it can work. People are coming to us, but we can't heal anybody or make them well! Eavesdropping on their problems to benefit them is one thing, but beyond that, there is nothing we can do for a lot of them—"

"Stop! Please stop arguing, both of you." Ray's strong and forceful voice filled the room.

Caught off guard, Buck and Susannah stopped talking and looked at Ray's reddening face.

"I think we're starting to cross the line here." Ray grimaced. "Buck has a good point. What are we going to do when we fail someone? Aren't we setting ourselves up for legal action or worse?"

Susannah's demeanor changed as though a switch had flipped. She reached out a hand, softly patting Ray on his forearm. "Ray, sweetheart, we're not going to guarantee that they'll recover. I'd be a fool to think we could do that. Focus on Jesus as healer and you as the instrument. What's the harm in trying that approach once?" Her voice was seductively soft; and from his vantage point, Buck could see Ray already starting to waver.

Ray put his hand over hers. "If we focus on the fact that Christ was a healer and cast out demons, I can see that. But I will not get up before this congregation and demand some poor disabled soul get up out of a wheelchair and walk. I'd feel like a carnival huckster."

"It's compassion that I'm referring to." She smiled. "We always connect our message to our Lord and Savior Jesus Christ, who was compassionate toward the outcasts and the sick."

"Are you gentlemen all right with that?" Ray asked, his gaze settling on Buck and Jeff's silent faces.

Buck fidgeted. "I'm not wild about the idea, but I'll give it one time. There are numerous Bible readings showing Jesus as a healer; if you fit the message into a sermon, I can live with it—one time."

"Jeff?"

His muscular arms folded across a solid chest. "Yeah, I guess I'm in."

Ray's shoulders rose and fell as he sighed. "While that approach has had success, it needs to be subtle. I can't guarantee anything," he said, squeezing Susannah's hand. "We seek out individuals with ailments who have a genuine chance at getting better. But as with Jim Jameson, they should be an active part of the process, willing to make lifestyle changes."

"Right." Susannah beamed. "We're taking one small step at a time."

†

Sunday morning, March 23, 2003
St. Louis, Missouri
The Road to Calvary set

Buck hadn't expected things to move along this quickly. Pretending to heal a parishioner, even if backed up with suggestions for how to improve their lives, still made him uncomfortable. There were risks, and he wanted a longer interval to iron out the details. Instead, during rehearsals, Ray informed him that he'd written a sermon focusing on genuine healing.

The money is coming in a steady stream, and regulars are starting to make larger donations, Buck reminded himself. Ruth Perkins donated $10,000 after Ray inquired again on the progress of solving her family difficulties, promising to pray for them. *One thing's for sure, the individualized touch of Ray answering those requests is paying off.*

Buck brought himself back to the task at hand, skimming through the congregation for potential healing candidates. One of the concessions Susannah had made was Ray would not pick out an audience member on every single broadcast, giving the timing of healings more mystery and a sense of divine intervention. And, Buck mused dryly, it kept viewers watching. The conversation of an elderly woman with a cane being assisted down the aisle by a younger man, who appeared to be her son, caught his attention as their voices crackled through his headphones.

"Oh, this knee is killing me. I can still barely walk. I thought you said a knee replacement would fix everything, Paul."

"Mom, you need to keep doing your exercises. You had surgery less than three months ago."

"When you're old, Paul Schaffer, you'll see what pain really is!" the woman replied crossly.

The agitated middle-aged man with thinning hair guided his mother to the front row.

†

Ray stood at the pulpit, perspiring. Watching him, Buck knew this was highly unusual, but he also realized Ray's next words would put a lot at stake, perhaps even *The Road to Calvary's* future.

"The Bible says that Jesus Christ is a healer—casting out demons, healing the sick, bringing Lazarus back from the dead. Jesus performed these healing miracles, just as he can perform them here today."

That was Buck's cue. "Okay, Ray," he whispered into the earpiece. "The heavy-set woman in the front row with the cane had knee surgery three months ago but is still in pain. She's sitting with her son, Paul. Last name is Schaffer."

Ray locked eyes with the old woman. "Mrs. Schaffer, I understand you're recovering from knee surgery. May the healing power of the Lord come upon you to relieve you of your knee pain, so that you might walk freely once more!" he thundered.

Mrs. Schaffer did nothing but stare back at Ray in dazed silence.

"My God," Buck muttered. "This is going to be a disaster."

"Mom, the reverend's talking to you. Stand up!" Paul implored.

Ray thrust out his hand to her, and Mrs. Schaffer rose from her seat, leaving her cane, and walked to meet him at the stage.

The audience held its collective breath as Mrs. Schaffer turned toward them. "These are the first steps I've taken on my own in months!" she explained. "Glory be to our Lord Jesus Christ."

"The Bible says to pray for divine healing!" Ray said, taking her hand. "Keep doing physical therapy, and the Lord will continue to help you heal."

Buck sighed in relief, and his fist punched the air in victory. That wasn't a total lie; he could live with that. Then his attention was diverted by another voice from the audience.

"Reverend Ray, I feel the power of the Lord upon me! He commands me to rise from this wheelchair prison and walk!"

On the monitor, Buck could see Ray struggle to keep his mouth from falling open. A younger woman wearing braids rose from her chair and met him and Mrs. Schaffer at the end of the aisle.

"Praise be to our Lord and Savior!" Ray said, clasping both women's hands and raising them heavenward. "God has a purpose for each of you in life, which you can accomplish with divine healing!" Ray brought them up onto the stage. "You ladies have shown God's power at work in the flesh. What are your names?"

He handed the microphone to the second woman, who spoke in a strong, clear voice. "Hallelujah! I am Dolores Reid, and I thank the Lord and the Reverend Ray for this glorious day!"

Passing the microphone to Mrs. Schaffer, Ray could see that she was almost embarrassed at having to announce her great fortune.

"Hello. My name is Rose Schaffer, and I too thank the Almighty God for ending this awful pain."

Staring at the monitor, Buck's mouth hung open, and he wrung his hands. This was exactly what Ray didn't want, but somehow, it had happened. Right before their eyes. And then he saw Susannah standing behind Ray, up on the stage, her lips curving in a subtle smile, as if she had known all along the "miraculous" event would occur.

Buck's shoulders sagged, his stomach twisting in knots. *I haven't a clue how she did this, but we've gotta find out.*

32

Wednesday, March 26, 2003
St. Louis, Missouri
Downtown police station

When it rains, it comes down in sheets, Jeff thought, sitting in the precinct of his former army buddy, Malachi Johnson. On Sunday, miracles had occurred. People got up from their wheelchairs and dropped their canes. He was still wondering how it had happened. He suspected there was a darker side to the story than what witnesses had seen. As he sat listening to Malachi tell him things he'd discovered about Susannah Baker, he knew this feeling of apprehension was justified.

They sat at Malachi's desk, stacked with files from other cases. His muscles rippled a short-sleeved shirt, and his badge hung around his neck. Jeff had forgotten what a commanding presence his six foot four friend was. "Sorry it's taken me so long to get back to you," Malachi said, selecting a slim manila folder off the top of the pile. "This isn't an active investigation, and I've had to do research on my own time."

The squad room was noisy, police officers talking and clattering on computer keyboards, phones ringing, and the smell of onion permeating the air.

Jeff nodded his appreciation. "It ain't like you got nothin' else to do, man. I'm just glad you're willin' to consider it."

"There isn't much, but what I do have is suspicious and certainly merits further investigation."

Jeff squirmed in his chair. "Whatever you got, I'm all ears."

Malachi opened the file, shuffling papers. "This Baker woman is absolutely committing identity theft. A friend of mine works at the *St. Louis Post Dispatch*, so I asked her to run the name through obituaries of women with the same name and close in age. The first couple of years she came up empty. But Anna, like any good reporter, is persistent and started looking at older obits."

Jeff frowned. "Doesn't sound so good."

Malachi smiled across his gray metal desk. "No. One of the most common ways of committing identity theft or assuming some-one else's identity is by obtaining the names and dates of deceased persons from obituaries and cemeteries. A lot of obits include pic-tures, making it easier to find a person who resembles the criminal." Malachi pushed the open folder toward Jeff. "When Anna searched older obits, she discovered a Susannah Baker who died in a single-car accident in 1995. She was thirty-three years old and looked like this." Jeff pondered the photograph of a smiling young woman with dark, wavy hair, high cheekbones, and full lips.

"She looks a whole lot like Ray's Susannah," Jeff said, the astonish-ment evident in his voice.

"That's the idea," Malachi explained. "Your preacher friend's fian-cée comes to St. Louis needing to be somebody else. Looking for someone she resembles, she picks this woman. From there, she con-tacts the DMV and says she's lost her driver's license. They replace it for a small charge and take her picture, so now she has a photo ID."

"Meanin' the real Susannah Baker is dead."

"Hey, Malachi!" It was another cop sitting one desk over.

Malachi slipped the folder under the ink blotter on his desk.

"You know the guy we arrested for burglary yesterday? Can you interview the suspect with me?"

"Sure, Phil. Is he here now?"

Phil, also a fit figure, walked over to Malachi's desk, standing behind Jeff. He stroked a thick mustache. "He's in holding, so we can talk as soon as you're through. Who's your friend?"

Malachi and Jeff both stood. "Phil Burt, this is Jeff Jones. We served in Iraq together."

Jeff extended a hand, and Phil responded with a strong grasp and hearty shake. "*The* Jeff Jones? Malachi tells me you won yourself a silver star for bravery. Congratulations."

Being made out the hero always flustered Jeff, and he stammered his reply, "Uh, thanks, man. I was um, protecting my unit. Malachi would've done the same for me."

Sensing Jeff's uneasiness, Malachi said to Phil, "Give us about ten minutes."

"No problem," Phil said. "Nice meeting you."

Once Phil was out of earshot, the men settled back into their seats, and Jeff spoke slightly above a whisper, "I don't want to get you in trouble, bro. I appreciate everything you've done."

"The thing is, she needs more than a driver's license to prove she's Susannah Baker. She can get a copy of the real Susannah Baker's birth certificate by saying she's lost it, too, and showing her new driver's license as ID." Malachi pointed to the obituary. "We discovered from the obit that Susannah Baker was a North Dakota native who moved to St. Louis as a young adult. The imposter goes to vital records for the county and asks for a copy. This is becoming a real problem with identity theft, and some counties ask for information on the birth certificate only the person would know. Or you can get a bored records clerk, who buys your story that you've been living overseas as a missionary."

Jeff clenched a fist. "This is exactly what me and Buck was thinkin'. Can't you arrest her for lyin' about who she is?"

Malachi raised hands. "For the most part, this is just speculation.

Yes, Anna found a Susannah Baker with a similar appearance and the same birth date who died in 1995. Is it suspicious? Absolutely. But weirder things have happened, Jeff. To prove this woman is masquerading as Susannah Baker, we need a birth certificate, credit cards, and a social security number. I did some investigating, and getting a dead person's social isn't that difficult. The Social Security Administration has what they call the Master Death Index database containing all previously used numbers. It's been computerized since the 1960s, and if your mystery woman has that, she has a new and improved identity."

"But ya'd think 9/11 would make stealin' someone's identity harder," Jeff said.

"For foreigners, sure," Malachi answered his friend. "Right now, that's what the focus is on, not US citizens in their own country. My guess is that she's done this before and knows how to avoid the pitfalls of electronic tracking."

"What'd ya mean?"

"In the old days before computers, criminals would get the name and birth dates of deceased babies from cemeteries. They'd get the birth certificate and build a new identity from scratch. They were called 'paper trappers' because it was all done on paper." Malachi paused, leaning back in his chair, hands clasped behind his head of tapered short black hair that faded into his skin. "How do you know she doesn't have an accomplice?"

"There ain't no accomplice, Malachi." Jeff huffed. "She and Ray are livin' together. Christ, they're hardly ever apart."

"That would make having a partner harder," Malachi acknowledged, leaning forward.

"Hell, all she talks about is how we should make more money. She's too damn greedy for there to be anybody else." Jeff stopped, looking at his friend's chiseled features. "There really ain't nothin' we can do?"

"Not without a lot more evidence." Malachi contemplated his

statement. "You know, there is one thing, but it's a stretch." His fingers clattered across the computer keyboard. "A while back, we were notified of a case in another state. Nebraska, I think. An email went out concerning an unsolved triple homicide involving kids and their father." Malachi typed quickly, scrolling down a screen. "Here it is. It was forwarded by the Assistant Chief, Roland Charlsen, who transferred from Lincoln, Nebraska, early in 2002."

Jeff sat upright. "Can ya tell me anything?"

"Only that the father was a pastor at the University Place Disciples of Christ Church. He and the children were found buried in the parsonage flower garden. It says here they're looking for the wife, a Nicole Hansen, who apparently disappeared and—"

Jeff was out of his chair standing over Malachi's desk. "Do you think she's involved? Do you think she's . . . a murderer?"

"Maybe, maybe not." Malachi motioned for Jeff to sit back down. "A couple of other things. We don't have an ounce of proof that Susannah Baker and this Nicole Hansen are the same person. To be honest, Jeff, that's a pretty big leap."

"But this woman just showed up one day with all these ideas to save *The Road to Calvary.* Like she knew the show was in trouble—"

"Jeff!" Malachi frowned. "As I said, is this suspicious? Yes. Do we have the necessary evidence? No. If you want to prove this woman is a killer, we can start by proving she stole Susannah Baker's identity. To do that, I'm gonna need a social security number. A friend of mine works at the SSA, so I'll give her a call. However, we still don't have a case; and everything I'm telling you, I'm getting on my own, so this isn't a top priority. I need you to be patient; it could take a while."

Jeff's shoulders slumped. Malachi was doing him an enormous favor. Much like setting a trap for the enemy in war, he would have to wait this out.

33

SATURDAY, MARCH 29, 2003
RICHMOND HEIGHTS, MISSOURI
RAY'S HOME

Ray and Susannah settled on the first Saturday in May for a wedding date. The scent on an early spring breeze of blooming flowers and freshly cut grass floated through open kitchen windows. It occurred to Ray he had much to discuss with Susannah, not only regarding their impending nuptials, but their new life together. With *The Road to Calvary* gaining in popularity and Easter fast approaching, winter had thawed into the symphony of spring without Ray even realizing it. On this afternoon, Ray decided now was the right moment to share his good news.

Susannah made ham and cheese quiche for their lunch. Ray carried two plates of quiche, the smell of ham filling the room, while his bride-to-be brought a plate of succulent fruit and a pitcher of iced tea to the table.

"My gosh, Ray, it's been forever since we've had a leisurely Saturday to ourselves," she said, pouring the tea into glasses filled with tinkling ice.

"Yes, it has. In fact, there's something I want to talk to you about." He sat down at the table, and she pulled out a chair to join him.

"This sounds serious," she teased, mock concern furrowing her brow. "Am I in trouble?"

He chuckled. "No, I have a few simple questions around the wedding and things to complete once we're married. Wills, finances, things like that."

"Umm, this sounds important."

"It is, but we'll get to that in a minute. I wanted to ask you a question about the wedding ceremony itself," he said, taking a forkful of quiche.

"You cannot see my dress until I walk down the aisle. Besides color scheme, flowers, the music, and my matron of honor, what else is there?" The ice in her glass sparkled in the sun when Susannah took a drink.

"This quiche is delicious," he said. He beheld her face, reaching for her hand. "I know we've talked about a small ceremony, inviting *The Road to Calvary* regulars. But I'm thinking that the way we're growing, it would be unfortunate if we left anyone out." Ray paused, basking in the beauty of her lovely face. "How would you feel about doing a special live broadcast of our wedding? I've spoken to KNSL, and they're open—"

Susannah hesitated and pulled her hand away from Ray, bringing it to her mouth. "I confess, I've never considered televising our wedding. I see can both sides. Broadcasting a wedding will surely give ratings a boost, but we're also giving up our privacy." She reclaimed Ray's hand. "I'm sorry, honey, but I need to think this over."

Ray hid his disappointment behind a loving smile. "No pressure, but KNSL will want an answer soon."

"Give me a week," she said, squeezing his hand. "This is something I've never given any thought to."

"Take your time, sweetheart. I was viewing this in terms of everybody likes a wedding, and it would give us greater exposure."

Susannah frowned, putting her chin in her hands. "What do Buck and Jeff think? I know they're always feeling I'm pushing too hard for exposure."

He reached for her hand again and kissed it. "Buck and Jeff will find out when we tell them. This is our wedding; and if they're opposed to it being on television, that's too bad. Which brings me to my next topic."

"My, you are just full of surprises, aren't you? You have my undivided attention," she said, wiping her mouth.

Ray put his fork down, folding his hands in a V-shape over the plate of food. "We realize already that we're cramped for space. I'm proposing that after Easter, we meet with an architect and discuss ideas for an expansion of the building. Karl Wilcox gave us a building and three acres of land, so there's room. We'll still keep the building we're in for Sunday school classes and other events, but I'm thinking we should undertake a capital campaign to build a larger worship space and hire additional staff." His smile was both tender and content. "I can't shake the feeling that this is what God wants our next step to be. It'd be a large undertaking, but your thoughts mean the world to me."

Susannah said nothing for a moment, deep in thought on this latest information. "I love it. We could call it the 'Growing in Christ Campaign' and provide incentives for large donors. One option could be putting their name on plaques recognizing what they paid for. Oh, Ray, this is fantastic!"

His face radiated contentment and he squeezed her manicured hand. "I was counting on your ideas and input. But Buck and Jeff aren't aware of this venture yet either. I wanted to talk with you first, seeing as how we'll soon be partners in this endeavor."

"I love how you say that—partners." She blushed.

"I'll tell them right after Easter, and I'll want them both to have input on the design process. This leads me to another decision as we get closer to becoming husband and wife." He drank more tea, setting down the glass. "One of the first things I should do is revise my will, because if something should happen—"

"Ray! Don't even think that way."

"I understand, it's not the happiest of topics, but we need to be realistic. Since everything will be in both our names, should I die first, everything will automatically go to you."

Susannah brushed away a stray tear with the back of her hand. "I know, but I want to enjoy being married first."

"We will. But we need to plan for the unforeseen. That said, I also need to let you know where we stand financially. I've mentioned occasionally that I spent five years in the corporate world, before the good Lord called me back to ministry."

Susannah interrupted him with an amen, and he grinned at her, so glad he was no longer working in corporate America. Ray laid down his fork. He wanted to be certain he had Susannah's full attention, when he shared his news with his bride-to-be.

"I also invested. It's been a constant bull market since the mid-1990s, and my money grew many times over. As of this moment, we have over three quarters of a million dollars in the bank."

She stared at him mutely, her mouth gaping in utter disbelief. "But . . . but the first time we met you said, as I recall, 'I'm just a poor preacher . . .'"

The character lines in his face deepened as he smiled at her. "For the most part, I still am a poor preacher. If I hadn't worked so long with Fidelity, I probably wouldn't have been able to keep my house. But the money gave me a good cushion and the chance for me—for us—to do some things like travel, that wouldn't be possible otherwise."

Susannah was tentative in her question. "Why is it so important for *The Road to Calvary* to be a success then? You actually could have ended the program and been quite comfortable."

Ray leaned back in his chair. "I put a lot of my own money into funding this program. We were still losing substantial amounts, at which point I knew we couldn't keep going. I also felt it wasn't fair to Jeff or Buck to keep stringing them along when they were working two jobs. Then you came into my life and gave plenty of good reasons why we should continue." He reached for her hand again, squeezing it tenderly. "We still have work to do before the show is solvent, and I think a larger worship space will allow us to achieve that."

"You are a genuine gentleman and a true believer, Ray Williams. I am so lucky to have found you." She smiled through her tears.

"*The Road to Calvary* provides the opportunity to spread the Word of God to more people than I ever dreamed. This is my mission, and I want us to continue it as partners. I also want us to be financially secure."

Susannah rose and walked to where Ray sat. She slid into his lap, putting her arms around his neck. "I love the way you say that." They kissed deeply, lost in the tenderness of the moment.

34

Monday, March 31
Lincoln, Nebraska
Northeast Police Headquarters

Ten months, seemingly a lifetime, had dragged by since the Hansen murders, and the fact that the LPD seemed no closer to solving them hung over Linda like an invisible weight or a self-inflicted burden. There were newer crimes to occupy her attention, and she had a team of seven to manage.

She kept trying to comprehend the unthinkable—a mother killing her children. Although Linda knew she shouldn't, she couldn't help researching other women who had committed the same inconceivable act, desperately trying to figure out the thought processes of Susan Smith, who had driven her young boys, still strapped into their car seats, into a South Carolina lake in 1994; or in 2001, when Andrea Yates had methodically drowned all five of her children in Texas. There had to be a common link with Nicole Hansen's motive. She needed to crawl inside her mind to understand the rationale of a homicidal mother.

†

Saturday, April 12, 2003
St. Louis, Missouri
The Road to Calvary Building

Ray took a long drink of coffee for fortification before he spoke with Buck and Jeff. He wasn't sure if the feeling in his stomach was nerves at sharing details of the wedding and capital campaign with them or his failure at making an omelet that morning. Susannah had left him on his own as she had an appointment for her final wedding dress fitting. He thought with anticipation that she would be the most beautiful of brides.

Fresh paint permeated the air because Ray had wanted to brighten the set for the Easter broadcast.

"One thing I do not want is any technical wizardry," he said, motioning to Buck. "Just a straightforward, joyful Easter celebration. I've sent an email to Ryan, and we'll run through rehearsal Saturday morning. But there's something else I want to discuss with both of you."

Ray could see curiosity on each man's face. "When Karl Wilcox donated this building, he also bequeathed the vacant lot next door. That's nearly three acres of land surrounding the structure so we would have the means to expand. And I'm pleased to tell you, we are at that point. Susannah and I have met with an architect to start drawing up plans for the worship space."

There was absolute silence; Buck and Jeff stared at Ray as though he were speaking a foreign language.

Disappointed at their lack of enthusiasm, Ray furrowed his brow. "Do either of you have anything to say?"

Buck's chair squeaked as his weight shifted, and he looked at Jeff, who squirmed uncomfortably. "Jeff and I are trying to process all of this."

Jeff nodded in concurrence.

Buck's voice took on a pained edge. "This is a huge decision, Ray, and you didn't even ask for our input. We've worked with you a long time, sometimes making great sacrifices so the program would succeed, and this is the thanks we get?"

What Ray was hearing was outrageous. He tried to keep his voice even, but knew it was betraying him. "Now wait a minute, Buck. You make it sound as if we deliberately left you out. For all the years you've worked for me, both you and Jeff have had other jobs. I didn't want to overwhelm you. We were trying to get plans in place before we told you."

Buck balled a fist on the table. "Aren't we getting ahead of ourselves? We're finally bringing in a healthy income, hiring additional staff, and making a name for ourselves. But can we afford to build a new space? And what would become of this building?"

Jeff coughed nervously. "Where are we gonna get the kind of money it takes to build a new church? What's wrong with what we got?"

Before Ray could answer, Buck shot off another question, waving his arms. "There's the loan you took out in your name to pay for necessities when we moved into this building. With another, much larger loan, that's going to be a lot of debt—"

Ray held up his hands as if he was surrendering. "Whoa, gentlemen! You need to hear me out."

Buck and Jeff both sat up straight, their complete attention directed at Ray.

"Okay," Buck said. "We're listening."

"The twenty-five thousand dollar loan I took out has been paid off—"

"With what?" Jeff demanded.

Buck agreed. "We have a right to know how finances are being handled."

Ray's voice took on a reprimanding tone. "It's a business matter that's taken care of."

Ray hadn't anticipated the conversation going this direction. He almost expected to see Buck and Jeff's breath steam with the hostile chill in the air.

Jeff leaned into the table. "Before we start talkin' about spending money we don't got, there's somethin' else we wanna talk to you about."

Ray could feel the flush of testiness rising in his cheeks. *What the hell is going on here? The campaign is good news!* He chose to ignore Jeff and focused on the campaign. "This is a marvelous opportunity for us! After all the time we've spent struggling, I thought you'd be excited."

Buck coughed into the curve of his elbow. "As Jeff said, there's something else we want to discuss with you that doesn't have anything to do with launching a fundraising campaign."

The pastor stared down the length of the table at the concerned faces of his employees. "All right, let's have it."

Jeff spoke again, his words coming quickly. "It's about Susannah. She ain't the woman she says she is, Ray. We think she's stolen someone else's identity—"

Ray stood up, nearly knocking his chair over. He paced back and forth in the cramped space. "That is absolute nonsense! How dare you—"

Boom! Buck slapped his clenched fist hard against the table. "Ray! It's time you hear us out. We have mounting proof. We don't want to see you get hurt or worse. Please. Just listen to what Jeff and I have to say."

Arms rigidly folded across his chest, eyes glowering, Ray said tersely, "Tell me."

"Hey, I'm sorry to interrupt, but is everything okay? I could hear raised voices down the hall." Susannah stood in the doorway, the soothing honeyed tones of her voice filling the room.

Ray spoke abruptly to Buck and Jeff, the anger mounting in his voice. "Why don't you gentlemen tell Susannah what you were telling me?"

All he got was strained silence. Ray felt himself seething, waiting for one of them to speak. "Well, if you won't tell her, I will. My darling, Susannah, Buck and Jeff here believe you have stolen another person's identity and are not the woman you say you are."

She smiled warmly at the disturbed faces, making herself comfortable among the men. "You have the story backwards. It was my identity that was stolen, following my divorce. It's literally taken years to get my good name back, and the stress of the situation is a small part of why I let alcohol take over my life." She steeled herself, grasping Ray's hand to continue. "All they needed to open charge accounts was my social security number, which they got by breaking into my house. I had to dig myself out of a mountain of debt I hadn't created and prove my identity had been taken by someone else. I was already dealing with the deaths of my children and a divorce, which were the beginning of my emotional collapse."

She paused, looking Buck and Jeff squarely in the eye, no tears, but her eyes glistened. "I appreciate that you're both leery of me because of the way I showed up here, and believe me, I understand. If I were either of you, I'd be suspicious, too. I have found true happiness with Ray, and my hope is that as we move into a new phase of our lives, you'll be a part of that."

As he beamed at Susannah, so proud to soon call her his wife, Ray observed his friends. He wanted to still be angry at them, but he knew they were not trying to cause him pain.

"I guess we owe you an apology," Buck said with a deep sigh. "I'm sorry we doubted you."

"Me too," Jeff acknowledged. "We made a mistake. Let's move on. Tell us your ideas for a capital campaign."

Ray's rigid face melted into a warm smile as he stroked Susannah's knuckles. "Susannah has come up with a terrific name for the campaign—the Growing in Christ Campaign. We want to officially launch after Easter."

"How much are you plannin' on raisin' for this campaign?" Jeff asked.

"We'll see what the architect has in mind. I want a beautiful place of worship, but not too extravagant. For a 17,000-square-foot addition, the architect estimates two and a half million dollars," Ray countered, still caressing Susannah's hand.

"Of course, that doesn't include the architect's fees, which we estimate will be around three hundred thousand dollars." Susannah smiled.

Buck coughed again. "Wow—that's a lot of space and money. This campaign could take years. I'm not convinced the congregation is big enough for either."

Next to him, Jeff nodded in agreement.

"But we're growing," Ray said. "Increasing numbers are attending in person and watching us on TV. We'll set a goal of two and a half million dollars and see where we are in a year."

"And then what?" Jeff wanted an answer.

Susannah pulled her hand from Ray's, spreading them wide. "God will let us know where we need to go. We want everyone to feel a part of this campaign, and to do that, we'll offer opportunities for congregation members to purchase things—a pew for instance—and as a donor, their name will be inscribed on a plaque. It gives members a sense of ownership."

Ray studied Buck and Jeff. As they contemplated this new development, he thought Buck remained agitated. He couldn't sit still and kept bouncing a knee under the table. After a long moment, Buck spoke. "Do you want our feedback on any of this, or is the deal done?"

Ray kept his tone measured. "Now, Buck, don't say it like that. We want your opinion on the new building; but as far as actually raising money, Susannah and I have that mapped out. And I'm hopeful a successful campaign will allow you both to come on board full time." He touched Susannah's hand again, grinning. "But there is something else we want to share with you."

Then, he had an epiphany. His employees and friends had given themselves wholly to his enterprise, his ministry. Ray recognized that Buck and Jeff were jealously protecting what was a huge part of their lives. Their actions also explained this nonsense of accusing Susannah of committing identity theft. They were fearful of the unknown, and Ray understood he would have to be cautious.

Ray gently introduced the next subject. "After much thought and prayer, Susannah and I feel it would be good to broadcast the wedding. KNSL has agreed, but of course, they're not doing it for free. This is a new beginning for Susannah and me, and *The Road to Calvary*. We do this right, and there will be other benefits."

"Such as a bump in the ratings," Buck said.

"Yes," Ray acknowledged, noting the tinge of sarcasm in his voice. "To be clear, no funds from the Growing in Christ Campaign will be used—I will spend my own money for the broadcast."

"It's just surprising, you know, having a personal event like your wedding on TV. Being the groom three times, I honestly can't imagine broadcasting my nuptials," Buck said. "Walk us through your plan, so we understand what's expected of us."

Everyone had calmed down, and the discussion focused on promotion. As he listened carefully to Buck and Jeff, Ray's thoughts kept returning to their assertion Susannah was using a stolen identity. What on earth would make them think such a thing? To Ray, she had honestly acknowledged the tension with the other two men early on and tried to rectify it. It was typical human nature, he mused. Buck and Jeff, as much as he cared for them, would have to adapt to the transitions that would benefit their futures—or they would part ways.

35

Later the Same Day
St. Louis, Missouri
Outside The Road to Calvary Building

In the open air of the parking lot standing by their cars, Jeff and Buck intently watched the building entrance for signs of Ray and Susannah.

Jeff cocked his head toward the door. "So, you believe her?"

Buck fiddled with his earring. "No, not for a second. I never thought I'd see Ray so angry and defensive. Nothing we can say will ever convince him that Susannah is anything short of perfection."

"Our best hope is that Malachi finds incriminatin' stuff on her." Jeff let out a breath.

"You realize Ray damn nearly fired us, right?" Buck put his hands on his hips. "Or if he didn't, he will if we ever bring this up again. No, Jeff—I'm sorry, buddy, but if you want to continue taking risks to find out her real identity, you're on your own."

Jeff stood there, shielding his eyes from the brightness of the setting sun, trying to see his friend through the hazy light. "But you said yourself, ya don't trust her."

"I don't. But this has gone on long enough. Everything we've tried has led to a dead end or turned out to be more complicated than we thought. I want to move on before we find ourselves in real trouble. I'm starting to look for another part-time job. You can wait on Malachi, but I'm done."

Jeff's shoulders sagged in disappointment. "You really thinkin' about leavin'?"

"I've put some feelers out. Let's face it—once they're married, Susannah's going to be in a position of power, and every step we take will be watched. You said so yourself. Maybe you do want to reenlist with the army. That's risky, too, but at least you know what you're up against. With Ray, and soon Susannah, we have no idea what we're fighting."

Jeff straightened to his full height. "Buck, damn it, we've been friends with Ray a long time. And you and I been friends a good long time, too." Jeff knew he was desperate; his voice was close to begging. "That's one of the reasons we can't desert Ray and just walk away. The other is that talkin' to Malachi about those unsolved murders of the pastor and his kids in Nebraska turned something over in me. I wanna know if Susannah was involved in these killings, Buck. I'll be goddamned if I'm gonna stand back and pretend this woman isn't up to somethin' terrible. You're a good guy. Don't leave. You might not say it, but you want the truth just as bad as me. If nothin' else, think about those little kids." Jeff felt completely spent, his body a limp rag. "Please, Buck."

Buck transferred his weight from one foot to the other, gazing at the dirty cement parking lot. "You're right," he said, raising his eyes to his friend. "We can't endanger Ray, or anyone else. I'm in."

Jeff grasped Buck's outstretched hand, and they shook on it.

36

Sunday, April 27, 2003
St. Charles, Missouri
Ruth Perkins's home

"We believe that the Growing in Christ Campaign is the next logical step for *The Road to Calvary*, providing us with added space and amenities for the entire family," Ray said, smiling into the camera, motioning to the blueprint displayed on a tripod. "In addition to the new church, the original space will house Sunday school classrooms, a Christian bookstore and music center, and a coffee shop and bakery—a place where Christians can come together with other members of this faith community."

Ruth scooted to the edge of her chair, peering intently at the blueprints of the proposed facility. "My, this is quite exciting," she said aloud. "And to think Emma pooh-poohed the Reverend Ray's good works."

"But we can't begin this large undertaking without the support of our wonderful viewers and church community," Susannah Baker purred. "We've set ambitious goals, but we have faith that, with your help, we can reach them."

The camera pulled back, revealing Ray in a sharp gray suit and Susannah wearing a red sheath standing center stage. "We recognize that two and a half million dollars is no small amount of money, and a year is a relatively brief period to raise that amount. Visit our website, where you can view the detailed building plans, get answers to your questions, see ways you can personalize your donation, and prayerfully consider how much *your* gift can be to realize this dream on *your* continuing journey of faith."

"Or you can start the ball rolling today by calling 1-800-HE-SAVES. So why don't you do that—help us kick off the Growing in Christ Campaign by donating right now?" Susannah added smiling. "1-800-HE-SAVES, and remember that He died to save us from our sins."

Susannah handed the microphone to Ray who began, "In Christ's name we pray . . ."

Ruth was jotting down figures on another piece of paper. *My house is paid for. Orville's life insurance policy, investments, and my retirement from teaching give me well over $750,000.* She paused, feeling rather guilty. *I should probably leave something to Emma, but I'm not sure she'd appreciate it.*

The television announcer's voice caught her attention.

"Mark your calendar to join the Reverend Williams and Miss Susannah Baker as they enter into the bond of holy matrimony on a very special live broadcast of *The Road to Calvary* on Saturday, the third of May, at seven in the evening," said a male announcer.

She sat back in her chair, contemplating this message. *I want to share in their happiness.* She didn't drive much anymore, especially at night. She hit the pen against paper—tap, tap, tap. *I don't want to bother the girls, and Emma certainly won't take me*, she thought. Considering various scenarios, Ruth beamed. *I'll take a cab. That way, I'm not a bother to anybody, and they won't even know I attended.*

†

Saturday evening, May 3, 2003
St. Louis, Missouri
The entrance to the Road to Calvary building

Ruth's yellow taxi pulled up to a single-level warehouse near the river-front and the silver metal curve of the Gateway Arch soaring skyward. Outside in the warm spring air, people wearing their Sunday best filed into the building as greeters opened the door. Ruth had selected a floral print dress and donned her pearls for this special occasion.

"Good evening," she said and smiled at the greeter. Inside, she was handed a program with "The Marriage of the Reverend Raymond Williams and Susannah Lynn Baker" written in script with entwined wedding bands on the cover.

An usher offered her his arm. "We are not a divided house, so I'll seat you in the best available spot."

"That sounds lovely," Ruth said.

He escorted her midway down the aisle to a spot near the row's end, which she thought was an excellent vantage point to watch the proceedings. Viewing the crowd, she saw persons of all different ages, races, genders, shapes, and sizes. The young blonde woman who took the seat next to her also seemed to be alone, and Ruth exchanged pleasantries with her.

"What a perfect day for a wedding. Are you a friend of the reverend or Miss Baker?" she inquired.

The blonde smiled in return. "My aunt Julia is a long-time parishioner, but she couldn't be here tonight due to illness."

Ruth held out her hand. "I've been following Reverend Ray since their early days myself. Ruth Perkins. Nice to meet you."

"Sally Sullivan. I sold Ray Miss Baker's engagement ring, and he's been praying for my aunt's health ever since."

"Oh, I hope it's nothing serious."

The blonde woman shrugged her shoulders. "Unfortunately, it is. My aunt had a second heart attack, and she's on life support. I truly thought if I asked the reverend to keep praying for her, this wouldn't happen again."

"Don't lose faith," Ruth said encouragingly and patted Sally's shoulder.

Ruth noted that the crowd was quite large, and every seat appeared to be filled. The beginning notes of Pachelbel's "Canon" filled the air as the processional began. The full choir assembled on the stage. Onto the stage walked the minister, whom Ruth barely recognized, then Ray in a black silk suit and pale rose tie, along with a younger best man in coordinating attire. They took their places at the front of the altar.

The matron of honor followed dressed in a dusty pink silk frock. The "Bridal Chorus" began, and everyone rose to their feet, turning toward the back of the church. Carrying a small bouquet of pink roses, Susannah entered wearing an ivory tulle-and-lace, tea-length dress.

At the altar, Susannah took Ray's arm, and they approached the minister.

The congregation took their seats, and Ruth fanned back tears. Sally handed her a tissue, and the minister beamed at the congregation. "Dearly beloved, we are gathered here today . . ."

They were married in little more than half an hour. By then, both Ruth and Sally were clutching tissues as the choir sung "The Wedding Song"; the Reverend Jacobson recounted how Ray and Susannah met and their personal stories of overcoming adversity to find each other.

"That was lovely, just lovely," Ruth said to Sally as they queued up in the reception line.

"I'm so sorry Aunt Julia had to miss it. She would have cried right along with us."

Meeting Ray and Susannah, Ruth grasped both their hands heartily. "Congratulations! I'm Ruth Perkins. It is a pleasure to finally meet you. Such a beautiful, solemn ceremony."

"It's a pleasure, indeed. I continue to pray for your family, Mrs. Perkins."

"Ray prays for your daughter, Emma, very hard," Susannah said, reaching for her hand.

"Our continued correspondence means so very much to me. I won't hold up the line, but best wishes for a long and happy marriage," Ruth said.

The newlyweds greeted Sally. Worry flashed over Ray's face. "It saddens me that Julia had another heart attack," he said. "Please know that I will continue to pray for her full recovery. Be sure to keep us posted."

The young woman brushed aside a tear. "I appreciate that, Reverend. Congratulations to the both of you."

As Ruth and Sally passed a white basket brimming with cards, Ruth deposited a wedding card. Inside was a check for fifteen thousand dollars.

37

Monday, June 2, 2003
Lincoln, Nebraska
Northeast Police Headquarters

There had been a match on ViCAP, followed by an intriguing email. Raymond Charlsen, now an assistant chief of police in St. Louis, had contacted Linda right after the ViCAP hit, providing further details.

She stared at her computer, reading Charlsen's words again. "The murder of Delores Reid, a homeless woman who was miraculously 'healed' on a religious program here, bears striking similarities to the Hansen murders. Lethal amounts of the drug Ambien were found in her system."

The exact same M.O., and very possibly the same used in killing Pamela Watts's parents. Linda returned to the email. "Detective Malachi Johnson is lead on the case, and I believe Detective Johnson has valuable material that can be of assistance to you. He's expecting your call." Linda wrote down the detective's number and dialed.

The voice on the other end was deep. "Detective Johnson, Homicide Division."

"Detective Johnson, this is Captain Linda Turner in Lincoln, Nebraska. I understand you're investigating a murder that is very similar to a triple homicide that occurred here thirteen months ago."

"That's right. I've been aware of the unsolved Hansen murders since Chief Charlsen transferred here from Lincoln. Horrific case, but I didn't expect to ever come across a connection. Until last week that is, when I was investigating what initially looked to be a suicide of a fifty-nine-year-old female. I got confirmation from the FBI that the common denominator between our cases is the large amount of Ambien present in our vic's system, the same drug used to kill the Hansen family."

"Correct. But what else made you suspicious?" she asked, hardly able to catch a breath.

"A couple of things. The substantial amount of Ambien present initially pointed to suicide. But while processing the scene, we discovered the prescription label on the bottle of pills was fake."

"And the second?" Linda could feel her heart beating faster.

"The victim was a down-on-her-luck former actress who was also sometimes homeless. She was living in a flophouse, renting a room by the week. According to three residents, Delores let it be known that in March, she was paid to pretend she was crippled, rise up out of a wheelchair, and walk on some local religious program. The pastor claims to perform healing miracles."

Linda tried not to get too excited. "In your professional opinion, Detective, why kill a homeless woman appearing on a fraudulent religious program?"

She heard shuffling of papers at the other end. "The neighbors I interviewed all said that she was paid and told to leave town. But Delores didn't leave; she lay low waiting. This program is now running a capital campaign asking for close to two and a half million in donations. Delores began talking about how being able to miraculously heal and walk was worth more than she was paid. She wanted additional money, or she'd go public with the truth about these healings."

"Good old-fashioned blackmail," Linda said. After all this time, another sour disappointment would do them no good, and she found herself questioning Detective Johnson's finding. "Or it's coincidence, and Ms. Reid could have overdosed on the Ambien?"

"Sure," Malachi acknowledged on the other end of the line. "But on the night Delores Reid died, another resident saw a figure leaving her room at around three in the morning."

"Did they get a description?"

"It was in a dimly lit hallway, and the person was dressed in dark clothing. The witness indicated the person's build was slight and thought it might have been a woman."

Linda took a drink from her water bottle. This was all circumstantial, but it was the best lead she'd had in months. "What was the name of the program Ms. Reid rose from a wheelchair on?"

"It's called *The Road to Calvary*, and here's why this may be a potential lead for you. The pastor has a new wife, maiden name was Susannah Baker. I've seen the program once and need to do further research, but she hasn't been around that long. They got married in a live broadcast in May. One of my army buddies works on the show. He's always been suspicious of Ms. Baker's intentions and brought me a copy of her driver's license. I also delved into the origin of her social, and the Susannah Baker issued this particular number died in 1995."

That statement grabbed Linda's attention hard. Her breathing was shallow, and she could hear her heart pounding in her ears. *Is this the break we've been looking for?*

There was utter silence on the line as the thoughts in Linda's mind competed for attention. *The mysterious woman showing up fit the pattern. The murder of Delores Reid fit the pattern.*

"Captain Turner?" Malachi inquired.

"Yes, I'm still here. Trying to process these findings. These months of having a heinous crime still unsolved have been unsettling for our department, and this would be a huge break. The woman we're looking for is very skilled at changing her appearance, so making a positive ID that way could be difficult. However, I do have forensic evidence in the form of a palm print. If we could get prints from this Susannah—what did you say her last name was?"

"It was Baker. But now it's Williams."

Linda scribbled the names across the page. "If we get her prints and DNA to make a positive ID, the Hansen case is back on. Before we rush into anything, I'd like you to come to Lincoln ASAP with all the materials you have. If you need me to speak with your superiors, I'm happy to do that."

"Chief Charlsen mentioned sharing evidence and discussed undertaking a joint investigation. I need time to gather what we have, but I can be in town the day after tomorrow."

"Great. We'll find you a place to stay." She paused, her mind running at full speed. "Besides case files and evidence, can you get me some of those TV tapes of this program? Those are crucial to making a positive identification."

"Sure, that's no problem. I'll contact you tomorrow with my flight itinerary."

"Thank you, Detective Johnson. I look forward to meeting you and our possible collaboration."

Linda hung up, her thoughts tripping over one another. The Hansen case was back on.

38

Linda liked Malachi Johnson immediately. His tall, muscular physique was evidence he worked out and, she thought, was perhaps a former athlete. In reviewing the cases, they found too many similarities for this to be coincidence. They had written the common aspects of both cases on a white board, and similarities were emerging.

Linda knocked on the board. "The mysterious woman showing up seemingly out of thin air fits the pattern. The murder of Delores Reid fits the pattern in the way she was killed. Still, it's all circumstantial."

Malachi reached into a bag and produced a half-dozen video tapes. "You asked for videos from the program. Any place we can look at these?"

A television and VCR were set up in Linda's office and Malachi queued the tape to an image of a woman with medium chestnut hair, ringlets framing her face. Linda motioned to photographs attached to a board. "As you can see, none of these women resemble each other. What matched were fingerprints and an odd half-moon hole on the inside of her right ear. We believe her real name is Pamela Jane Watts. In this photo taken by Catholic Charities we have an overweight girl, with blue eyes, short red hair, and an identifying mole." Linda pointed to an enhanced photo of the hole. "This appears on every photo except her mug shot. I confirmed the shape was present from birth. At nineteen her hair is shoulder length, a mixture of platinum blonde and black streaks. Again, the mole is present. After her release from prison, she marries her first husband. Her hair is bright copper and the style quite short on her Minnesota driver's license." She moved down the row of photos. "Pamela weds her second husband using an assumed name of Susan Nichols. You can see her appearance is strikingly different. She's wearing a tight blonde perm, big glasses, and she's heavier, making her look older. On her Nebraska driver's license she transforms again. As Nicole Hansen, the mole is gone, her nose is smaller, her eyes seem brighter, and her weight is 40 pounds less. She looks closer to her real age and the shag haircut is very flattering in contrast to the perm. I believe she underwent plastic surgery to alter her looks permanently, a nose job and eye lift for sure. Three of her identities involved financial crimes, mainly check forgery and embezzlement. Additionally, embezzling money would provide her with the funds for this type of surgery. If we can determine from these films that Susannah Williams is left-handed, there's a stronger chance our killers are one and the same."

"Ah, a southpaw," Malachi said knowingly. "There was no indication from the ME's report if Delores's killer was right- or left-handed."

The pair began studying the videos. When Susannah appeared facing the camera straight-on, Linda paused the tape and held up the various photos. "We need to find evidence of that shape within her ear."

"Your hunch about plastic surgery makes sense. I can't imagine one single person looking so different without surgical help." Malachi took the remote and fast-forwarded.

"Stop and go back," Linda commanded, moving in closer to the screen. "There. You can barely see it under the cuff of her blouse, but Mrs. Williams is wearing a watch on her right wrist." She pointed to the flash of a gold watchband.

"Left-handed," Malachi said, stroking his neatly trimmed black beard. "Still, we need a person on the inside. I'm thinking an undercover cop who's familiar with her MO."

Linda stared at Susannah Williams's frozen image. "I have an idea, but it may take a few days. Can you stay longer?"

"Sure," Malachi said.

39

Thursday, June 5
St. Louis, Missouri
The Road to Calvary offices

Cole Leon opened another envelope, looking for a prayer request or donation. Instead all he found was a letter—a very angry letter. He scanned the contents briefly before calling Seth over.

"Hey, Seth, look at this," he said and scooted his chair closer, so both men could read the missive.

"'To Whatever the Hell Your Name Is: My name is Michelle Thomas and I'm putting your program, *The Road to Calvary* on notice that I have filed a complaint with the Missouri Attorney General's Office, regarding the fraudulent practices of your organization. For the past year, my roommate, Jeanette Morelli, has given nearly every penny she makes to your program, believing your outrageous claims that healing and prosperity will come to those who believe.'"

Cole paused. "I've never seen a letter like this before."

"I don't think we're supposed to," Seth whispered. He read on in low tones. "'Belief in such nonsense has caused her to be unable to pay rent, help buy groceries, or get her car fixed. I'm not a heartless woman, so instead of kicking Jeanette out, I'm letting her stay. However, I'm using her as an example of how your program, Reverend, along with that cunning wife of yours, prey on the vulnerable. You give people false hope, and I won't rest until the world knows the truth about you and your program.'"

Cole folded the letter, holding it in his hand ready to speak, but an anxious Seth cut him off. "What are we supposed to do with this?"

Still holding the letter, Cole glanced around the empty mailroom. Satisfied they were alone, he lowered his voice further. "I'm not convinced Ray is at fault here; in fact, he may not even know what's going on." He ran a hand over his thinning brown hair. "There's something I should tell you. I'm picking up extra shifts for more money. I want outta the halfway house." Cole stopped and pulled his thoughts back on track. "I started noticing late at night Susannah going through the prayer requests being sent to Ray. It started right after they were married. She was here every night I worked. One night, after she'd gone, I went through the requests again, and a third of them were gone. Anything Susannah doesn't want Ray to see, she removes. I'm betting Ray will never see this letter."

Susannah's strong, condescending voice startled them both. "My, but that's quite the story you've concocted, Cole. Given your history, I guess I shouldn't be surprised. The truth is that Ray can't possibly answer every prayer request. I'm only trying to be a helpful spouse." Her face showed no emotion, except perhaps contempt.

Seth's raised voice was angry. "We're both turning our lives around; we're not using anymore. We're grateful for the opportunity we've been given. But, please, don't patronize us."

Susannah sneered at Cole and Seth. "You don't even know what patronizing means."

Seth began to protest, but Cole raised a hand, stopping him. He held the letter between his index and middle fingers, speaking very calmly, trying to sound as professional as he could. "We came across this irate letter and thought you should see it. It's from a woman filing a complaint with the attorney general against us. She's talking about fraud."

Susannah snatched the paper away without looking at it and addressed both men. "I'm not buying your 'we were just bringing it to you' story for a second. But here's what I do buy," she hissed and moved toward them. "You're both nothing more than heroin junkies who every day are this close to falling back into your old ways." She held her index finger and thumb a fraction of an inch apart.

"But," Cole protested, "you were once an addict yourself, saved by this very program—"

"Shut up," she snarled and moved in even closer. "I was never on the level of you two losers. I was a drunk, and in case you've forgotten, alcohol is legal. Heroin, on the other hand, is not. Let me be very clear—read one more letter, and you're gone tomorrow. And what would your probation officers think when I tell them you were caught using again, and we had no choice but to let you go?" Susannah taunted them. "This letter or any other letter is none of your concern. Take my advice—do your fucking jobs and pull the checks."

Cole's spine straightened, bringing him to his full height. Eye-to-eye with Susannah, the edge in his voice was angry. "Are you threatening us? I'm not afraid to tell Ray this woman has grave concerns."

Her lips curled into a nasty smirk. "And who do you think he'll believe? Two grungy junkies or his good Christian wife?"

"Susannah! Sweetheart, where are you? I'm ready to leave," Ray's voice called from down the hall.

Cole witnessed her transformation with terrified awe. "In a minute, sweetheart. I'm finishing pulling your prayer requests." Her voice turned from icy hatred to honey sweet and then back to the former. She put the letter in her purse and leaned in over the desk, separating them. "You mention this to anyone, and I can make you both disappear. Not a fucking word." As Susannah left the room, the men overheard her coo, "Sorry, darling. I'm ready to go now."

As their voices faded, Cole huffed angrily, "Jesus, we have got to tell somebody about this."

Seth looked at him as if he were crazy. "Are you kidding me? You heard what that bitch said! We can't tell Ray. What the fuck's the matter with you!"

Cole tapped nervous fingers on Seth's desk. Then he walked to his workspace, fishing in the wastebasket till he found what he was searching for. "We're not going to tell Ray," he said, waving the envelope. "But there are others we can trust. And . . . we have this."

†

Later the same day
St. Louis, Missouri
Buck's home

Buck leaned forward in his living room recliner, listening to Cole and Seth, who sat on the couch and finished the story of their encounter with Susannah. He had never asked their ages, but looking at their scared, unlined faces, he figured early- to mid-twenties at most.

Cole and Seth waited expectantly for Buck to speak, and he reprimanded himself for ever having doubted he could trust them. "Susannah took the letter, so we can't even contact this Michelle Thomas, correct?"

Rising from the sofa, Cole removed a crumpled envelope from his back jeans pocket. "Not quite. I had tossed the envelope in the trash, and Susannah never asked for it. Ms. Thomas included a return address."

Buck smoothed out the crinkled envelope, postmarked St. Louis. "Well, she's local with a legible address, which is all very helpful. I'm glad you thought enough to save this."

"So now what?" Cole was apprehensive about meeting Buck at his home and rubbed his fingers along the back of his tense neck.

Buck put an elbow across his knee. "First, I want you both to know you can trust Jeff and me implicitly. The next few days will be difficult, but be as nice to Susannah as possible without raising her suspicions."

Seth crinkled his forehead, gulping air. "I'm not a good enough actor to pull that off."

Buck sat up straight, eyeing the young men. "You're gonna have to be. What I'm going to tell you cannot leave this room," Buck said, leaning in. "Jeff and I have been working with the St. Louis PD trying to figure out who Susannah Williams is. Jeff's old Iraq War buddy is a homicide detective, and it was Jeff who made contact."

Cole nodded. "We heard the argument you had with Ray that Susannah had stolen someone's identity. Then she twists the story that she is the victim. I'll be honest—Susannah scares me."

"We all have to be on guard at the office," Buck said. He held up the envelope. "In the meantime, I'm going to pay a visit to Ms. Thomas."

40

Friday, June 6, 2003
Lincoln, Nebraska
Chief Langston's office

"Your idea for a joint investigation is a good one," Chief Langston said, looking from Linda to Malachi. "What are you proposing?"

"Sir, we need to get close to Mrs. Williams. Put a cop on the inside who gains her trust. Not only a joint investigation, but an undercover operation. Detectives from your department have more experience working this case, and I'm suggesting it be an officer from the LPD."

Langston tented his hands, elbows propped on his desk. "It's an unusual request, and a joint investigation limits our legal capacity in your jurisdiction. Captain Turner, who do you think would be the best officer to go to St. Louis in that capacity? Dale?"

Linda cleared her throat, feeling her insides tingle. "Chief, with all due respect, I believe that officer should be me."

There was quiet, Chief Langston mulling over this suggestion. The longer the silence, Linda worried, the less chance Langston would go for the plan.

"You definitely have the most expertise," he finally agreed. "You're also a captain and one of the best officers I have. The Northeast Sector needs a leader."

Linda brought her shoulders forward, her posture straight. "Lyle Dale has the knowledge and experience to step in for me temporarily. I realize that a ranking officer being gone for a lengthy period might be tough on the department." She stopped, taking in some air. "Therefore, I suggest we limit my undercover stretch to a relatively brief period."

Malachi's head jerked toward her. "How long, and will limited time give us the chance for you to build a relationship?"

"Captain Turner has a point, Detective," Chief Langston interrupted. "We've worked this case for over a year, and it needs to be wrapped."

Linda spoke, facing Malachi. "I didn't mean to catch you off guard, but these murders are a stain on our department. Mrs. Williams is a newlywed, and they've got the capital campaign underway. Both those things will keep her in town. I think we can undertake a shorter operation, but our planning would need to be detailed. We'd rely on your jurisdiction to have all elements in place."

"How long would I have?" the detective inquired.

Langston spoke up. "Four to six weeks planning time. Captain, you and Detective Johnson choose the most feasible identity. Once we have a backstory in place, she'll come to St. Louis." Langston pointed his pen at dates on a desk calendar. "Six weeks out is July eighteenth. From there, I'll okay slightly over six weeks."

This was going to be tight. Linda could feel her heart flutter. She hoped Malachi was on board.

"I always have liked a challenge." Malachi grinned. "And this will definitely be that."

They ordered in Chinese take-out and squeezed around the table in Linda's office.

"I could be divorced, the same as her," Linda said. "My professional background should be horticulture; maybe I've worked at a garden center. Common denominators right off the bat." She scooped up a mouthful of shrimp fried rice with chopsticks. "I can start researching that."

"That's good," Malachi replied. "Langston said I've got six weeks max to get you set up with documents, housing, IDs, all that. I'll work with our undercover unit. I've got a flight for late tomorrow out of Omaha."

They continued their discussion until they had filled yellow pages on a legal pad. The conversation took on a personal tone.

"Are you married?" Linda asked.

"Was married," Malachi corrected. "My ex and I are on friendly terms and have two beautiful girls ages sixteen and eighteen." The corners of his mouth turned down into a melancholy smile. "They're growing up too fast and are both dating, a father's worst nightmare. I wanted them to wait till they were at least thirty."

Linda wiped her mouth. "I'm sorry. Have you been divorced long?"

"Our second daughter, Sasha, was born while I was in Iraq. That was a tough adjustment. Then I joined the police force, and you know what a toll this job can take on families. I was always working, missing too many family functions, dance recitals, regular dinners at home. I see my girls on a consistent basis, but Michelle and I decided we were better off leading separate lives. How about you?"

"I'm widowed. My husband, Tom, died six years ago."

"Can I ask what happened?" Malachi took a sip of soda.

"Tom dropped dead of an embolism at thirty-seven. It changed my perspective on a lot of things, especially religion. This case only adds to my cynicism because it's revealed the scars left from preying on the gullible and the dirty secret of organized religion. The individuals involved here not only haven't proven me wrong but have shown there's a very dark side to believing in something without question." Linda stopped herself. "I hope I haven't offended you."

Malachi took another gulp of his drink. "Not in the slightest. I've been thinking much the same, regarding religion in general, and whether I even believe in the idea of a Supreme Being."

Linda wiped the remainder of her lipstick off, thinking how comfortable it was to have this conversation with someone who had the same doubts. "After my husband died, I was certain there was no God, at least not for me. Yes, there's still good in the world, however buried it might sometimes be. I always thought that if there was a God, the world would be a better place. Chalk it up to free will, a concept I remember from my Catholic school days."

He nodded in agreement. "We tried to raise Sasha and Lauren to be good, honest, moral people, but I wasn't convinced we needed religion to accomplish that." He took another scoop of rice and looked Linda straight in the eye. "Do you believe in God? If that's too personal a question, please tell me to take a hike."

Condensation formed on Linda's glass. "No, that's a perfectly reasonable question, given that this case deals with persons of supposed faith who have lied and cheated those who trust them. I was raised Catholic. It didn't make sense to me that only men could be in charge and that you absolutely had to believe certain things, so I walked away. I consider myself an agnostic, but the people we deal with make me question it every day."

"Yeah, this line of work can jade a person pretty damn quick." He swirled the remaining soda in the bottom of his glass.

Linda wiped her mouth once again. "I'm not a theologian, but I think some people just want to be given the answers. They don't want any tough questions to deal with, just tell them what to believe straight up. I have confidence that's what's happening here. We'll see how this plays out. Even if this program is a fraud, some members will still choose to keep believing."

Finished with his meal, Malachi placed his chopsticks crosswise on his plate, returning the conversation to the job. "My sources on the program say Susannah Williams talked about suffering a major tragedy."

Linda made certain her gaze didn't linger too long on Malachi's handsome features. "What sort of tragedy?"

"She claimed that her two children were killed in a car accident. Sister-in-law picking them up from daycare. She's never provided enough details for us to check the authenticity."

Linda held her chopsticks aloft. "That is one of the most revolting things I've ever heard. Jacob and Elizabeth Hansen are those dead children. The image of those small bodies clad in their torn Disney pajamas will never leave me. I will do whatever it takes to catch this bitch."

41

Thursday evening, June 12, 2003
Glendale, Missouri
Michelle Thomas's home

It was after nine o'clock when Michelle Thomas's doorbell rang, interrupting a crucial moment in her favorite TV show, *Survivor.* "Damn!" she huffed, rolling off her living room couch to answer.

Michelle tied the belt of her robe around her waist, flipping on the porch light. A woman dressed in dark clothing stood alone. She unlocked the bolt lock but kept the chain in place, opening the door as far as the chain would allow. "Can I help you?"

"I am so sorry to bother you," the woman apologized. "But can I use your phone? My car won't start, and my cell phone is completely out of bars." She held up her useless cell.

Michelle was hesitant at first. It was dark and late with a stranger on her doorstep. "Okay," Michelle said and unchained the door.

"Thanks so much. One call, and I'll be on my way."

Michelle led the way to the wall phone in the kitchen, her slippers shuffling along the floor. Turning toward the woman, Michelle pointed to the phone. "If someone needs to come and get you—"

"That won't be necessary," the woman replied abruptly, holding a thick throw pillow from the sofa across her body. "You won't be filing a complaint against us."

Two muffled pops, and Michelle clutched her hemorrhaging abdomen, falling to the floor in excruciating pain. She gasped trying to breathe and was still cognizant enough to realize she hadn't noticed the stranger's gloved hands in the dark. Michelle observed the profuse amount of dark blood spurting from her midriff. She tried to cover the hole in her stomach with her trembling hands, but the tacky substance soaked them in red. The woman climbed the bedroom stairs, and Michelle heard a single *pop*.

In a few seconds, the woman returned from upstairs, heading toward the sliding back door.

Michelle used her waning energy to speak three words. "Help me. *Please!*"

The woman turned toward her, the gun still in her hand. "No."

Michelle felt the room fading away. She was losing consciousness, blood pooling on the vinyl. As her world fell into blackness, the last sound she would ever hear was the slamming of the patio door.

42

Saturday, June 14, 2003
Glendale, Missouri
Michelle Thomas's home

Buck drove to the Glendale suburb, thankful that Michelle Thomas's phone number was listed and that she was willing to talk to him. He had a disturbing feeling that Susannah wasn't going to stop at threatening Cole and Seth's jobs. His visit was twofold. He wanted to confirm whether Susannah's constant appeals were driving her roommate to give all her money to the church. He also felt the need to apologize in person to Ms. Thomas. They had talked on Thursday and agreed to meet Saturday evening. Buck didn't know if it would make any difference, and perhaps he was the one looking to assuage his guilt.

Turning down a block where tree branches arched over the street, he spied the 1950s brick rambler, set back on an expansive lot, under a canopy of trees. He parked and went to the front door and rang the bell. He heard talking inside, but no answer. *She must be home.* Buck rang the bell a second time. Still no answer.

After the third ring, Buck peered in the bay window and viewed the flickering blue light of a television set in the living room. That explained the voices he'd heard, but where was Ms. Thomas? He stepped off the porch, walked past the attached garage, and made his way to the back, where there was a cozy patio with sliding glass doors. Buck went to peer inside.

He gasped and jumped back from the door, fumbling for his cell phone. "Oh shit! Jesus!" A woman's body lay on the vinyl floor of the kitchen in a congealed spatter of blood.

He took a deep breath, trying to compose himself. He attempted to dial 911. In his state of shock, Buck's fingers seemed enormous as he misdialed yet again.

Goddamn it, Buck, focus! Deliberately he punched in the three digits. An operator answered on the second ring.

"911, what's your emergency?"

Holding his phone in one hand, he tugged on the sliding door with the other. As soon as the door was ajar, a foul odor filled his nostrils, and Buck realized by the darkening of her body that the woman was dead.

"I came to visit Ms. Thomas and found a body. I'm pretty certain she's dead."

"Are you sure, sir?" the operator asked.

"Yeah, the odor's terrible—" Buck gagged and closed the sliding door.

"Are you all right, sir?"

Buck covered his mouth and nose. "The smell is ghastly, and her skin is very dark."

"Sir, are you on a cell phone?"

"Y-yes," he stuttered. "Yes, I am."

"I need you to tell me the address for first responders."

He was shaking so violently, Buck was afraid he would drop his phone. He gave the dispatcher the address.

"I need you to stay where you're at until the police and fire arrive," the calm dispatcher instructed.

"Sure," Buck managed, his legs wobbling. "I'm not going anywhere."

†

Buck paced the length of the driveway, leaving a voicemail for Jeff to call him right away. Within minutes, wailing sirens filled the air—first the police, followed closely by the fire department. Flashing lights lit up the street. As emergency responders entered the front door, Buck surveyed the winding block as curious neighbors came outside, gathering in small groups, scrutinizing the scene and murmuring among themselves.

A female officer walked toward Buck. "Did you call this in, sir?"

"Yes." Instinctively, Buck reached for his driver's license in his back pocket.

The officer asked him routine questions on the nature of his visit, and he noted her nameplate read "Lane." When she asked Buck whether he had entered the house and disturbed anything, Buck felt intimidated, but he tried hard to steady his voice and remain calm.

"Once I opened the sliding door, I knew by the smell that something was horribly wrong."

"What exactly did you see?"

"A woman—at least I think it's a woman—lying in a pool of blood. I think she had a gunshot wound to the chest, but to be honest, I can't be sure. I've never seen someone who's been murdered before, and it freaked me out."

"How did you know she was deceased?" Officer Lane asked, taking notes.

"There was so much blood, and the smell—" Buck searched for the right word. "Foul. It smelled like something was rotten."

"We're going to need you to come to the station and give a statement, Mr. Neal. You've experienced a huge trauma, so a squad car will bring you." Then she pointed to Buck's Taurus. "Is that your vehicle?"

"Yes."

"It's just standard procedure, but we'll need to have a look inside."

He gulped, feeling his Adam's apple hard against his throat. "Am I a suspect?"

Officer Lane smiled in empathy. "I realize this is hard for you, Mr. Neal, but part of our job is eliminating you as a suspect."

Buck inhaled deeply. Other officers were now sealing the area off with yellow crime tape. "You're right," he said, and Officer Lane led him to the back seat of a squad car.

†

WEDNESDAY, JUNE 17, 2003
LATE AFTERNOON
St. Louis, Missouri
Downtown Police Precinct

Malachi provided Buck and Jeff with limited information on the unfolding investigation. No longer working a speculative crime on his own time, Malachi had given his superiors the material Jeff and Buck had gathered. Buck, however, was reliving the scene in a continuous stream of nightmares. Susannah, he felt sure, was behind this.

"Both women were shot with a nine-millimeter." In a drab interrogation room, Malachi relayed the women's fate. He nodded toward Buck. "The woman you found was Michelle Thomas. Jeanette Morelli had been upstairs apparently asleep. She was found in her bed."

Recognition registered across Buck's face. "Morelli. Isn't that the name of the family that owns the upscale liquor stores?"

Malachi acknowledged Buck's question with a nod. "Yes, Jeanette was one of the daughters. Not long ago, her family cut her off because

she kept giving copious amounts of money to various religious organizations, most recently *The Road to Calvary*."

Buck groaned, his head dropping into his large hands.

Jeff scratched his chin. "But wouldn't she or the neighbors have
heard those gun shots? Guns ain't exactly quiet."

"We found feathers at the scene that came from a pillow used to
muffle the shots," Malachi explained. "The poor man's silencer."

Racked by shock and guilt, Buck pulled at his hair. "If I hadn't asked
Michelle Thomas to talk to me, this never would have happened." His
eyes were wet, and Malachi put a comforting hand on his forearm.

"Not necessarily, Buck. This wasn't your fault. If it's any small con-
solation, this may actually be of help. It's the adage that criminals
eventually make mistakes."

But Buck was distraught, thrashing his arms. "Two more persons
died, Malachi! I can't stop thinking about Michelle. She seemed so
nice and glad somebody was willing to listen to her. She laughed
when I told her I was concerned for her safety. She didn't believe me,
and now she and Jeanette are dead. How can this be helpful?"

He started sobbing, his shoulders heaving, and his head fell to the
table.

"Hey," Jeff said, putting an arm around his friend's shoulders.
"Malachi's right. This ain't your fault."

A box of Kleenex sat on the gray metal table, and Malachi pushed
it toward Buck.

Eyes red and puffy, Buck took a wad of Kleenex and wiped his
eyes. "I'm so sorry, but I can't help feeling somehow responsible. If I
hadn't called her—"

"No, no," Jeff was saying as Malachi brought his hand forward.

"The moment Cole and Seth came to you," Malachi said, "those
women were in danger. There is nothing you could have done. Had
you not gone there, the bodies might not have been found until someone noticed they were missing."

Buck inhaled a breath and sniffled. "I guess you could look at it that way."

Malachi sat erect, hands folded on the table. "There's one other thing. You both have always suspected Susannah of being involved with other crimes before she came to *The Road to Calvary*. I can't go into a lot of detail, but I'm going to be working with an officer from another jurisdiction on a joint operation that directly involves this program."

Buck's eyes widened with this revelation, and he saw the same expression on Jeff's face.

"You can't tell us nothin'?" Jeff said after a minute.

"Not until the plan is in place. In the meantime, you both need to be very cautious around Susannah and Ray. Be careful not to ruffle any feathers. Neither of you knows anything about a letter. Same goes for the deaths."

The lines across Buck's forehead creased, an ominous thought filling his mind. "But what happens to Cole and Seth?"

Malachi slid a yellow legal pad over to Buck. "Write down their full names, addresses, and phone numbers. They need to be interviewed."

Buck's hands still trembled as he struggled to hold the pencil. His writing was unusually sloppy. "Can you read all that?" he asked the detective.

"Yep. We will be in contact, and if we think they're in any danger, we'll take them into protective custody. We're pros and can keep Cole and Seth safe."

Outside the precinct, Buck found he was still a mass of nerves, agonizing over Seth and Cole and the plan Malachi couldn't divulge.

He took his keys out of his pocket, and they jangled in his hand. "Why do you suppose a police officer from another department is coming here?"

Jeff unlocked the door of his VW Golf. "I won't be surprised if there are others dead. But I can tell ya one thing for certain, Malachi knows what he's doing. We need to follow his instructions and do exactly as he says."

Buck's keys jiggled as he watched Jeff climb into the front seat. "This is much worse than we ever thought, and I can't shake the feeling that Susannah's watching us, too."

Jeff started the engine, closing the door. "We can't do anything stupid. We gotta be on our guard twenty-four seven—the same as in the military."

43

Saturday, June 21, 2003
St. Charles, Missouri
Ruth Perkins's home

Ruth listened intently as Susannah spoke of dedicating a stained-glass window in her name.

"Each of these custom windows depicts an important part of Christ's life," Susannah said. "These contemporary panels are one-of-a-kind, and as a donor, your name would appear on a permanent brass plaque underneath."

"How much would I need to contribute for my name to be on a window?"

She noticed that Ray had started to speak, but Susannah cut him off as he opened his mouth. "A window is fifty thousand dollars, which we understand is a large amount of money. But think of it as an investment and one that will be in your memory for generations."

"Please understand that we're extremely appreciative of the large donation you've already given us," Ray said, his handsome face beaming. "If purchasing a window is too much, please tell us. We do have other donors."

Ruth saw Susannah give her husband a gently reprimanding look in the vein of, "If you would just let me finish!" and realized the newlyweds were still getting used to being united. She smiled at them both. "Oh, I know you appreciate my giving, and it's my decision how much I donate." Ruth removed her glasses absentmindedly as she thought about what she wanted to say. The room remained silent. "Ever since my eightieth birthday party, Emma has barely spoken to me." She looked at Ray, brushing away a tear. "It's because I asked you to recommend a family counselor. She was furious and left the party in a huff. Since then, our conversations have been terse, at best. She insisted I stop writing and watching your program because in her words, 'He is nothing but a fraud.'"

Susannah's eyes narrowed, and Ray took Ruth's hand. "I feel terrible that it's come to this. Why didn't you say something? Is Emma upset about the donation you made?"

Ruth laughed sadly. "Emma knows nothing about my continued support. And that's the way it must stay."

Ray voiced his unease. "I think we've asked for all the money we're going to."

"Nonsense. Don't get me wrong, Reverend and Mrs. Williams, I love my daughter and don't want to lose her completely. A few weeks ago, I told Emma a little white lie—that I wasn't interested in *The Road to Calvary* any longer. Since then, we've begun to make amends. As far as how I spend or donate my money, Emma has no say. So I wish to be your first donor to purchase one of these beautiful windows."

Susannah clapped her hands together in delight. "That's wonderful, Mrs. Perkins! This will be such an inspiring legacy."

Ruth could see that Ray wasn't quite convinced. "Are you sure? Fifty thousand on top of what you've already contributed?"

Ruth eyed the couple. "I wouldn't be doing this if I didn't truly believe in your Christian endeavors. And Emma failed to mention that she and Jack continue to see the therapist you suggested. You have made an impact, whether Emma admits it or not. As for the money, you know as well as I that you can't take it with you."

Ray chuckled, and Susannah smiled her agreement.

That settled, Ruth switched into hostess mode. "Who can I interest in some homemade apple pie and fresh coffee?"

They both raised their hands, and Ruth motioned to Susannah. "Come with me into the kitchen, dear, and help me serve, will you?"

"Certainly," she said, following Ruth out of the room.

Ruth had set out her best silver coffee service and china plates and cups. "Susannah, you cut the pie, and I'll pour. Then we'll serve off this silver tray."

"What will happen to your beautiful house when you pass away? Of course, obviously, that's a long way off."

Ruth considered Susannah's question as she poured. "I haven't given it much thought. It's paid for, so I imagine Emma would sell it and keep the proceeds. Why?"

"This is delicious," Susannah said and licked apple filling off her finger. She went to the sink and washed her hands. "Here's something for you to think over. Rather than keeping so much of your money in savings accounts with the bank, another option could be investing your money in a new fund the church is developing for members only. We're calling it Jesus Saves Investments, which has both a secular and religious meaning. If you're interested, I'd be happy to explain the particulars."

Ruth placed the coffee service on a tray and carried it across the room, where Susannah added the plates of pie. "I would definitely be attracted to spreading my money around for a better return. We can discuss it tonight, if you and Ray have the time."

Susannah glanced over her shoulder at her husband on the couch, flipping pages in a magazine. She smiled warmly at Ruth. "He is so busy with his regular ministry and this campaign; I hate to add more to his plate. How about you and I meet first, next week, say on Tuesday or Wednesday? Ray will be out of town, and I can give you further details about the fund and answer any questions. Let's have lunch, and it will give us a chance to get better acquainted."

Ruth studied the vivacious Susannah. *Such a lovely, caring woman.* "That sounds delightful!"

"Do you like seafood? We could go to Steamers. I can explain the benefits and the steps involved. The final decision, of course, is up to you."

Ruth looked at the calendar on the wall next to the phone. "I love seafood. Tuesday is good for me. Say around eleven thirty?"

"That time is perfect," Susannah replied. "I'll pick you up. But for now, why don't we keep this between you and me? Ray is meeting with an organization in Oklahoma City about possible national syndication, and I don't want him under any more pressure."

"How exciting!" Ruth exclaimed and put a finger to her lips. "I won't say a word."

44

Tuesday, June 24, 2003
St. Louis, Missouri
Buck's Home

When Buck answered the jangling telephone, Seth's frightened, panting breath filled his ears. "You gotta come quick, Buck! Cole's real sick, and they've taken him to St. Joe's Hospital, and he might die and—"

"Slow down, son! You called 911?"

"Y-yes," Seth stuttered. "Cole wasn't breathing when I found him, and there was vomit all over and—"

This was surreal. Buck felt his chest tighten, preparing for the ultimate disappointment. "When you found him, were there drugs near Cole?"

"No, no. Nothing. Some stuff was knocked over, like he was stumbling around the apartment. But there's no smack anywhere. Cole won't even take aspirin."

"Alcohol? Maybe Cole went on a bender after our meeting."

"Buck!" Seth shouted into the phone. "There is nothing here except some spilled orange juice."

The police have got to be at the apartment. "Put the officer in charge on the phone. I'll meet you in the emergency room."

†

Malachi was seated on a vinyl sofa talking to Seth when Buck arrived. He excused himself to greet his friend.

"Thanks for coming," Buck said, gasping for breath. He spoke fast, his sentences running together. "I can't get ahold of Jeff. Have you talked to the EMTs? How's Cole?"

"Let's take a walk," Malachi said, guiding him by the elbow into a hallway.

Buck ran a hand over his mullet, shaking his head apologetically. "Sorry. This has rattled me as much as the murders of those poor women. None of this seems real. You talk, and I'll listen."

"Cole's in a coma. I had CSI bag all the foods in his refrigerator for testing, after you mentioned the orange juice. I'm speculating here, but given what you and Seth have told me, Cole could have been poisoned. The lab's running every test imaginable. I'm on my way to the crime scene. Officer Buchner is taking Seth downtown to get his statement."

"Goddamnit. I didn't take them seriously enough," Buck said, shoulders drooping under the strain. "You said Cole's in a coma. How bad?"

Malachi patted Buck's back. "The doctors indicated it will be a couple of days before the extent of the damage is known. But you did everything you could."

†

St. Louis, Missouri
Ray and Susannah's home

Later that evening when Ray pulled into the driveway, he saw Susannah pulling weeds in the flower garden. Even dressed in overalls, her hair tied back, and covered in dirt, she was beautiful. He sat there for a moment just watching her, thinking how very lucky he was. In the driver's side mirror, he caught his own reflection—wistful yet scowling. He needed to give her the news.

"Hello, my love," he said, stepping from the car.

Susannah got up off her knees, wiping sweat from her brow with a gloved hand. "Whew! It's getting warm out here. I think I'm ready for some iced tea." She came to Ray and kissed him on the cheek.

Ray viewed the tall plants, spiked pink and yellow flowers with massive leaves at the back border of the garden. "What are your new plants?"

She peeled off her gardening gloves and slipped an arm through his. "Castor oil plants. I like them because they're ornamental and give a nice balance to the rest of the garden. The drawback is the seeds are toxic if you eat them."

They walked to the back door, Susannah entering ahead. "Well, so is the lovely oleander plant," Ray said. "Gardening can be a dangerous business."

Susannah laughed. "You are so clever."

In the kitchen, Susannah poured iced tea from a pitcher. "Do you want a glass?" Ray declined, and she joined him at the table. She took a long drink, set down her glass, and reached out a hand. "Why did Doug Snyder want to see you? Did Seth and Cole get into trouble?"

Ray noted the sarcasm in her voice. He knew Susannah had never been a fan of hiring recovering addicts, worried that they might slip back into using or stealing from them. But he had found Seth and Cole to be hardworking, dependable employees determined to take their lives back and be productive members of society. That had made today's events greatly disturbing.

"I'm not sure. Neither Cole or Seth came in today. That's highly unusual behavior for them. This afternoon, Doug called me and said not to expect to see them again."

Susannah mulled over the news, slowly running a finger around the rim of her glass. Her reply brimmed with contempt. "I'm not shocked. That's junkies for you, Ray. After all you've done for Cole and Seth, we always knew they could revert to their drug habit any time."

Ray sighed, wishing his wife would give recovering addicts the benefit of the doubt, since she was one herself. But he kept these thoughts to himself. "Remember that there are two sides to every story, and the truth is somewhere in the middle."

Susannah finished her iced tea, the cubes tinkling in her glass, and changed the subject. "I need to get these dirty clothes off and shower. Then we can discuss the parishioners we're approaching for donations." She placed the glass in the sink and let an overall strap slide off her shoulder. "Care to join me?" She smiled, unhooking the overalls.

Ray stood, and she took him by the hand, leading him upstairs to the shower.

✝

Monday, June 30, evening
Lincoln, Nebraka
Linda's home

For over two weeks, Linda had immersed herself in the world of horticulture while memorizing key details of her new life story. She felt confident.

She had stepped from a warm, bubbly bath when her police cell rang. Throwing on a robe over her slender body, Linda ran to her bedroom. She was surprised to see Malachi's name on the caller ID and wondered why he was calling.

"Hello?"

"Hi, Captain Turner, this is Detective Johnson. We have a major change of plans."

All business—Captain Turner versus an informal Linda. Her stomach sank. He sounded as if the undercover operation were being scratched. She braced herself for his news. "What kind of changes?"

He breathed heavily. "Hope I'm not calling too late; but in the last fourteen days, crimes have been committed that are directly related to our investigation."

Linda reached for the glass of water on her nightstand, her insides twisting into tight bunches of anxiety.

"Two women, one of whom was threatening legal action against *The Road to Calvary,* were found shot to death. That was on the fourteenth. A week later, a *Calvary* employee was found with severe antifreeze poisoning."

Still clutching the water glass, Linda asked, "Is he okay?"

Malachi's voice was grave. "He ingested a lot of antifreeze; all the food in his refrigerator had been tainted. If he'd not been found promptly, there's a good chance he'd be dead, too. As it is, he'll have permanent health issues."

Linda groaned in sadness and sympathy. "I am so sorry. What can I do?"

"I need you in St. Louis as soon as possible. It's essential we get a person on the inside. I realize this alters Chief Langston's timeline, and we're not ready—but we can't wait."

Linda bit her bottom lip. "I'll talk to the chief. Give me a couple of days."

45

Friday, July 4, 2003
St. Louis, Missouri
Downtown Precinct

Malachi and his team wanted Linda to be on set for the Sunday morning service. They had been questioning her on various details of her new persona for hours until it slid off her tongue as though it had been a part of her life for years.

Situated in an airless interview room, Malachi wanted one last run. "Ms. Sinclair, tell me about yourself. What brings you to St. Louis?"

Linda threw back her shoulders, inhaling deeply. "I moved to St. Louis after a messy divorce. It was final in February of this year in Illinois."

Malachi crossed his arms, his expression that of a cop listening for any inconsistencies in her answers. "Where did you live in Illinois?"

"The town of Geneva, a quaint historical village considered an outer suburb of Chicago. I worked as a plant specialist for Gethsemane Garden Center on Clark Street in Chicago proper."

Malachi's partner, Phil Burt, launched the next question. "I see you've got some pretty swell digs in the Marquette Building on Broadway in a tenth floor corner condo. You made out well in your divorce. What did your ex do for a living?"

She composed her thoughts and met Phil's gaze. "He's a psychiatrist at Cook County Hospital, Dr. Ray Mohan. I got a substantial settlement in the divorce."

"Where did you meet Dr. Mohan?" Malachi quizzed her, his brown eyes intense.

"We were college sweethearts at the University of Illinois. I was at the College of Agriculture, studying horticulture, and he was at the College of Medicine."

Phil asked Linda a question that still made her stop and carefully recall each digit. "What's your home phone number?"

She grimaced. "How about my social security number; I definitely remember that."

"You've got to know your phone number. Yes, you're new in town, but it needs to trip off your tongue like you've had it for years," Phil said, tapping his pencil. The smell of his cheap Brut cologne wafted under Linda's nose. *How does his wife stand it?*

She focused, feeling as though she was taxing every single brain cell. She slowly recalled the number and, for good measure, rattled off her social as well.

"Keep practicing that phone number," Phil said.

Malachi observed her closely. "About your appearance—do you want to change it even further than just glasses?

"No. Glasses alter my appearance quite a bit. I'm styling my hair differently and dressing in far pricier clothes than I'm used to."

The detectives took turns lobbing questions—everything from Linda Sinclair's birth date, mother's middle name, where she grew up, to the mundane details of her favorite color and baseball team. She passed them all.

It was her turn to ask a question. "Where will the surveillance team be?"

"We'll be in a van, up the street, listening in," Phil said.

Linda's brow creased. "The service starts at eleven o'clock, correct?"

"Yep, but with the crowds they've been drawing, you'll want to get there early and familiarize yourself with the layout," Malachi answered.

He pushed a stack of legal documents, a set of house and car keys, and electronic devices on the table. "That brings us again to backup and surveillance," Malachi said. He picked up a box off the table and handed it to her. "This is your earpiece. You'll want to wear it the next couple of days and get comfortable."

Linda opened the box, noting the earpiece was for the right. It felt odd, the sensation of her ear plugged with water.

Malachi asked another question. "Where's the parking garage we'll meet up in for updates?"

Linda leaned back in her chair, watching both officers. "Three blocks north of the Marquette Building. Lower level, underground parking."

Phil stroked his mustache. "Malachi hasn't asked you this yet, so I will. What are the names of the two employees at *The Road to Calvary* we are working with and briefly describe them?"

Linda caught a breath. "Jeff Jones is Malachi's army buddy from the Gulf War. He's physically fit, has short cropped hair, and is the camera operator. Buck Neal is their stage director and IT guru. He wears a mullet and has a pierced ear. Both men are aware I'm coming, and the code for urgent is either Jeff or Buck wearing a red plastic bracelet."

"Good. I also need to give you these," Malachi said, handing her two cell phones. "You may not have seen one of these, but this is a burner cell, popular among drug dealers. It's a secure line and is the phone you call Phil or me on. Keep it in a safe place. This second one is your personal cell with GPS. Keep it on you always, so we can track you. They're marked—red for burner, green for personal." He showed the bottoms of the phones.

Linda looked over the multiple piles. "Even though we're rushed, it feels great to start. I realize we have limited time; but when I become Linda Sinclair, all I have to do is remember Gregory Hansen and those children to make this a success."

46

Sunday, July 6, 2003
St. Louis, Missouri
The Road to Calvary building

Linda pulled into *The Road to Calvary* parking lot at 10:15 a.m. It was already three-quarters full. She cut the engine, observing throngs streaming into what appeared to be an industrial warehouse.

"Can you hear me?" she said.

Malachi's voice filled her head. "Loud and clear. We'll check the reception once you're inside. Take your time. Introduce yourself and get comfortable with the surroundings. Good luck."

Linda had carefully considered her new persona's appearance. Her glasses and a loose updo gave her a bookish appearance, still attractive but nonthreatening to someone like Susannah.

The humidity seared her lungs as she walked across the parking lot. She shook hands with greeters at the entrance and searched the crowd for an empty seat. There was no sign of the Reverend Ray, his wife, or the guy with the mullet. From behind a camera, she spotted a buff male with a near buzz cut. She breathed more easily as she spotted a lone chair at the end of a row.

"Is this seat taken?" she asked an obese middle-aged couple.

"Oh no," the large woman answered. "Happy to have you join us."

"Thank you."

The woman's husband leaned across his wife, addressing Linda. "Are you a new member? We've been growing so fast, it's hard to keep track of the regulars and who's new. We're the Carlsons, Bob and Billie."

Linda smiled, happy at her good fortune, striking up a conversation with parishioners on her first try. She extended her hand. "I'm Linda Sinclair, and I'm new, both to St. Louis and *The Road to Calvary*."

"Welcome," Billie said, shaking her hand firmly. "The Reverend Williams and his wife, Susannah, are wonderful people. You can definitely feel God's presence here."

"St. Louis is a great city," Bob said. "You'll have to visit the Riverfront."

"I have a lovely view of it from my condo," Linda replied modestly. "I love to walk on the paths there in the morning," she lied. Her residence wouldn't be ready for a week.

"Oh, that is so nice." Billie said. "Can I ask what brought you to our fine city?"

"Billie!" Bob voiced irritation. "That's none of our business."

"It's quite all right." Linda said. "A divorce, unfortunately. I felt St. Louis was a good place to begin my life anew."

"I'm terribly sorry," Billie soothed. "Were you married long?"

Billie's question sent Linda's mind racing. After all the prep, the length of Linda's marriage had never been discussed. Quick calculations were worked out in her frenzied brain. "We were college sweethearts and were married fifteen years."

"That's no short period," Billie said, and Bob nodded sympathetically.

Perfect, Linda thought. *My first visit and I not only meet members, but nosy ones, who might just direct me to Mrs. Williams.*

Someone yelled, "Two minutes to air!" The stragglers found seats, and the room fell into silence.

The choir walked out onto the stage and sang the first hymn, the words flashing up on a screen behind the stage. Ray and Susannah came to center stage, holding hands.

Linda's trained eye zeroed in on Susannah's presence. She played the devoted wife, holding Ray's microphone when he handed it off, doting attentively during his sermon, motioning for the congregation to rise during the prayer of deliverance. Near the end, Susannah implored the congregation for donations.

"As most of you know, we are already a quarter of the way toward our capital campaign goal, which is great and glorious news. But we can do better."

Linda watched Susannah make deliberate eye contact with each segment of the audience.

"As a special gift from us to you, receive Scriptures of Encouragement from the Reverend Ray when you contribute to the Growing in Christ Campaign."

Linda glanced around the studio, noticing the audience's rapt attention on Susannah.

"Even if you've already donated, won't you pick up the phone, write that check, or use a credit card? This is *your* church, and all the wonderful works we do are possible because of your support. Help us continue our mission to preach and live the Gospel of our Lord Jesus Christ."

When the final prayer was said, the crowd flowed toward the doors and queued up to shake Ray and Susannah's hands, like bees trying to get to the hive. Linda stayed with her new acquaintances as they quizzed her on her past, and she asked the couple questions in return. Bob brought Linda forward for the personal introduction she had hoped for.

"Reverend Ray and Mrs. Williams, this is our friend, Linda Sinclair. She's just moved to town, recently divorced, and is looking for a church. Billie and I told her she couldn't find a better one."

Linda exchanged pleasantries, shaking both Ray and Susannah's hands, but didn't hear a word Ray said. At the comments "just moved to town" and "recently divorced," Susannah decisively grasped Linda's forearm.

"I've been in the same position and know what you're going through. If there's anything I can do to help, please call me."

Smiling warmly, Linda said, "I would love to talk with someone who's had the same experience. Maybe we could get coffee sometime."

"I'd love to," Susannah replied. She grabbed a program from a table and asked for a pen. She scribbled a number—with her left hand. "Here's my home phone. I'd love to chat."

She's Pamela Watts. Linda forced her brightest smile. "I'll give you a call next week."

47

Wednesday, July 9, 2003
St. Louis, Missouri
Linda's condo

Linda was torn between seeming too anxious to contact Susannah, her need to bring justice to the Hansen family, and the limited time to accomplish their goal. *Deep breath. Take your shot and ask her to meet. There isn't much time.*

She inhaled and called. Susannah was very enthusiastic, suggesting lunch the next day and proposing a restaurant. "I can pick you up," Susannah offered, but Linda wasn't quite yet ready to be alone with the killer of at least six. That simple number sent a prickly chill up her spine, as she politely declined.

"Thanks for the generous offer, but I have some errands to run first. Give me the address, and I'll meet you."

†

THURSDAY, JULY 10, 2003
St. Louis, Missouri
Downtown café

Their meeting place, a small café not far from her hotel, allowed Linda the chance to walk. She arrived ahead of Susannah, dressed in white slacks and a linen jacket over a turquoise shell. She looked polished, but casual. Linda caught her reflection in a window and observed that the glasses and having her hair up made her resemble a staid librarian. Up the city block, she spotted the nondescript van in which Malachi and Phil had set up surveillance.

Linda went into the empty ladies' room. Casually checking her makeup, she said, "How do I sound?"

Malachi's voice filled her right ear. "Great. As though you're here in the van."

She walked to the hostess stand, explaining she was waiting for a guest.

Susannah arrived a few minutes late. "I hope you haven't been here long," she apologized.

"I just got here myself. Thanks so much for agreeing to talk with me," Linda said, slipping out of her linen jacket. "It is warm out there today."

"I hope you don't hate the heat," Susannah offered sympathetically. "St. Louis summers can be hot and humid. Took me a while to get used to it."

They settled into a booth, and Linda seized on Susannah's comment. "You're not a native?"

"No. Like you, I moved here after my divorce to start over. Must be the Gateway Arch with all its promise. St. Louis appealed to me as the right place to live."

Linda pretended to peruse the menu, while carefully making

mental notes of everything Susannah said. "Where are you from originally?"

Susannah paused, looking over the top. "I'm from North Dakota. My dad worked in the oil fields, and Mom was a housewife. Things were good until the 1980s when the oil boom went bust. But let's talk about you!"

That's a new spin, Linda thought, confident that Malachi and Phil were recording every word. She decided not to push Susannah on personal details so quickly, asking for luncheon suggestions instead.

Susannah related some favorites, and they ordered iced tea and salads. She was quickly probing Linda on her personal life.

"Your divorce—how are you doing? Is it final yet?"

Oh, yes, my divorce. "I'm doing pretty well, now that I'm living in another city. I waited to move until the divorce was final; but even then, there are things, like changing my name back, that are so time consuming."

"That's the worst," Susannah agreed. "There are so many different documents that you forget have your old married name on them and need to be revised. If you get married again, you have to do it all over." Susannah shook her curls and sipped her tea.

"Have you and Reverend Ray been married long?" Linda asked.

"A little over three months. It's so nice to find the love of your life after losing both your children and watching your marriage crumble because of it."

"I am so sorry for your loss," Linda said, reaching for her own glass. "We didn't have children, so no custody to fight over. But losing a child, much less two, I can't imagine the trauma you went through."

Susannah's eyes were wet, and she brushed away a tear. "It was very, very difficult. But, my goodness we're not here to talk about me. Where are you from?"

You are a fiend—using your children's deaths, children you most likely murdered, to garner sympathy. Linda maintained a poker face.

She regarded Susannah while eyeing a tiny scar above her lip where a mole—exactly like the one Darryl Patterson had mentioned—could have been removed, and smiled even if she didn't have an unobstructed view to her right ear. *Still, this was more proof.* "We, I mean, I'm from Illinois. I grew up there, as did my ex-husband."

"What did your husband do?" she asked, taking another sip of tea.

"He was a psychiatrist at Cook County Hospital in Chicago. He still is."

Susannah was impressed. "A doctor! Where did you meet?"

Linda knew Susannah would ask questions, but she wanted to get back to talking about her. "We met in college at the University of Illinois. He was in med school, and I was studying agronomy and horticulture."

Susannah swirled the tea in her glass. "Are you an avid gardener? I love working in mine and being outside with God and nature."

"Living in a high-rise doesn't allow for much gardening, but I worked at a large nursery for years."

A middle-aged waitress came bearing the spinach-cranberry salads, and Linda was pleased the conversation reverted to the mundane for a few minutes. She needed a minute to contemplate her next move.

After a few bites, Linda steered the focus back to Susannah. "The hardest thing for me is dealing with the loneliness." Her tone was one of taking Susannah into her confidence. "Was it that way for you, too?"

Susannah finished a bite of salad. "I won't lie—the loneliness and dealing with the loss of my kids was unbearable. At least until I met Ray. This program literally saved my life, and I thank God every single day."

She reached out, touching the top of Linda's hand. It felt as if electricity were spiking in her veins.

"It will get better, and the pain won't feel like it's breaking your heart. But you have to keep busy and be around those who support you." Susannah withdrew her hand, resuming the topic of Linda's past. "You said you're in a condo. If you don't mind my asking, are you renting, or did you buy?"

The ice cubes in Linda's glass clinked. She took a long drink. "I bought a unit, in a building not very far from here. The Marquette Building—have you heard of it? I'm on the tenth floor with a view overlooking the Arch and the river."

Susannah nodded appreciatively. "Very nice. You must have come out pretty well financially." She wiped her mouth using her napkin.

Linda's smile was tinged with melancholy. "I always wonder if I could have done something differently to salvage the marriage." She threw Susannah a crucial tidbit of personal data. "I was able to pay for my condo and car in cash, still leaving me very comfortable financially. But I want to make a difference. I'm researching causes and organizations, several of which I was involved with in Illinois. I'd welcome any suggestions you might have."

Susannah put her fork down slowly, her face beaming. "The Good Lord must have brought us together for a special reason. Our Growing in Christ Campaign launched recently. Have you received our materials?"

"Oh, yes! You mentioned it last week. I took a donor package."

Susannah raised her glass, deliberately eyeballing Linda. "Wonderful! You asked for suggestions of places to contribute your money, and of course, I am somewhat biased. As we work to raise funds, one of the things Ray and I are stressing to potential donors is that they are not only celebrating the work of Jesus Christ, but also creating a legacy that will live on indefinitely."

Linda finished her salad, smearing off the remainder of her lipstick with the napkin. "I'd like to hear more of these special opportunities."

"Everyone who donates will have their name inscribed on a plaque, so future generations will know who built this church, tying into the idea of a legacy. For those with the financial means, and this may be exactly what you're looking for, there is the chance to purchase one of twelve custom-made stained-glassed windows depicting key scenes in Christ's life. There will also be the option to purchase pews as an individual, family, or group. This is *your* church, and we want you to have every opportunity to be a part of it."

Susannah was a master manipulator, making her would-be victims feel how special they were. Linda speculated on Ray's involvement. "This is impressive. Let me review the materials, and I'll get back to you in a few days. This could be exactly what I'm looking for."

They finished lunch, which Linda insisted on buying. "It's been so helpful talking to you," she lied.

They parted, with Susannah giving her a hug. "It is so nice to visit and make new friends. Call me if you have any questions on the campaign. I'd be happy to meet again."

Linda bobbed her head in agreement.

She walked a full block before saying a word, looking behind her to make certain she wasn't being followed. "That was noteworthy," she finally said aloud.

Malachi's voice occupied her head. "Let's meet in the parking garage at eight when it starts getting dark to review."

48

Later that evening
St. Louis, Missouri
Downtown parking garage

Linda spotted Malachi beyond the garish yellow light of the garage that illuminated the fringes of a dark corner.

She checked her surroundings, meeting him in the shadows. "Susannah didn't waste any time asking for a donation." Linda removed the slick four-color brochure from her bag.

"Ah, the Growing in Christ Campaign," Malachi acknowledged. He accepted the brochure, casually flipping the pages.

"Right. Susannah's peddling these as custom-made at fifty thousand each. I don't believe her for a second. She and possibly Ray are running a scam. Susannah will want a decision soon. I realize I'm asking a lot, but I need the money ASAP to make the purchase and collect her DNA all at once."

"When can you meet for lunch again?"

"Susannah wants to see my condo. Fantastic opportunity to invite them for dessert and coffee, as a friendly get-to-know-you gesture. Obtain both their DNA by next week, if the money can be approved."

"I'll start the paperwork tomorrow."

The sound of screeching tires startled them both. A car careened up the ramp, heading directly toward Linda and Malachi. Linda felt him grabbing her around the waist, pulling her deeper into the darkness.

She felt Malachi's rapid breath at the back of her neck, muscular arms holding her close. Taking the corner at high speed, the car slammed into a cement pillar.

Without thinking, they sprinted to the smashed car, black smoke curling from under the hood. Malachi reached the vehicle first, and with force, pried the door open, where the bloody driver slumped over the steering wheel.

Dialing 911, Linda spoke urgently, "A car has crashed in the Commons parking garage."

"Driver's unresponsive," Malachi called out.

She rattled off pertinent details. "ETA less than a minute."

As witnesses, they would have to provide statements to police. Malachi silently revealed his badge to officers on the scene. Firefighters sprayed foam to put out any fire, while the victim was taken away by ambulance.

Nearly an hour passed before they returned to their conversation. "It's as if this case is drenched in death," Linda remarked glumly.

"Yeah, things have been pretty weird." Malachi was saddened, too.

"He must have experienced a medical crisis of some kind."

Malachi's strong hand grasped hers, drawing Linda into the shadows again. "Let's wrap this up. I'll work on the money aspect and what else?"

She motioned toward the brochure inside his coat. "The company supposedly making these windows is American Stained Glass. Let's find out if they're working with Susannah or ever heard of her. We should also start investigating Ray Williams. They could be in this together."

"You got it," Malachi nodded. "I'll leave a message on the burner once the money's in your account."

They left the garage separately. Close to ten now, the air was heavy with humidity, the night steamy. On her three-block journey, Linda's mind kept returning to Malachi holding her. It had felt natural, which surprised her. She chided herself. *He's your partner. Don't see things where nothing exists.*

49

Sunday, July 13, 2003
St. Louis, Missouri
The Road to Calvary set

The confirmation call from Malachi came three days later. He did not, however, have information on the glass company. Every day lost came closer to her six-week deadline. It was nerve-racking to move so quickly, but getting the money was a temporary relief. Linda wondered who else was being suckered for fifty thousand dollars.

Billie and Bob Carlson seemed exactly the type who would want to invest heavily in the building campaign. Prior to the next service, Linda broached the subject as though she were consulting them for advice.

"I'm considering purchasing one of the stained-glass windows," she confided in a whisper to the couple. "But I want your thoughts, since you've been around longer."

Bob laughed jovially. "We believe buying a window is a terrific investment. We've already selected ours."

Billie fanned her girth with the program. "We're dipping into our 401(k). But this is the opportunity of a lifetime."

"Billie's right," Bob said. He patted his wife on her plump knee. "This will be a part of our legacy."

Linda concurred. "Thanks, I'll do that, right after the show."

"Two minutes to air!"

Linda recognized Buck Neal giving the command as people scurried to find seats and the lights went down.

Paying little attention to Ray's sermon, Linda kept going over what she would say to Susannah. She wanted to seem excited, but not overly so. From experience she knew someone as calculating as Susannah constantly suspected others.

At the show's conclusion, Linda made her move, taking Susannah aside. "I wanted you to know I've decided on my financial contribution. I'd prefer to discuss this with you and the reverend privately."

Susannah grasped her forearm excitedly and squeezed it. "That's wonderful, Linda! Is tonight too soon? We have space available to talk here. Or we could come to your place."

Linda's brain was in overdrive. She hadn't even had to offer an invitation. "Coming over to my place would be lovely. Why don't we say six-ish? I'll have dessert and coffee."

"I can't wait to see your place. The view sounds fabulous." Susannah waved Ray over. "Great news. Linda has made a decision regarding her donation. We'll be going to her condo this evening to present the options."

Ray clutched Linda's hand. "That is wonderful. I haven't been in the Marquette Building since its renovation into condos, but I understand it's one of the premier addresses in St. Louis."

Susannah nodded enthusiastically. "I told Linda I've been dying to see it!"

Linda felt goose bumps tickle her skin. She was both excited and slightly apprehensive. "Well then, tonight it is."

"Look closely at the patterns on the china," Malachi instructed over the burner. "One is a lighter shade of blue than all the others. That's the coffee cup you want to give Susannah."

Linda held the flip-phone to her ear and pulled the four place settings from the china cabinet. "Okay, I see which one. I'll keep her dishes and silverware separate from the rest without being obvious."

"Repeat the code phrase should anything go wrong."

"Yep. 'My sister called.'" Linda lined up the dishes on the counter.

"Phil and I were able to get access to a vacant condo, so we're in the building. We can be at your apartment in seconds."

It unnerved her ever so slightly that Malachi kept reminding Linda this in-home meeting had the potential for danger. But she thought that of every meeting with Susannah. Ray's presence made her feel more at ease. "Listen, I need to get going. They'll be here in less than a half hour."

Malachi hung up, and Linda hid the phone.

She stacked the china on the counter rather than setting a formal table, so she would control who got what cup and plate. Linda had purchased a summer centerpiece and napkins for a festive, hospitable décor.

Ray and Susannah arrived promptly at six, and Ray carried a large portfolio under one arm. They settled in the living room.

"Your donation will be instrumental in helping us reach our goal. We're excited to know what choice you've made."

Linda didn't want to drag this out. "I have decided to purchase a stained-glass window. How many are left?"

"Four," Susannah said with mounting excitement.

"You'll have to forgive me," Ray said, looking over at Linda. "Susannah is handling finding donors for the windows and pews, as well as getting them ordered and made. We've split responsibilities. She has a gift for marketing ideas, in case you haven't noticed. I let her take the reins and chair the Growing in Christ Campaign giving committee, while I handle all the logistics."

"I'm not dealing with the land and meeting city codes," Susannah said cheerfully, shaking her head. "I enjoy overseeing fundraising."

Linda retained every word. *And being in direct contact with the money.* "Of course." She looked at the couple with a hint of inquisitiveness. "This is a huge undertaking, and I can imagine you need to spread things out. What else does the committee do?"

"We're also responsible for the land and making sure we meet other city requirements," Ray said, spreading his hands out. "Our building and three acres of land were donated by Mr. Karl Wilcox. He and several parishioners with city hall connections assist us with building permits, code specifications, and such."

Linda played ignorant. "Where are we in terms of raising money? It sounds as if we still have a ways to go until we can break ground." She put on a face of mock unease. "Of course, it's not any of my business."

Ray grinned at Linda. "Yes, it *is* your business! You're a member of this church."

"*Absolutely.* Without the contributions of members like you, we wouldn't be where we are!" Susannah once again pontificated on how the gifts of people like Linda were making this endeavor possible. The captain wasn't buying.

Ray came forward on the sofa, folding his large hands across his knees. "You know we have to have half the money in place—in this case just over a million. Right now, we have donations totaling four hundred fifty thousand."

Linda coughed. "Let's get started. What are my choices for a window, seeing as there are now only four remaining?"

"You have several options. Some donors don't care what scene their window portrays. These are larger, detailed photos than in the brochure." Susannah opened the portfolio. "We also have a prototype, although it's not to scale."

The glass window gleamed under the bright lights of the room. Linda had to admit it was stunning.

For the next fifteen minutes, Susannah and Ray pointed out Jesus's baptism, his walking on water, miracle at Cana, driving the moneychangers from the Temple, and other scenes for windows. Linda knew these stories from an education in Catholic schools, and she was getting antsy to finalize the deal. She decided to do just that.

"This is all very overwhelming with so many choices," Linda said, interrupting the spiel. "I'll tell you what. I trust your judgment implicitly, so why don't you choose the scene depicted in my window?"

"We appreciate your faith in us," Ray replied. He turned on the sofa toward his wife. "I think we should check with these other folks and make certain they want us to choose. After all, this is a large investment."

From the corner of her eye, Linda saw Susannah's eyes narrow at her husband's statement. Ever the manipulator, in the next sentence, Susannah was cheerfully agreeing with him. "Certainly, we'll double-check with donors on their selection. As Ray said, fifty thousand dollars is no small amount of money."

Linda rose from the overstuffed chair and retrieved her purse from the open-concept kitchen, switching on the coffee maker. "Well, other members definitely trust you. What I wish to do tonight before indulging in some apple cobbler and coffee is to finalize my contribution." She rummaged through her purse for a checkbook. "I'll give you the check tonight, but if I decide in the upcoming weeks that I do want a voice in the selection process, can I still make the change, and how long would I have?"

Ray's response was emphatic. "You certainly will have that option! It will be months before these windows are complete, right, sweetheart? And you won't have to pay the full amount up front. I'm sure some folks will want to pay in installments."

Linda wasn't paying much attention to Ray, but to the scowl creasing his wife's forehead. *She does not look pleased.*

"Susannah," Ray said. "Linda asked us a question. There will be several weeks for her to decide if she wants to choose her window and a down payment will be fine."

Linda looked at the reverend's sincere face. *Ray doesn't seem to have any fraudulent intent; he appears to believe this campaign is legit.*

Susannah shook her head, as if she were bringing herself out of a trance. "I am so very sorry. Yes, of course you can ask for input. Paying all at once means a nice tax break."

Linda rose and handed her check to Susannah.

"Let me help you," Susannah said, trying to follow her.

"You and Ray are my guests. Think of this as my inaugural hosting of friends." Linda eyed the coffee cups and poured. She felt almost giddy as Susannah's red lipstick made a perfect imprint when she took her first sip. Apple cobbler and ice cream were served.

It didn't appear as though Ray and Susannah had discussed Linda in any depth beyond her divorce and subsequent move. When the reverend began inquiring about her family, she deftly turned the conversation toward the story of how Ray and Susannah met.

At around eight-thirty, well after Linda had hoped they would have departed, Ray and Susannah started saying their good-byes.

Ray stood, waiting for his wife. "Well, I think we should bid Linda good night and be on our way. Thank you for your hospitality and a most generous donation."

"This was such a lovely evening," Susannah cooed. She clasped Linda's hand and spoke of her deep generosity again. She asked Ray to say a prayer before they departed.

The three of them held hands as Ray blessed the evening and their blossoming friendship, and Linda didn't remember what all. She could barely touch Susannah's flesh without squirming because she was confident Susannah Williams was their killer.

Linda cared about one single thing. *We've got her DNA.*

"I hate leaving you with all these dirty dishes," Susannah said. "Let me help you clean up. *Please.*"

"Next time," Linda promised, holding a firm open palm against Susannah's chest. She ushered the couple out into the hall. "See you Sunday."

The door closed behind her, and she crumbled against it exhausted. Linda exhaled, imagining a balloon deflating. "We've got her."

"Roger that," Malachi's deep voice crackled in her earpiece.

50

MONDAY, JULY 14, 2003
ST. CHARLES, MISSOURI
RUTH PERKINS'S HOME

Emma arrived promptly at noon for lunch with her mother. *At least we're speaking again,* Emma thought with a sigh of relief. She parked and immediately saw that the drapes were still drawn. Her mother always liked lots of light coming into her house. She rang the bell and waited. Minutes passed, and her mother didn't appear. Emma noticed her hands quivering.

She had a key, but hardly ever used it. She dug deep into her purse to retrieve it. The door unlocked with a loud *click,* and Emma stepped inside.

"Mom? It's Emma. Did you forget we're going to lunch? Mom!" Her words reverberated inside the house. Emma walked toward the back of the house to Ruth's bedroom. She caught a glimpse of her mother's makeup on the bathroom counter. She surmised her mother was in the process of getting ready and simply didn't hear her.

"Mom! It's Emma. Where are you?"

Emma moved into the bedroom, her level of anxiety increasing. The bed was made, Ruth's clothes laid out. Then she viewed feet sticking out along the other side of the bed and rushed to her mother's side.

Crumbled on the floor and still in her bathrobe, Ruth stared blankly at her daughter.

"My God, what happened to you?" Emma knelt beside her mom, but only incoherent words came from Ruth's mouth.

"Jesus!" Emma grabbed the phone off the nightstand, calling 911. "It's my elderly mother. She's fallen or something. I don't know what's happened! She needs help. Please hurry!"

The dispatcher calmly verified Ruth's address and stayed on the line with Emma.

"They're on the way, ma'am. I need you to listen to me."

Emma sputtered. "Uh—of course! She's my mother! Should I move her?"

"No, no. I need you to take her pulse. Do you have a watch with a second hand?"

"Y-yes," she stammered.

"Put your middle and index fingers on the inside of her wrist, below her thumb. You should feel her pulse."

Emma cradled the receiver under her chin. "Yes, I feel it."

"Count your mother's pulse for sixty seconds," the dispatcher instructed. "A normal pulse should be from sixty to a hundred beats per minute."

The beats seemed very fast. Emma had difficulty keeping up. At the end of a minute, she told the dispatcher, "Very fast—two forty."

"I'll alert the paramedics. Is the door locked or can the EMTs walk right in?" the dispatcher inquired.

Emma felt as though her next breath was out of reach. "The door's unlocked. They can come on in."

"What are her symptoms?"

Emma looked closely at her mother and exhaled loudly into the phone. "She was talking gibberish, and there's liquid coming out of her mouth. The left side of her face is drooping."

"When the EMTs get there, you need to get all of her medications and bring them to the hospital. Can you do that?"

She kept tripping over her words. "S-Sure, I can do that." Emma scribbled that note on a piece of paper on her mother's nightstand. She held Ruth's hand. "I'm here, Mom. It's me, Emma."

The sound of wailing sirens in the driveway announced the arrival of the EMTs. Emma stepped aside as her mother was moved to a stretcher. When they asked Emma what had happened, she explained her mother's speech was garbled and her face drooping. Oxygen and an IV were started.

Jim was the senior EMT, a middle-aged man with a mustache. He questioned Emma about her mother's medications and medical history.

Emma was relieved that she knew the answers but had plenty of questions for them. "Mom turned eighty in March; and other than the usual signs of getting older, she's healthy as a horse. Walks every day, plays bridge at the senior center twice a week, and loves to work in her garden. What's happened to her?"

"Our preliminary observation is that your mother suffered a stroke. We're taking her to St. Joe's."

The day had started like any other ordinary Monday, but this sultry summer afternoon had turned into anything but unremarkable. "Can I come along in the ambulance?"

"No," Jim said, politely, but firmly. "Your mother's vitals have to be monitored, and a lot could change in route. Meet us at the hospital. Bring all of her medications."

The three paramedics brought the stretcher up as a pale and confused Ruth stared at the emergency equipment and people she didn't recognize. Emma watched them load her mother into the ambulance, departing with emergency lights flashing and sirens blaring.

Emma stood motionless in the driveway, oblivious to the neighbors gawking and whispering among themselves as the ambulance pulled away.

51

Saturday, July 19, 2003
St. Louis, Missouri
Linda's condominium

Linda turned the key in the lock and slowly opened the door. Malachi had left a message earlier that he would meet at her condo. He'd let himself in and was waiting in the living room.

She dropped her purse on the floor. "Hi. This must be important for you to want to meet in person."

He removed wrap-around sunglasses, and she noticed his eyes were dull, not lively as they normally were. He also carried a large courier's pouch. "I've got news, both good and bad." He set the glasses and baseball cap on the coffee table and opened the pouch.

Linda shrugged out of her coat, tossing it over the back of a chair. Her mind immediately focused on the word "bad."

"Can I get you something to drink?"

Malachi placed sheets of numbers and photos into neat stacks on the table. "I'm good. I'll dive right into the serious stuff." The muscles tensed into a frown on his face.

Linda crossed the room and seated herself next to Malachi on the cream sofa. "What's happened?"

Malachi rubbed his bearded chin, brown eyes intense. "Susannah's

DNA was apparently contaminated in the lab. It matched another individual whose DNA was being tested at the same time." He exhaled in irritation. "The crime lab has a huge backlog, and not to make excuses, but that may have contributed to sloppy procedures. We're going to need to get her DNA again."

Linda slumped against the cushions, not believing what Malachi was telling her. "Get her DNA again? That makes me very uncomfortable."

He sat forward. "I am truly sorry about this. Use the excuse that you've decided you want to choose your window after all. Meet in a public place, preferably a restaurant. We'll cause a distraction to obtain her DNA."

Concoct another lie. Linda raised her hands. "I'll call her tonight and ask to meet again for lunch. Telling her I've changed my mind may raise her suspicions."

"You're gonna have to trust me on this." He tapped the sunglasses against the table. "Here's what I've discovered."

Linda looked at the documents Malachi had spread over the coffee table. He selected a typed page, his mouth curling into a knowing smirk. "I contacted American Stained Glass and spoke with the president, Steve Jacobson. The windows featured here are custom, and they cost from fifty to a hundred grand a piece. However, they've never heard of *The Road to Calvary.*"

Linda's forehead wrinkled. "I can't fathom Susannah pulling these figures from thin air. Not everyone in this church can be blind fools; somebody is going to want additional information."

"I hope not," Malachi admitted. He flicked pages, finding a piece of yellow legal paper with detailed notes. "Steve recalled he received a call three months ago, from a woman named Lorraine McArthur. She was interested in a prototype, and Jacobson had the sales team build one, paid for with a cashier's check. They haven't heard from her since."

"Who is Lorraine McArthur?"

"I knew I recognized the name but couldn't remember from where. I went back over my notes. Jeff told me Lorraine was the name of Ray's deceased wife. Recalling that, I did some research and discovered McArthur was her maiden name."

Linda's head dropped into her hands. "That explains why there's a prototype. With a sample to touch and see, it closes the deal. If I were gullible and desperate to believe, it would have sold me. Susannah showed it the night they were here."

"Another thought," Malachi said, his fingers tapping the table. "We have no idea how many of these she's selling. Your idea that Susannah could take orders for more than twelve and disappear before this church is ever built has merit."

Linda hated when her mind darted around from one dark possibility to an even bleaker thought. "I believe this scam has turned into the biggest score of her life, a possibility she perhaps hadn't foreseen. Like many criminals who haven't been caught, she's grown overly confident. That would explain why appearing on TV, even with her changing appearance, isn't an issue for her." She reined in her thoughts, focusing on the windows. "Hypothetically, let's say she takes money for twelve windows. That's six hundred thousand in donations she's overseeing. We have no idea how much money she has; but when she does, Susannah fades into the wind."

Malachi reached for his notes. "Ray has had financial success, too. Jeff told me that after he lost his wife, Ray left the ministry and went to work for a large corporation." Malachi shuffled papers, removing a national financial publication. "In the mid-1990s, Ray was a handsomely paid ethics consultant for a Fortune 500 corporation. This magazine wrote an extensive profile about him. I contacted some of his former coworkers. All said he was a great guy, hard worker, et cetera. I called in some favors to access his financials; in a five-year period, Ray Williams made over two and a half million."

Her thoughts were overlapping, one half-finished on top of another one forming. Mentally, Linda forced herself to slow down. "How much is Ray worth?"

Malachi sat forward on the couch and found a page. "Currently, he has over a half-million in the bank, and no mortgage or loans. There's a stock portfolio worth close to a million."

She could almost feel the color drain from her face. "And now that he and Susannah are husband and wife, she likely has access."

Malachi stretched muscular arms over his head. "I fear that Ray may be her next victim. They probably have joint accounts; and if he's dead, it's simpler for her to take possession. Then add on all the money she's keeping from the window sales—which could be all of it—and she's gone. It'll be somewhere we can't find her or have jurisdiction." His knuckles cracked.

"Some foreign country," Linda said forlornly. "I'll call her tonight."

Malachi stood his tall frame, replacing the baseball cap and sunglasses. "As soon as you've set up a date, call me. I'll explain the plan in detail. I'll leave this information here for your review. I agree with you; Susannah is planning to leave soon."

Linda walked him into the foyer. He opened the door slowly, surveying the hallway. Without a word, he slipped into the stairwell.

She closed the door behind him, feeling the rapid beat of her heart and quickened breathing. *How could this have happened?*

52

TUESDAY, JULY 22, 2003
St. Louis, Missouri
Downtown restaurant

Numerous what-ifs ran through Linda's mind as she asked Susannah to review the prototype. The stress of having to covertly gain her DNA once again and the tightening schedule was keeping her awake at night. Luck had sided with them once, but twice?

"Everything set?" Linda asked casually, entering a restaurant close to the studio.

Malachi's voice entered her head. "Yep. Phil is already there, sitting at a table toward the back, reading the *St. Louis Dispatch*. He's carrying a leather shoulder bag. Just follow the plan."

This was really happening, no going back. They were either successful, or they weren't, and then what? Her palms were sweating, and she casually wiped them along the pleats in her skirt.

Linda pleaded with herself. *Please, please, do not fail at this.* She twisted the watchband on her wrist, observing Susannah on her way up the street, prototype tucked under her arm. "She's here." She waited until Susannah reached the entrance and held the door open. "Hello. I so appreciate your flexibility at my indecision."

Susannah smiled. "Not a problem. Most individuals couldn't give this much. We understand you want to spend it wisely."

Eyes darting around the room, Linda found Phil seated in a booth. Susannah requested a table nowhere near him. "A table in the middle," she told the hostess.

Oh, for the love of God. "Susannah, would you mind if we took a booth instead? That one by the window will give us plenty of light and room to spread out." Linda kept her tone amiable.

Susannah spied the booth, being cleared of dishes. "Sure, if it's clean."

"It will be a couple of minutes," the hostess said.

They chatted while they waited, but to Linda, it was just noise. When the hostess brought the women to their seats, Linda made certain that Susannah's back was toward Phil. He would pass by the women when he left the restaurant as discussed. Linda felt a surge of energy.

Susannah pointed to the prototype. "Do you want to eat first or get right down to business?"

Despite experience as a cop in varied positions, Linda could feel the tremors of her rapid heartbeat. Impatient to move into the action phase, she wanted this charade over with. "Let's get business taken care of and then enjoy a leisurely lunch."

Susannah approved. She spread the accompanying brochure. "These are all exceptional windows, and, as I mentioned, three couples have chosen specific scenes. You have nine options."

She removed the prototype window from the pouch, holding the glass with both hands. Linda realized it depicted Christ's baptism. Feigning passionate interest, Linda listened to Susannah's well-rehearsed spiel on celebrating the glory of God.

"After you called, I got to thinking about which of these scenes might have meaning for you personally, and it occurred to me that our Lord's baptism might be the most meaningful. I didn't think of that when I initially showed you this."

Abhorrence was Linda's gut response. There was sad mockery in the notion that this woman of endless schemes of deception and betrayal, all leading to nefarious secrets, was speaking to her about the ultimate act of forgiveness. Linda suppressed her fury and queried Susannah. "Why do you feel this represents me?"

Susannah reached across the table, grasping Linda's forearm, her small fingers too tight around her arm. "First, we're all sinners. When I thought of Christ's baptism, I think it also signifies new beginnings. That's what I believe you are doing by moving to St. Louis after your divorce, finding us as a faith community, making a new life—just as baptism symbolizes."

Tremors ran the length of her body. Linda forced a smile that showed she understood. Her lie sounded natural and heartfelt. "That makes sense, and you put it so elegantly. Your suggestions are very important to me."

Susannah spoke in honeyed tones, pulling Linda into her confidence. "It's the right choice. Since meeting you, I've watched you blossom into your own person. I've seen how destructive divorce can be, and I'm happy you're making a life for yourself."

"I appreciate that," Linda continued to lie, wishing this was behind her. "Ready to order some lunch?"

Susannah returned the glass prototype to the pouch, propping it next to her.

The waitress brought menus and water. Linda felt the tightness of her insides tied in knots. Casually, she glanced in Phil's direction and noted he nonchalantly continued to read his paper. Waiting for him to move was nerve-racking, and Linda took the table's edge to steady her hands.

Their food arrived, and she endeavored to stop thinking of the coming event. Susannah chattered on about her garden. She talked of distinctive flora and shrubberies making the parcel her sanctuary. Her mention of castor oil plants caught Linda's notice. "Aren't those poisonous if ingested?" Linda asked.

Susannah wiped her lips. "Only if they're ground into powder. But who does that? In most gardens, they're lovely ornamental plants. Because they grow so tall, they give a garden a nice balance."

Over her shoulder, Linda saw Phil rise from his seat.

"I should have you over to see the garden in full bloom," Susannah continued.

Phil strode past, bumping their table hard, and glasses fell, spilling water all over Susannah.

"Ma'am, I am so sorry," he apologized, grabbing a napkin from a vacant table.

"Why don't you watch where you're going?" Linda said sharply.

When Phil attempted to dry off Susannah's soaking dress with a napkin, she swatted him away like an annoying insect. "Don't touch me! My friend is right—watch where you're going!"

"I apologize. Let me at least buy you ladies lunch," he offered.

Susannah stood up, seething. "I'm going to the restroom to dry off. I'll be back in a minute."

Once she was out of sight, Linda stood, facing him, blocking people's view of the open satchel. She gripped Susannah's empty glass and silverware. In one smooth motion, they dropped into the open plastic evidence bags.

He nodded his head curtly and hurried toward the cashier where he asked the manager for the women's bill.

A waitress approached Linda with towels. "Can I take these dishes? I'll be back to clean up."

"Thank you," Linda replied, accepting towels to mop up the remaining water. She should have begun to relax—their plan to retrieve Susannah's fingerprints and DNA had gone off without a glitch, but instead, her hands were shaking. Phil was paying the bill as Susannah came out of the bathroom.

"What an ass, pardon my French." Susannah turned toward Linda, her eyes narrowing. "I recognize that guy from somewhere."

Shit! Linda felt nauseous. *Think.* "He's got one of those familiar faces. He actually reminds me of my old neighbor."

"No, I recognize that face." Her voice callous, she jabbed an index finger toward Linda. "I know where I've seen him—hanging around the parking lot on Sunday mornings before the broadcast. As if he's waiting for something to happen."

Don't lose your composure. "Come to think of it, I've seen him, too. In fact, I spoke with him once. He asked if Reverend Ray performed miracles every Sunday. I told him he should come and find out. He seemed weighed down by guilt, embarrassment, I don't know. He thanked me and walked away. I haven't seen him since."

Susannah contemplated Linda's statement. "Maybe you're right. A lost soul pondering coming to services."

At the counter, the manager informed them that their lunches had been paid for.

"Well, that takes the sting out of getting water spilled all over me," Susannah said.

They wandered the block together, Susannah chatting mindlessly, parting ways at the corner light.

On the spur of the moment, Linda chose to walk out of her way. She strolled along leisurely before speaking. "Did Phil get what you need?"

"He did. I'll send it to the lab with orders to expedite testing. Still, it will probably take a couple of weeks. We can't risk her DNA being contaminated again. I'm also getting my sergeant involved as an extra precaution."

As she stepped down the crowded street, Linda realized her hands were still shaking.

53

Friday, July 25, 2003
St. Charles, Missouri
Ruth Perkins's home

After eleven long days, Ruth was still in the hospital, and Emma was bone tired. She was having difficulty accepting her mother's stroke had been more severe than originally diagnosed. Her mother couldn't speak and had difficulty swallowing. The paralysis worsened the situation. Emma visited every morning and evening, often tenderly feeding her mother a meal. She talked to her constantly, but Ruth's distant eyes told Emma she didn't recognize her only daughter.

She sat at Ruth's upstairs desk. The reality was setting in—she and Jack knew little about her mother's finances. She opened a drawer, looking deep into the space. Emma recognized her father's gun case. It was unlocked; the Smith and Wesson was tucked inside. She laid the gun and ammunition on the desk. Handling the gun, Emma thought back to her father teaching her to shoot. She smiled at the memory of Sunday afternoon outings of target practice, shooting tin cans off a country fence.

The revolver's chamber was fully loaded. Shocked, Emma removed the bullets and yelled for Jack to join her.

"Jack!"

Emma held the gun, dropping the bullets into the pocket of her sweater and walked out to the hall. She peered at her spouse below. He held an open manila file folder on his lap; when he looked up at her, his brow furrowed in distress.

"You need to come down here."

Emma walked the carpeted steps fast. "What is it?"

Jack saw the Smith and Wesson in Emma's hand. "Isn't that your dad's gun? I hope it isn't loaded."

"It was." She moved closer to Jack. "What have you found?"

"Ruth's bank accounts, and she doesn't have as much money as we thought. The file had fallen behind the drawer. Look at this."

He handed Emma the folder, and she sat down hard in the chair crosswise from him.

Labeled "Donations," Emma mutely flicked through the letters of thanks for her generous contributions to *The Road to Calvary*: ten thousand dollars, fifteen thousand dollars, and fifty thousand dollars for a stained-glass window written in July. Emma's chest was tight, the air dry. Jack pushed another folder titled JSI toward her.

Emma opened it and huffed. Inside laid a check photocopy for two-hundred thousand dollars, written to JSI. "Damn it!" she screamed, and tears of fury sprang from her eyes. "She *promised me* she wouldn't have any more to do with them. My own mother lied to me!"

Jack reached out and put a hand on Emma's quaking forearm. "I know this looks damaging, Em. But I thought your dad invested in blue-chip stocks, leaving Ruth secure. We'll have to meet with her financial team."

The manila file shook in her hands. "I think I figured out what the JSI stands for," Emma sniffled.

He patted her arm. "What?"

"Jesus Saves Investments," she stated flatly. "It's hard to accept she could fall prey to schemes like this. Mom is going to need every cent just to live in a decent place with excellent care. We can sell the house, sure, but how long will that take? My mother shouldn't live in some hell-hole shack. She deserves better." She pulled a tissue from her pocket to blow her nose.

"Let's arrange a meeting with her legal and financial advisors. They'll have a better idea of her real assets." He took the revolver out of his wife's quivering hands. "Give me that and all the bullets, too. Emotions are running high, and access to a firearm is not a good idea."

Emma glowered at her husband in irritation. She couldn't believe what he was insinuating and dumped the gun in his lap. "Jesus, Jack, you're being ridiculous."

54

THURSDAY, JULY 31, 2003
St. Louis, Missouri
LEGAL OFFICES OF BAYLOR AND WHITE

Emma and Jack walked out of the elevator into the sleek offices of Baylor and White and let the brisk receptionist know they had a ten o'clock appointment.

"Mr. and Mrs. Duncan, there's drinks at the coffee bar. Have a seat. Mr. Osborne will be with you shortly."

Sleep had not found Emma easily. Any rest was transient at best. With so much at risk, she had lain awake for nights worried about what the future might bring. She declined the receptionist's offer of coffee—she was wound up enough.

"Remember," Jack whispered. "Let's hear what they have to say before we start making demands."

Emma grudgingly shrugged her shoulders. "Yes, I know."

Mr. White didn't keep them waiting. "Both your mother's accountant, Louis Osborne, and financial planner, Raymond Kyle, are here." He motioned for Emma and Jack to follow him past busy junior associates to a glass-walled conference room.

Introductions were exchanged, and Emma noted no small talk ensued as Mr. White got right to business. "Mrs. Duncan, your mother made some changes to her will in June. I apologize for not having gotten copies sent to the house yet, which is why you couldn't find it." He shoved documents toward them.

"What kind of changes?" Emma asked, trying to keep the testiness out of her voice.

The attorney directed them to page seven. "Ruth is no longer giving you any proceeds from the sale of her home in the event of her death. Instead, that money is to be donated to a religious organization she's listed, *The Road to Calvary*."

Emma looked at Jack wide-eyed. "What? It's not a religious organization. It's a program, run by a fucking televangelist here in St. Louis. I will contest this will in court!"

Mr. White forced a smile. "I'm sorry this is upsetting to you, but—"

She cut him off and zeroed in on the accountant and Mr. Kyle. "My mother also gave this organization over one hundred thousand dollars in less than eighteen months, Mr. Osborne. And then, we found paperwork that she invested two-hundred thousand in a fund called Jesus Saves Investments. Did either of you know about this?"

Mr. Osborne folded his hands. "Only recently was I made aware of your mother's intentions. After she had given the first one hundred thousand, she asked me if she could comfortably continue contributing—"

"And you didn't think to stop her?" To her dismay, Emma saw spittle flying out of her mouth.

Raymond Kyle spoke up, his palms open. "I did know of the investing, and I strongly counseled Ruth against it. But, the client has the final say. However, I have additional unfortunate news."

Jack put a protective arm around Emma's shoulder, and she fought to keep her voice from cracking. "Let's have it then."

Mr. Kyle spread manicured hands over a file. "Three factors converged for a 'perfect storm' if you will, to severely impact

Mrs. Perkins's finances. Are either of you familiar with the Enron Corporation and the ensuing collapse?"

Emma knew she'd heard the name somewhere—the news maybe? She frowned and looked at her husband for input.

Jack squeezed her shoulders tenderly as he spoke. "Enron was an energy company that filed for bankruptcy last year. I believe they were the largest American company to ever do so."

"That's correct. Your father bought Enron stock in the 1980s when the company was starting out." Kyle slid a colored graph over to Emma and Jack. "For years, Enron was a superior investment. Orville continued to buy the stock until his death, making him and Ruth millionaires on paper."

Emma viewed the graph of Enron stock soaring upward until December 2001. She felt her skin becoming wet and clammy, but she nodded for Kyle to continue.

"At the time, I suggested Ruth dump her Enron stock, explaining she would take a substantial loss. Your mother is of the generation where women often didn't get involved in the financial aspects of things. She insisted that since Orville had been right for such a long stretch, the stock was sure to rebound once Enron was sold. That deal fell through; and by the time Ruth understood the gravity of the situation, the stock was worthless."

Emma fought back tears. She recalled her mother hadn't written her first check until after her father died, a process Emma had to school her in. Her bottom lip trembling, she posed a statement and a question. "She never spoke of losing the Enron money to anyone. But I thought she had other investments and her pension from teaching. Is that money gone, too?"

Mr. Osborne's face was sympathetic. "I am so sorry. I understand this isn't what you wanted to hear."

Raymond Kyle's tan features were troubled. "The news is not going to get better," he said, his voice solemn. "Up until 2002, Ruth still had a large amount of money in the stock market outside of Enron. Last year was a bear market. She sold off a larger portion of her portfolio than either Louis or I recommended; but in 2003, the market has been on the upswing, and she was making gains. Then we discovered Ruth had taken out two hundred thousand to invest in the religious-based JSI fund you mentioned."

Emma's wailing cries interrupted him. "I knew it! Oh, my God, Jack, what has she done?"

Jack enveloped his sobbing wife in his strong arms.

Mr. White poured Emma a glass of water, and she drank it down.

"We believe this entire organization is fraudulent, taking advantage of people," Jack said, gently rocking Emma back and forth.

Mr. White took notes on a rapidly filling legal pad. "We need the names of others who invested in this fund who can corroborate that the organization is fraudulent. If it's a Ponzi-type scheme, it could be awhile before other investors come forward. The IRS will review their 501(c)(3) status. We may have a chance at getting some of the funds Ruth donated back. I can't promise the outcome will be in our favor, but we'll pursue it."

Emma dabbed at her moist eyes with a tissue. "How can we do that?"

The lawyer stopped writing for a moment, facing them squarely. "Historically, US law operated on the principle that once a gift was given, it couldn't be taken back. Around ten years ago that started to change, with some courts giving donors greater control over their gifts, but enforcement varies by state. Let me research this, starting with whether Missouri has a Uniform Trust Code."

"Even a ballpark figure of the money Ruth has left would be helpful," Jack said, releasing Emma from his hold.

"We understand the urgency," Mr. Osborne added. "Raymond and I will begin a thorough accounting of Mrs. Perkins's assets. The estate isn't terribly large, so we'll have numbers to you in a matter of days."

Emma realized she was panting. Grabbing Jack's hand again, she thanked the men. "The state of my mother's finances has been a great shock. I'm desperately hoping you find more money."

55

Friday, August 8, 2003
St. Louis, Missouri
Ray and Susannah's home

Ray was home early, hoping to surprise his bride. He thought they might have dinner at a restaurant they had been wanting to try, and then . . . He smiled to himself as he reached the mailbox.

He sorted the pile—the usual bills, magazines, and a letter from his financial advisor. *That's odd. I already got my quarterly statement,* Ray thought. He carried the stack into the house, found a letter opener, and slit it open.

Ray read the statement twice. This was a confirmation letter that twenty-five thousand dollars had been withdrawn from the account. *What the hell?* It was a beautiful Friday in late summer, and his financial advisor was probably on a golf course. Nevertheless, he called the office number.

His advisor, Shaun, hadn't left yet.

"Hi, Shaun. This is Ray Williams, and I have a question."

"Sure," the young man said. "What can I do for you?"

"I received a confirmation notice in today's mail that I withdrew twenty-five thousand from my portfolio. I don't recall that being discussed at our quarterly meeting."

"Right. The plan was to keep your holdings as is. I'll pull up your account," Shaun said as computer keys clacked in Ray's ear. "Susannah Williams made the withdrawal on Thursday, July thirty-first. Mrs. Williams met with Amy Schultz."

"Can I speak with Ms. Schultz please?" Ray was infuriated.

"Amy's on vacation until Tuesday the twelfth. I can give you her voicemail or find another associate. Both your names are on the account," Shaun said, as if trying to calm Ray by reminding him that Ray was not the sole person with access.

"Give me her voicemail," Ray responded briskly. "Thanks for your assistance."

✝

That evening, Ray sat in the living room recliner, listening to his wife trying to explain why the funds were missing.

"We're married, Ray! I shouldn't have to ask permission to withdraw our money!" Susannah was defensive, arms tight over her chest, standing rigidly before him.

"Susannah, twenty-five thousand dollars is a lot of money. It has nothing to do with your asking my permission—"

"Oh, I think it does," she replied sharply. "You don't trust me, Ray. I was going to tell you, but not now."

Ray felt the clench of his jaw tighten. "I do trust you. But as your husband, I have a right to know how our money is being spent. And why not tell me now?"

"Because it's for us," she spat. "If I tell you too soon, it will ruin everything."

Ray stood. "Tell me!" he nearly shouted at her.

Susannah waved him off. "I can't talk to you right now," she yelled, stomping from the room.

He decided against following her, mulling over her words, their screaming argument on endless repeat in his head.

A few minutes later, Susannah handed him a large whiskey and 7 Up. "I'm going out for a long walk. Maybe this will calm you down."

Ray accepted the glass and heard the back door slam. He needed to be reasonable and work this out. He drank deeply. The Marker's Mark was strong, the drink was sweet, and he relaxed.

✝

Saturday morning, August 9, 2003
St. Louis, Missouri
Linda's condo

Linda had found a Pilates class she enjoyed and was happy to keep her exercise routine consistent. Waiting for DNA confirmation became excruciating, as was watching the days slip by. She had returned home, still dressed in workout clothes, when the doorbell rang.

That's interesting, Malachi didn't mention anything about meeting. Who else could it be?

She peered through the peephole to see a deliveryman holding an exquisite arrangement of brilliantly hued flowers. Embarrassed her attire wasn't more appropriate, she cracked the door a sliver.

"Ms. Sinclair?"

"That's me," she responded cheerfully. Gorgeous flowers were arranged in a crystal vase. *These must be from Ray and Susannah for my donation.*

"Quite beautiful," the deliveryman commented. "Enjoy them."

Linda brought the arrangement into the kitchen, gingerly

removing it from the plastic bag. She opened the card, expecting a note from the Williamses.

> *Linda,*
>
> *Thought some fresh flowers would give your spirits a lift. It's been a tough haul, but we're almost there. You've done an outstanding job.*
>
> *M*

The last person to send her flowers had been Tom. Linda wasn't sure what to think. This was a lovely gesture on Malachi's part, but was it an implication of something deeper? She had feelings for him that went beyond just being partners. Linda had known since that night in the parking garage when the out-of-control car nearly hit them. He'd pulled her aside and held her so tenderly. She had been comfortable in his arms, placing shaking hands on his forearm without realizing it until later. Did Malachi have feelings for her, too?

She caught herself spinning fantasies, admonishing herself to stop. *We are caring partners, nothing else.*

Placing the flowers in the dining room, Linda pushed any thoughts of romance aside and went to shower.

56

Saturday, August 9, early afternoon
St. Louis, Missouri
Ray and Susannah's home

Ray woke up in the leather living room recliner with a blanket tucked around him. He pushed the chair into an upright position and rubbed the back of his neck. His muscles were stiff and sore. *How long had he been here?*

He let out a long sigh, trying to shake off the cobwebs of deep slumber and looked around. There was an empty highball glass on the end table next to his chair. *What time is it?* Ray looked at his watch—one thirty. Glancing into the kitchen, he saw brilliant sunshine against an indigo sky. *So, it must be one thirty in the afternoon on Saturday?*

His thoughts were muddled, and he realized he was wearing clothes from the day before. *What on earth?* Ray's memory was a blank; he had no recollection of the past several hours.

The house was quiet, and he called out for his wife. "Susannah! Honey, where are you?"

Ray tried to rise from the recliner and was overcome with dizziness. He fell back hard. *Why couldn't he remember anything? And where was Susannah?*

Ray picked up the empty glass and smelled it—maybe that would trigger his memory. The oaky whiff of Maker's Mark filled his nostrils. That was unusual in itself; he rarely drank alcohol.

He called for Susannah again. Getting no response, he rose slowly from the chair and dragged his heavy feet into the kitchen. Ray steadied himself on the kitchen counter. *What the hell was happening?*

A memory flickered. In Friday's mail, a letter had arrived confirming a large withdrawal from their stock portfolio. He vaguely recalled a confrontation. They had argued. He thought he remembered her insisting she'd withdrawn the money for them but wouldn't explain further. Susannah refused to talk with him until he calmed down. She had poured him a whiskey and soda—he recalled the drink being stiff on the whiskey—and announced she was going for a walk until he could be reasoned with. *Where was she?*

The last thing Ray remembered was accepting the drink.

Slowly, he walked out the back door. The garage was open, and both their cars were there. *She must be here somewhere.*

Ray hollered at the top of his lungs for his wife. "Susannah! Susannah, are you here?"

It was a glorious August day, and sounds of active neighbors filled the air. Kids rode their bikes, while parents mowed lawns and tended to vegetable and flower gardens.

"Good afternoon, sleepyhead!" Susannah's cheerful voice came from outside the shed where they stored yard equipment.

Ray shielded his eyes from the bright sun, watching her close the door of the shed. She ambled across the yard, wearing her gardening clothes and carrying a basket of dead flowers. As she approached, dry grass crunched under her feet.

"How long have you been out here?" Ray still felt confused about where he was or the day of the week.

She held out the basket. "Just cutting back some plants."

He met her at the halfway point of the yard.

"How are you feeling? I was worried about you last night." She came alongside him, planting a soft kiss on Ray's cheek and slipped her arm through his.

He had no idea what she was referring to. "I'm still a little groggy. How long did I sleep?"

She stopped and turned to look at him, her brow crinkled. "Sweetheart, can't you remember? We had a spat yesterday, over our financial portfolio. You accused me of withdrawing money without telling you. I was disturbed. I've never seen you that angry. After dinner, you made yourself a drink, which you almost *never* do, and you wouldn't speak to me. Around ten o'clock, you said you didn't feel well and were going to bed. But you fell asleep in the recliner instead."

He listened keenly. What Susannah was telling him was fuzzy at best. "I remember our argument. I thought you made me a drink, then went for a walk in the heat of things—"

"No, Ray, I never made you a drink or left the house. You were very upset—I mean, honey, you hardly ever drink. Anyway, I went up to get ready for bed, and when I came back downstairs, you were out cold." She reached up to massage his aching shoulders. "I shouldn't have let you spend the night in the recliner. I tried to wake you, but you were sound asleep."

He could not remember any of this, and it bothered him. Ray opened the back door, and they entered the kitchen. "I do want to discuss this portfolio matter further—"

Susannah held a finger up to his lips. "We're going to have that conversation right now. I'll come clean and tell you my surprise."

Ray joined her at the kitchen table, where she had laid out glossy travel brochures, presenting the majestic white sails of a windjammer cruiser amid a stunning tropical locale displaying blue sky, white sandy beaches, pristine aqua waters, and swaying palm trees. "What is all this?" he asked, his curiosity piqued.

"It's a Windstar cruise to French Polynesia. The cruise itself is eleven days, and I propose that we stay at least two weeks. I withdrew the money for a substantial down payment to reserve us a spot for next March. How long has it been since you've had a real vacation? Think of all the things we can do—snorkeling, windsailing, kayaking, walking along the beach. Yes, I realize a trip of this nature is expensive and requires detailed planning, which I am happy to undertake. We didn't take a honeymoon, and after all the work we've put in to make *The Road to Calvary* a success, we deserve a moment for ourselves. It would be a once-in-a-lifetime journey."

Ray reviewed the breathtaking brochures. He had been untrusting, just as Susannah had said. He felt like a complete ass and reached for her hand. "Forgive me for doubting you. This would be an amazing adventure, and you're right, we need a proper honeymoon."

Susannah came around the table and settled into Ray's lap. He was a pushover for her soft touch and kisses. "I need a shower after working in the yard," she said. "You could use one, too." Arms around his neck, she pulled Ray close for a deep kiss.

"That I could." He kissed her passionately.

She smiled seductively and tugged at his shirt.

His grogginess was eroding as her small hands slid into his trousers. Ray began unbuttoning her top, and they climbed the stairs, roaming hands all over one another's bodies.

Susannah had certainly opened Ray's sexual horizons to new possibilities, and lovemaking in a warm shower was one of them. Dressed, he called out to her before heading downstairs, "Want to try Charlie Gitto's?"

"That would be great," she said, and the blow dryer ramped into high gear.

He had forgotten a belt and returned to the walk-in closet.

While he was threading the belt through the loops, he noticed that Susannah's side of the closet seemed to have far fewer clothes than he remembered. Maybe his night sleeping in a recliner was still affecting him. Surveying the clothes rack, he was positive her favorite outfits were missing.

"Honey, why are almost half your clothes gone?" he asked casually.

Finished drying her hair, Susannah came into the bedroom. "Oh, darn! I wanted my purge to be another surprise. I have far too many clothes, so I'm donating anything I haven't worn in the last year. I thought, why not give them to women who need business attire for a job or an interview?" She kissed him again. "Why don't you make reservations for dinner, and I'll be right down."

He pulled her close for another kiss. Lost in a tight embrace and deep, moist kisses, Ray knew he was the luckiest man in the world.

57

Sunday, August 10, 2003
St. Louis, Missouri
The Road to Calvary set

Making her way up the aisle, Linda searched for the Carlsons. *Everything must seem normal.* From the corner of her eye, Linda spied Malachi accompanied by a female officer sitting toward the middle. Other officers she knew by sight took seats, spreading out through the audience.

The Carlsons sat in their usual seats close to the stage, their obese bodies spilling out of their chairs.

"Good morning," Linda said in greeting. She took off her light coat, draping it over the back of her chair as pleasantries were exchanged. She silently took in the scene of the buzzing crowd, counting seven officers in the room.

Settling into her spot, Linda was eager for this ruse to be over. She wanted to be Captain Linda Turner again. They were almost to the finish, after so many months of dead ends and false hope. *The stress of the fast-approaching deadline hasn't helped. After today . . .*

The lights went down, and Jeff yelled for quiet on the set. As the choir sang the opening hymn, Linda noticed a harried woman come up the darkened aisle and take a seat in the second row, one of the last available.

Billie leaned over and whispered in her ear. "I hate people who come late to church. Especially when we're on live TV!"

†

Ray's sermon could have communicated the world would be coming to an end today for all Linda knew. Minutes seemingly went every direction but forward. Linda glanced at her watch every thirty seconds, which made the minutes tick by even more slowly.

The service was finally coming to a close. She felt the adrenaline course through her veins, as the reverend invited the congregation to recite the prayer of deliverance. *Let's get this wrapped up.*

The large crowd stood.

Ray signaled for Susannah to join him, and they clasped hands.

As the congregation reached the line, "You died for my sins and rose again to save me from a world mired in sin—" an incensed woman's voice rang out.

"You're the sinners!" She was steps from the stage, pointing at Ray and Susannah. Linda moved into the aisle to see her. "Taking advantage of people, conning them out of their hard-earned money for the promise of salvation? The way I was taught, salvation didn't require you to write a check! Reverend Ray and his wife are frauds, and they're scamming all of you!"

Linda observed the woman, every muscle in her body on full alert. Saliva flew from the woman's mouth as she talked.

The crowd was eerily silent. Linda saw Jeff making a frantic slashing motion across his throat.

An attractive brunette in her late thirties, the woman continued her tirade. "Reverend Ray stole over three hundred thousand dollars from my mother, Ruth Perkins, leaving her practically destitute."

Linda had seen this kind of wrath before—a fury so blind that even the most level-headed person could cross into madness. She inched closer to Ruth's daughter.

The woman assessed the stunned crowd, waving her hands wildly. "I'm sure my mother wasn't the only person suckered into buying a custom-made stained-glass window for your new church," she sneered. "Sure, they're one-of-a-kind and cost fifty thousand dollars, but you'll never see them! How do I know this? I called the manufacturer. They've never heard of this church." Emma made quotation marks with her fingers when she said *church*. "A prototype was ordered to make you believe windows were being made. Reverend Ray and this evil woman destroyed my mother's life. Someone needs to be held accountable!"

Behind the slight woman, Linda saw the gleam of silver in her hand. She shouted into the crowd, "Gun!"

Two loud *pops* like firecrackers going off filled the air with haze and the smell of gunpowder. Linda dove toward the petite woman. As she brought her to the floor, the woman still held the gun, pointing it toward the ceiling. Two additional shots shattered lights above, chunks of glass spraying the crowd. Pieces sliced Linda's arm open as she wrestled the weapon away.

58

SECONDS LATER

Ray saw flashes when the gun fired and heard the pops. Falling shards of glass cut some of the parishioners directly under the shattered lights. A few bled profusely. *Oh my God!* He could hear the beat of his heart in his ears. People were screaming. He thought he glimpsed uniformed police swarming into the space. *What the—*

Holding Susannah's hand, he was terrified, but tried desperately to stay composed. *Get off the stage,* he thought and moved to the left. Then, he felt his wife tug awkwardly on his arm as she toppled to the floor. Crimson blood rapidly soaked her dress. Gurgling noises came from her throat, her eyes rolling back.

"Susannah!" he yelled in anguish, kneeling next to her. From the stage, he looked out at the chaos of bodies running, armed police surrounding them. "My wife has been shot! Call an ambulance!"

Ray held Susannah tightly, her blood staining his suit. He felt a strong tug on his shoulder, and a deep voice said, "Sir, you need to step back."

Angry and fearful, Ray shouted at the strangers. "No. She's my wife!"

"Sir!" the large, muscular male commanded. "Step back."

Authoritative voices rose, yelling for the congregation to stay calm and show their hands. Ray heard the screech of sirens growing closer. The cops surrounding Susannah knew what they were doing, trying to stem the bleeding. Others attended to the injured parishioners. The same officer spoke into a microphone. "EMTs are on their way."

Ray felt his knees buckle as he stumbled into a seat. The cut to Linda Sinclair's arm was deep, blood soaking the makeshift tourniquet the officer kneeling next to her ripped from her jacket.

Behind him, Ray heard the shooter's erupting words directed at him. "You bastard! My mother trusted you and your wife! You're not a man of God; you're a con artist. I hope you burn in hell!"

Ray turned to see the woman being brought to her feet, arms handcuffed behind her back. Plainclothes officers marched her toward the stage.

The throng of police parted for the EMTs jogging up the aisle. Ray's attention returned to his wounded wife. With military precision, Susannah was placed on a stretcher, an oxygen mask placed over her face, an IV started in her arm. In seconds, the paramedics had sealed off the wound with what looked to be plastic.

He watched in astonishment. A paramedic shouted, "Let's go, folks! We have ten minutes max!"

Bodies and equipment surrounding Susannah made it impossible for Ray to see her.

He was desperate to be with his wife. "I want to go to St. Alexius with her!" he shouted. He was startled by a woman's voice.

"No, Ray. You have to come with us." He stared dumbfounded at Linda Sinclair's pallid face. The muscular police officer, his closely cropped black hair damp, gently brought her upright.

Dazed, Ray tried to connect missing pieces. "Are you a cop?"

"Yes, she is." The officer's voice was tense. "Captain Turner also requires medical attention. I'm Detective Malachi Johnson. We're bringing you downtown."

"I want to be with my wife!"

Ray's head was bursting with conflicting and alarming information; he couldn't comprehend it at all.

59

Four hours later

Detective Johnson handed Ray a ceramic mug of hot coffee, which he gratefully accepted.

Linda Sinclair, or rather Captain Turner, from somewhere in Nebraska, held her left arm in a sling. She was seated already as Ray was escorted into the interview room.

He stirred in sugar. Detective Johnson stood.

"I sure hope you can tell me just what the hell bringing me here is all about," Ray told them. "Let me get to the hospital."

"We have other items requiring our immediate attention," Detective Johnson replied.

It bothered Ray greatly that the police seemed more concerned with asking him questions than the prognosis of his wife. Incensed, he shouted, "My wife was shot by a disturbed woman, and the police want to talk to me. Why? What do you think I've done?"

Malachi opened a file, removing several pictures of women he didn't recognize. "Captain Turner is investigating a triple murder in Nebraska, and I'm probing three similar homicides here. I am also charged with finding Cole Leon's attacker."

Ray was stupefied. Doug Snyder had told him Cole had died of a heroin overdose. "Attacker? Cole's alive?"

"We'll get to that. What you need to know is after months of working undercover, we've matched Susannah Williams's DNA and fingerprints to our murder suspects in both cases—"

"That's ridiculous! You obviously have made a terrible mistake. Susannah is the most loving, wonderful person—"

Linda Turner interrupted him. "Almost as wonderful as your late wife, Lorraine, who died from ovarian cancer. Susannah Baker knew all the details of her death. She also identified all the previous churches you'd served in Illinois, Kentucky, and Iowa."

Ray was indignant. "Susannah was completely honest that she'd done some research on my past. That's not a crime."

"But it is when Susannah Baker isn't her real name, and she's responsible for the murders of at least six people." Linda held the photos of a young woman's mug shot, a smiling young family, and a promotional shot from *The Road to Calvary*. "Susannah Baker's real name is Pamela Jane Watts. She's had numerous aliases and marriages. The common denominator that led us to you is her penchant for preying on widowed pastors."

Yes, there was a resemblance, he conceded. But his darling Susannah could not possibly be the person they were looking for. He was confident he could explain all of this. Ray picked up the picture with the two young children. "This must be her children who were killed in a car accident. That's her first husband, and they divorced after the accident. She was devastated—"

Linda's enraged voice shocked him into reality. "These children, Jacob and Elizabeth Hansen, and their father, Gregory, were *murdered*, Ray. She slaughtered her own family, and then she buried them in the parsonage garden. Susannah's DNA verifies that *she* is the biological mother of the Hansen children. Your wife is a vicious killer."

"No, no. That can't be true," he protested.

Detective Johnson shoved three new photos at him. "This is Delores Reid, whom you may remember as your first 'miracle.' She was found dead in a flophouse. There was a large amount of the sleep aid Ambien in her system. We can't prove Susannah's involvement beyond a reasonable doubt, but we are going to. The other women, Michelle Thomas and Jeanette Morelli, had a connection to your wife as well. Ms. Thomas wrote an angry letter to *The Road to Calvary* that she was planning to sue you for fraud. Susannah discovered that your former employees, Cole and Seth, read the letter, which caused them to question the honesty of the organization they worked for. Before we could get them into protective custody, someone tampered with Cole's food, lacing it with antifreeze. He is now blind, and I intend to charge Mrs. Williams with attempted murder as well. We have reason to believe, Reverend, that you would have been her next victim."

Ray's stomach clenched as his mind rushed over events in the past six months. Listening to the detectives, he sensed nauseating suspicion and dread. It did seem more than coincidence when Susannah abruptly appeared with her ideas to "save" *The Road to Calvary*. He hadn't questioned it then, but her detailed knowledge of Lorraine's illness and his past now seemed unusual. But most alarming was yesterday's strange incident, Ray having no memory, and her vanished clothing.

The police were telling him that the woman he trusted and loved with his entire being was a suspect in multiple murders, and he, too, had been in danger. Ray sensed he had stepped outside of his body, detached from the proceedings. Susannah's voice played in his head. *After dinner, you made yourself a drink . . .* The clarity of his memory became distinct—his wife handing him the drink.

He heard Linda say something about gathering DNA. Shaking himself out of fogginess, he accepted the reports she handed him. Ray studied the fingerprints and DNA results, detailing the matches between Susannah and several other names. Malachi laid other enlarged photos of her in a line. The reverend reviewed all the documents carefully, comparing the pictures closely. Ray nearly missed it. The odd hole in a moon shape on all of the women's right earlobes. He couldn't deny the truth any longer.

Ray dropped his head into shaking hands.

The howling sobs escaping his lips racked his entire body. He felt his shoulders pitching and tears streaming down his face. He thought about Susannah's betrayal and his own role in a massive deception. In a way, his tears were the beginning of cleansing his soul.

A gentle hand on his back brought Ray face to face with Officer Johnson, who handed him a box of tissues.

He would tell them everything. Pulling a tissue from the box, he blew his nose. "My God, I've been an absolute fool. I should have known when Buck and Jeff were so suspicious because she seemingly showed up out of nowhere. They never trusted her. I want it on record that they questioned everything we ever did to 'help' the show."

Malachi smiled sadly. "I know. For now, let's focus on their distrust of Susannah."

Ray nodded. "A few months back, they confronted me. They told me Susannah was not who she claimed, and they had proof she had committed identity theft. I, of course, didn't believe them."

Malachi met Ray's distressed gaze. "I can confirm every word is true. Jeff and Buck came to me months ago with their concerns and asked me to investigate. I didn't have anything to go on until Delores Reid was killed, and then I found a link to Linda's case in Nebraska. Tell us the timeline from the moment you met Susannah. I also need your permission to search your home. Otherwise, we'll get a warrant."

Ray felt as if he'd taken a brutal punch to the stomach. He seized a deep breath. "Yes, you can search the house, the set. Whatever you need, I will cooperate fully."

He closed his eyes tightly, the image of Susannah's blood-spattered dress and limp body appearing before him, a vision he couldn't erase. *She was my wife. I want to know if she's going to die. I need to pray for her,* he thought. Ray addressed both detectives. "Tell me the extent of Susannah's wounds and her prognosis."

Malachi folded his large hands and spoke solemnly. "She took two bullets to the abdomen and is undergoing emergency surgery. Doctors won't know the extent of the damage until they open her up."

"What if she dies? Then what happens?" Ray witnessed the gravity of the situation in both officers' faces.

Linda spoke first. "If that happens, at least six innocent individuals will have died in vain. As horrific as this is, we need her to survive and be prosecuted."

Malachi handed Ray a yellow legal pad and pencil. "It will be easier for you to recall details writing them down—dates, times, locations—everything."

Ray took the pencil in his apprehensive hands and began to write.

60

Monday, August 11, 2003
EARLY MORNING

St. Louis, Missouri
Linda's condominium

Linda returned to her condominium well after midnight, her adrenaline still surging. An emergency room doctor had given her painkillers, but she was loath to take them, even as her arm throbbed. She needed to stay sharp. She parted the drapes for a view of the city skyline and slouched on the sofa consumed in thought. Malachi and she would go to Ray's home in Richmond Heights that morning, but Linda knew she wouldn't be able to sleep.

Ray's anguished face appeared before her, as the realization sunk in that Susannah had led him down a path of fraud and deceit. How horrible it must feel to realize you'd been taken in by a cold-blooded killer. Linda knew the guilt, present in his eyes every instant he returned to the photo of the Hansen family, would not dissipate soon.

She recalled the forlorn sound in Ray's voice when Malachi asked if he had any family in the area he could stay with.

The words were whispered to the walls, not to them. "No. Buck, Jeff, and Susannah are the closest to family that I have."

The department placed him in a hotel.

Rising from the sofa, Linda went to the window. The lights of the city reflected off the river. At least Susannah had survived surgery. She kept hearing the surgeon telling her and Malachi the prognosis. *"She's lost a great amount of blood and flatlined in surgery. Getting through the night will be an enormous hurdle. I've placed her in a medically-induced coma. We're doing all we can."* Malachi contacted the Feds, and US marshals stood round-the-clock guard.

Linda's mind returned to the shooting. The police had never thought about the possibility that an angry relative of a bilked parishioner would shoot Susannah just as they were closing in to arrest her. *Maybe we should have,* she berated herself. *There hadn't even been the chance to question Emily, or was it Emma?* Linda couldn't recall. She had been taken to county, and Phil was overseeing interviewing her.

✝

Later Monday morning, August 11, 2003
Richmond Heights, Missouri
Ray's home

Chief Langston was pushing for Linda to wrap up the investigation, but she had argued they were right at the six-week time limit. After so much work, she wanted to be the one to end this.

At Ray's brick home, Linda pointed out the castor oil plants to Malachi. "Those tall plants are extremely poisonous. Susannah admitted as much, and I think she may have been making ricin. Be on the lookout for typical stuff found in every home—pots, coffee filters, and solvents to unclog drains. Completely innocuous products on their own."

In the kitchen, Malachi opened drawers and cupboards. "I've got coffee filters and pots. "

A female CSI technician named Sanders walked through the kitchen door. "Detectives, I've found something you need to see."

Outside in the stifling detached garage, they listened.

"I'm processing Mrs. Williams's car," Sanders said. "At first glance, everything appears normal. But I noticed the glove compartment seemed small. I did some knocking around and sure enough, there was a false bottom hiding a box." The tech had laid out her findings on the hood of the car. "Here's what I found—a hypodermic needle, a large amount of the sleep aid Ambien, a loaded nine-millimeter, and travel brochures for Tahiti."

Malachi's deep voice raised a notch. "A nine-millimeter was used to kill Michelle Thomas and Jeanette Morelli. If we prove this is the same gun, that gives us the connection we need," he told the women, but he looked puzzled. "I understand that Susannah used the Ambien to drug Ray, and it knocked him out, leaving him with no memory, particularly when combined with alcohol. But the syringe?"

Linda's smile tightened, mentally returning to her research. "Because the most lethal method of ricin delivery is by injection."

"Why not use the combination of Ambien and alcohol if she wanted to kill Ray?" Malachi said. His forehead creased.

Linda's gaze was steely, observing Malachi and Sanders. "Ricin is nearly impossible to discover in an autopsy unless you're looking for it. I think Susannah was planning to drug Ray before injecting him with the ricin, which would cause his heart to stop, looking to all appearances like a heart attack."

"We gotta keep hoping she lives," Malachi said and pointed toward the backyard. "Ray mentioned the maintenance shed. Let's have a look." He paused. "Nice work, Sanders."

"Yes, Sanders, this is fantastic," Linda enthused.

They headed toward the wooden shed at the far corner of the

property. The ground was soft from recent rainfall. Malachi handed her gloves as they walked. "How's the financial review coming?"

"I haven't heard back from Phil. It shouldn't be much longer," Malachi said, reaching for the door of the maintenance shed.

It was stuck; using his shoulder, Malachi pushed it open. Sunlight filtered into the small dark space. Linda felt around for a light switch, careful not to bump her injured arm. She found the toggle, and a stark yellow bulb illuminated the murky angles.

Garden tools hung on the walls. A partially covered lawn mower and snow blower stood in the corner. Linda's attention was drawn to cupboards above and drawers below a small counter area. She pulled a flashlight from her inside jacket pocket. Opening the cupboards first, she saw a large plastic watering can and various holiday decorations, the ordinary implements found in countless backyard sheds across the country.

Malachi whipped off the vast tarp that covered the lawn equipment, sending a cloud of dust into the air. Dirty air parched their throats, causing spasms of coughing. Linda covered her mouth. Malachi glanced over a shoulder. "We've got suitcases—two." Dragging one out from behind the snow blower, he tried to open it. "It's heavy and locked. "

Linda turned back toward the tools. "Maybe there's a crowbar in here."

"On your upper right," Malachi said. He placed the bar between the lids. His muscles bulged as he popped the suitcase open, and women's clothing scattered on the floor.

"Susannah was very close to leaving," Linda said, surveying the clothing. "She kills Ray and goes to Tahiti with plenty of money to begin life under another identity."

"We need evidence bags for all this," he said and left the shed.

She turned on the flashlight in her hand and observed the dimly lit room. Rummaging through the suitcase, Linda discovered a one-way first-class airline ticket to Tahiti. She used a knife from the shed to rip the suitcase lining, where various envelopes were hidden, each stuffed with cash, and there was a passport under a new name.

She bent down to open the lower cupboards, shining the light inside. Seasonal wreaths, Halloween pumpkins, Christmas lights. Her good arm stretched farther back, touching some type of plastic bag and metal.

Linda's stitches tugged in protest; the wound hurt like hell. She sat back on her heels, sweat beading on her forehead. The heat and humidity left her gasping.

On her stomach and stretching as deep as she could, Linda illuminated an obscure corner of the cabinet—a clear Ziploc bag filled with a ground substance and, next to it, a food processor. *An efficient way to pulverize castor oil seeds.*

Linda heard rapidly approaching footsteps and pulled her body from the cabinet, her blouse and pants encrusted with grime.

"I think I've found ricin but can't reach it. I also found scads of cash and a passport in the suitcase lining."

"Holy shit." On his knees, Malachi reached into the corner, removing the bag.

"There's also a food processor we need," Linda said, taking the bag.

They bagged as much of the evidence as they could before running out of bags. "Too much money," Malachi said, wiping his wet brow. His cell rang.

"Great. Phil's finished reviewing Ray's financials. I'll get CSI to bag the rest."

61

Phil handed the detectives a sheet of numbers.

"The account listed under Susannah Baker must be where she kept the window donations," Linda said, skimming the columns of a separate account. "There's over half a million dollars."

Malachi cocked his head at Phil. "Where's the reverend?"

"He's waiting in Interview Room 3."

Malachi held the door for her. "I feel for the pastor."

Ray sat at the gray metal interview table with another cup of hot coffee. Linda searched his lined face and thought the pastor looked as though he had aged fifteen years overnight. "Good afternoon, Reverend," she said as she pulled out an empty chair. "Pardon our appearance."

"Any news on Susannah's prognosis?" he inquired tentatively.

Malachi sat next to Linda. "No change since we last spoke. She's still in critical condition. However, we can prove our theory she was planning to leave soon."

Linda watched Ray's gloomy face sag. She tried to make her voice soothing. "Reverend, we threw a massive amount of data at you last night. Do you remember us explaining her embezzlement activities with the other churches she became involved with?"

"Yes, I remember everything."

She moved the pages of financial data toward Ray. "We assembled the capital campaign finances as well as personal money. Let's start with the church campaign. We've discovered that American Stained Glass made one prototype for a Lorraine McArthur, whom they never heard from again."

The pastor inhaled, color seeping from his stunned face. "That's my late wife's name. My God!" Ray struggled to compose himself, his voice shaky. "What happened to the money Susannah collected for those windows?"

The legs of Malachi's chair screeched across the floor. "We traced the donations to a small local bank. Over five hundred thousand dollars was deposited into an account under the name Susannah Baker, a name you know well. Reviewing the list of donors, Susannah had collected either partial or full amounts for sixteen such windows, none of which was ever going to be built. In your maintenance shed, Captain Turner discovered a packed suitcase with a hundred thousand in cash and a fake passport."

They explained the discovery of the gun, Ambien, travel brochures, and tools for making ricin.

Ray's body went limp in the chair, and Linda watched his eyes enlarge as he realized he had been mere days away from death.

Linda gazed keenly at his pale face. "Are you all right, Reverend?"

He stared into space, talking as if to himself. "The purple spiky flowers in the garden—Susannah said they were poisonous. We joked about it." Ray's eyes returned to face them. "Could you give me a moment alone, officers?"

"Certainly," Malachi answered.

As they left the room, Linda looked over her shoulder. Ray had lowered his head back onto the table, his body shuddering in waves of sobs.

62

Friday, August 15, 2003, early morning

Linda's condominium

Linda fumbled for the receiver as the ringing phone woke her from a deep slumber. She dropped it on the floor and through blurry eyes, glanced at the clock. Six o'clock. Damn it! "Hello?"

"Morning, sleepyhead," Malachi said cheerily. "Our girl survived. The doctors are bringing her out of the coma this morning. If Susannah breathes on her own once they take her off the ventilator, they'll stop the drugs and gradually get her to wake up. In any case, I'll pick you up in an hour."

Still groggy, Linda sat up in bed against the pillows, her arm throbbing. The alarm was buzzing from some unseen hiding place. She must have knocked the clock off the nightstand, too. "Okay. What time will you be here?"

"Seven. I'll bring you coffee."

Linda sprang out of bed, wide awake. Closing this case and going home were within reach. Racing energy surged through her body. For months, she had waited for this moment.

†

St. Alexius Hospital
St. Louis, Missouri
7:30 a.m.

As promised, Malachi arrived at her condo with a Starbucks venti-sized latte.

"Skim milk, extra shot, no froth, just the way you like it," he said, pulling the car away from the curb.

"Bless you," Linda replied, drinking deeply from the tall cup.

The drive was short, and they talked of bringing this horrendous case to an end. At the hospital, they rode the elevator to the hushed floor of the ICU. Outside the closed door of Susannah's room, US marshals stood guard. A nurse came out, at which point Linda heard gagging noises coming from inside.

The nurse noticed their police badges. "It will take a while for her to get used to not having a tube down her throat," she whispered. "She'll be hoarse and may have difficulty speaking. I'll let Dr. Maynard, the attending physician, know you're here."

In a vacant office, Linda and Malachi went over their strategy. It was agreed they would take a tag-team approach in the presentation of evidence, with Linda starting off. Three hours later, Dr. Maynard knocked at the door.

"Susannah is coherent, but I want you to back off if this becomes too much for her," he declared.

"I understand. However, Susannah Williams is the prime suspect in several homicides," Malachi bluntly informed the physician. "She'll be questioned, but we have the proof to arrest her."

The doctor glared at Malachi. "You can't do that!"

"Yes, we can," Linda added briskly. "You've done your job; now you need to let us do ours."

She watched Malachi's handsome face break into a smile. "We're pros, Doc," he said. "I promise you we won't cause a scene in the ICU."

✝

Clad in a hospital gown, left wrist handcuffed to the bed frame, Susannah sat upright, a tray of soft foods on her lap. An IV dripped in her left arm, and machines displayed her vitals.

Recognizing Linda, Susannah spoke softly, her voice weak. "Linda, it's so nice to see a familiar face. Do you know where Ray is?" She pointed at Malachi. "Why am I handcuffed to the bed?"

Linda approached, unzipping her portfolio. "This isn't a social call, Susannah. I'm Captain Linda Turner from Lincoln, Nebraska. I'm here to chat with you about your deceased husband, Gregory Hansen, and your children, Jacob and Elizabeth."

Susannah laid down a spoon, watching the detectives without a sound.

Next to Linda, Malachi's powerful frame towered over her. "And I'm Detective Johnson from the St. Louis PD. I'll be discussing the murders of Dolores Reid, Jeanette Morelli, Michelle Thomas, and Cole Leon with you. But, first, you have the right to remain silent. Anything you say can and will be used against you in a court of law. . . ."

Linda watched Malachi read Susannah her Miranda rights. As she suspected, Susannah's facial features betrayed no emotion. She pleaded ignorance, shaking her head. "Why are you reading me my rights? Where'd you say you're from—Nebraska? I've never even been there. I thought you were from Illinois."

Linda moved the food tray aside and laid out pictures of the smiling Hansen family in Disneyland and photos of their remains. "You have a long criminal history, preying on recently widowed pastors and embezzling. But in March of last year, as the wife of Gregory

Hansen at the Disciples of Christ University Place Church in Lincoln, Nebraska, you murdered your husband and two small children, burying them in the parsonage flower garden. Gregory's plan to do missionary work in Africa wasn't part of your scheme, so you killed *your own family*."

Susannah glanced at the photos before recoiling in horror. "You've made a terrible mistake. My husband and I divorced because our children died in a car accident. If I knew where he was, you could ask him yourself."

Linda was incredulous, hitting a fist against the tray. "Isn't that convenient? 'If I only knew where my husband was.' There is no husband, and I can prove it. Look at the photos, Susannah! These are your children and husband. We have evidence that you cannot deny—the DNA you share with Jacob and Elizabeth is proof you're their mother."

"What do you mean my husband and children? None of this is true or even makes sense!" Susannah gasped hoarsely. Her tears rushed down her pallid face in streams.

Her heart and blood pressure monitors began beeping loudly. Dr. Maynard quickly spoke up. "You're upsetting Mrs. Williams. I'm going to have to ask you to leave."

Malachi's muscular frame faced the physician, his voice firm. "We're not going to do that, Doctor. The truth can be very upsetting. You may remain present through the remainder of this conversation." He nodded for Linda to continue.

She took a breath. "You can lie all you want, but I've learned all about you, Pamela Jane Watts. You were abandoned at birth on the steps of St. Stephen's Catholic Church in Minneapolis. That must have taken your very soul, or maybe you never had one because there were people who loved you. From all accounts, your adoptive parents, Margaret and Paul Watts, adored their only child. No one could ever prove that you were responsible for the suspicious fire that killed them when you were thirteen. I'm convinced that you were."

Susannah fell against the pillows, shaking her head. "Why are you doing this? I'm Susannah Williams, wife of Reverend Ray. You're a member of our church, for heaven's sake! To say that I'm some sort of psychopath is a horrible lie."

Malachi spoke up. "If pictures of your dead children—a three-year-old and a toddler—won't elicit a response, I can't imagine these will make an impact either." He forcibly slapped crime scene photos of the other four victims across the bed.

From the corner of her eye, Linda saw Dr. Maynard holding his chin in his hand, listening intently. He stepped back from Susannah's bed.

Her wet eyes blinked. "They did! They make me sick to my stomach! Who could possibly do such a hideous thing? I've never seen any of these people!"

"*You did this!*" Linda snapped, her voice impatient.

Susannah's response was shrill. "No, no, no! That's not me!"

Linda and Malachi exchanged glances, and she retrieved an evidence bag holding the signed U-Haul return contract and three surveillance photos from the Cleveland video. Malachi removed the food tray.

"Emotion won't do it, so let's try some hard facts." Linda pointed to the contract. "This is the contract you signed when you returned the U-Haul trailer in Cleveland, Ohio, using the alias Nicole Hansen. The time stamp is 1:07 p.m., on Monday, April first, 2002. That's seven days after you fled Lincoln, Nebraska, towing a U-Haul trailer behind your beige 1995 Toyota Corolla. You'll also note in these still photographs that you laid your right hand on the paper to hold it while you signed with your left. Only ten percent of individuals are left-handed. You also made a palm print. It took us a while, but we matched that print to you, Susannah. You, Pamela Watts, Susan Patterson, and Nicole Hansen, who murdered her family in cold blood, are all the same person."

"You're upsetting me," Susannah wailed. "The doctor's right. I need to rest. I won't talk to you anymore!"

Linda calmly folded her arms. "Your turn, Detective Johnson."

She watched as Malachi's eyes zeroed in on Susannah, his look one of cool assurance. "Killing Delores Reid was a big mistake. Ms. Reid was a talker and wasn't going to shut up that you ripped her off. You used the same drugs to murder the Hansen family, providing a connection between our cases. Your next murders were a bit harder to prove. The footprints of size eleven men's athletic shoes initially threw us off. Ballistics matched the bullets that killed Jeanette Haskell and Michelle Thomas to the nine-millimeter we found in your vehicle."

Tears running down her face, Susannah pleaded with Dr. Maynard. "Please, Doctor, tell them to stop! None of what they're saying is true! They're harassing me for someone else's terrible crimes."

Malachi addressed the physician. "One last thing, Doctor, and then, we agree Mrs. Williams needs to rest."

Linda moved to the entrance, drawing the curtain open. She offered her arm to steady the gait of a young man whom she walked to the foot of the bed. Linda watched Susannah's face turn from a blank façade to one of horror.

"Hello, Susannah," Cole Leon greeted her, his voice steadfast. "I'm supposed to be dead. But I'm just blind, thanks to you." His vacant eyes looked in Susannah's direction, but stared into empty space. "You almost fucking killed me because your plan was coming apart! You know who saved me?" he taunted her. "Seth."

"You thought the antifreeze lacing Mr. Leon's orange juice would kill him and keep him from disclosing to Ray Ms. Thomas's plan to sue." Malachi's voice was smooth and even. "Even if you had succeeded, you were getting sloppy. You see, Susannah, when we searched your home, we found antifreeze hidden in the maintenance shed and a pair of your shoes also tested positive for it."

A hoarse scream emanated from Susannah as her arms swung wildly, the loosening IV setting off alarms. "Go away! All of you—go away!"

Clutching Cole's arm, Linda maneuvered his body toward the door as Susannah's cries echoed down the hall.

63

Emma had been in jail for five days. This was a life she had never, ever thought would be hers, but she would have to accept it.

She hadn't known what to expect, but certainly not this. There were no guards posted outside barred cells, as she had imagined. Instead, they mingled with the inmates in what she had been told was the "direct supervision" model. Cameras and computer screens monitored guards' and inmates' every move.

The food wasn't that bad. There was only one item so far that she couldn't stomach—powdered scrambled eggs. Their rubbery texture made her gag.

Emma stretched out on her bunk. Sleeping was almost impossible, even with lights out at nine o'clock. There were three other women in her "pod," most here on drug-related charges. Their every restless movement kept her wide awake, giving her too many stretches of watching herself shooting Susannah Williams again and again.

Learning that Susannah was not just guilty of fraud but had also been arrested and charged with multiple homicides didn't give Emma any sense that her deed had been a virtuous one. In fact, the truth sickened her and made her regret her actions more. *I should have let the authorities handle her.* She figured dealing with the "I should haves" was part of her punishment.

The charges were attempted murder in the first degree, and Emma knew jail was inevitable. Her lawyer, Maya Holbeck, initially thought an insanity defense was an option, but a psychiatric evaluation determined Emma knew right from wrong. She herself recognized that she wasn't insane.

She leaned her head against the cool brick wall and closed her eyes. The thoughts wouldn't stop. *What in God's name have I done? Poor Jack. The milestones I'll miss—Elizabeth and Katrina's college graduations, weddings, grandchildren. And the worst part is Mom's financial situation is the same. I'm grateful she doesn't know her daughter tried to commit murder.*

Emma was startled at the sound of the pod door unlocking via the click of a computer. A female guard named Sykes entered to escort her to a private room for the meeting.

"Okay, Duncan, your attorney is here. I'll take you downstairs."

Emma slid off her bunk in her beige prison jumpsuit. That was interesting—Maya was early, over an hour.

"Give me a minute, will you?" At the stainless-steel sink, Emma splashed water on her face to wash the tear stains away. She dried her face and ran a comb through her wavy hair.

Sykes led her into the hallway. Talk filled the air as they passed the dayroom. Inmates lounged on gray sofas watching *The Oprah Winfrey Show* on the big screen television or engaging in games at the recreation tables. She noticed a guard playing along.

Everything is so, so bright, Emma thought. Light filled the great room. They walked across the room and past the main guard stationed at a podium and computer screen.

On the floor holding the interview rooms, Sykes punched in a code on the keypad to open the door. Emma wasn't expecting to see Jack with Maya.

"Call if you need anything, Counselor," Sykes said to Maya. The door shut behind her.

The metal furniture seemed molded to the floor. The walls and doors were almost blinding in their sheer whiteness. Instinctively, Emma reached for Jack. She hugged him tight and pulled back. "Not that I don't love to see you, but this is unexpected."

"I have some news," he said. The somber look across Jack's features told her the news was not good.

Emma's temple furrowed in concern. "Are Elizabeth and Katrina all right?"

"Yes, they're fine." Jack said quietly. "It's Ruth."

Relief that the girls were all right tugged against the apprehension in Jack's words regarding her mother. "What is it—another stroke?"

Jack grasped her hand, his fingers caressing her knuckles. "Em, yes, it was another stroke—'a massive hemispheric infarction' is what the doctors called it. Ruth died early this morning."

Ruth died early this morning. Jack's words kept repeating themselves in Emma's head. She remained motionless, trying to make sense of this.

When the words finally came, they squeaked out of her dry mouth. "She's gone, and I didn't even get to say good-bye." Sobs shook Emma's body. She pulled her hand out of Jack's tender grasp, dropping her head into her own open hands.

Jack moved closer, and Emma felt his large arms envelop her trembling body. "Get it all out, Em," he whispered, gently rocking her.

For several minutes, the only sounds in the confines of the small room were Emma's sobs.

"If I had just kept my anger under control, I could have been there for Mom in her final days. Now she's gone, and I'm in jail charged with attempted murder. Why the hell did I think shooting Susannah Williams would get Mom her money back?" Emma's face was wet.

Her shoulders heaved up and down as another wave of sobs engulfed her. She laid her head on Jack's shoulder.

Maya handed Emma a Kleenex. "I think I may have some reasonably good news, given the circumstances."

Emma lifted her head, accepting Maya's tissue, and dabbed at her glistening eyes. "I guess it can't be much worse." She sniffled and wiped her nose.

The lawyer removed a folder from her leather briefcase. "You could be facing life in prison, but there's a deal on the table. The DA agrees that there are clearly extenuating circumstances that led to your actions."

Holding Emma close, Jack asked for clarification. "What does 'extenuating circumstances' mean?"

"In the simplest of terms," Maya said, "extenuating circumstances mean facts surrounding a crime that lessen or mitigate it. In your case, you were reacting to your mother being bilked out of most her life's savings by Susannah Williams and, you thought, the reverend. Extenuating circumstances don't lessen the degree of the crime but are applicable in the sentencing phase."

Emma felt the twinges of a headache start to appear in her temples, but she had to pay attention. She couldn't face spending the rest of her life locked up; yet, she understood it was a distinct possibility. "You said the DA is open to a deal."

Maya laid out the preliminary agreement. "Susannah Williams survived and is expected to make a full recovery from her injuries. Your charges have been lessened—instead of first-degree murder or attempted murder, it's now second-degree attempted murder. This is where extenuating circumstances and a plea bargain come in. If you plead guilty to second-degree attempted murder, the DA is offering ten years in prison, max. Part of the deal is mandatory anger management therapy. Given that you also have no criminal history and were essentially sent over the brink by fraud, there is also the potential for early parole and time off for good behavior. Or you have the option of taking your chances with a jury and going to trial."

The data piled up in Emma's brain. She knew that this was far better news than a life sentence, but that ten-year period in prison weighed on her. *How could I have been so rash?* She looked at Jack to gauge his reaction.

He touched her hair. "I don't want a trial, and I don't think you do either. I think this is the best offer we're going to get. But I'm not the one who will be in prison. Tell me what you want to do."

Emma was quiet for a few minutes, contemplating what she would say next. "I don't want a trial. I'm guilty. I'll take the plea bargain," she said without the slightest hesitation. "I'll pay my debt to society. But I have a favor to ask you, Maya."

Maya bobbed her head. Her face was one of compassion. "I think I know what it is. You want to tell your mother good-bye and go to her funeral, like any loving daughter."

Emma started to cry again. "Yes, I want to attend my mother's funeral."

"Let me present your request. I will also tell the DA you've accepted the plea deal. A lot of times a request to a family member's funeral is denied, but again there are extenuating circumstances." Maya returned the file to her briefcase and rose to depart. "I'll contact the DA as soon as I leave. I should have an answer in the morning."

Maya shook both of their hands, and the door opened. Sykes took the attorney's place, standing guard, her hands clasped in front.

Emma turned to Jack. She put her hands on both his shoulders, the tears running down her cheeks. She searched his face, considering his dark eyes for an answer. "Jack, do you still love me? I miss you all so much!" She buried her face in her husband's chest, the sobs overtaking her again.

She felt his lips whispering into her hair. "Shh, Emma. Shh. I love you more than you will ever realize."

64

Saturday, August 23, 2003
St. Louis, Missouri
Linda's condominium

Chief Langston relayed news that prosecutors in Missouri and Nebraska were working out the details of how the trials would proceed, extradition, and eventual incarceration. Linda knew that she would testify at all the trials, and there could be as many as six.

Tomorrow, she was flying home. Malachi was dropping by with dinner and to say a temporary good-bye. *Malachi.* Linda smiled at his name. Their budding romance had been a lovely development in a sea of darkness. On Wednesday they had found several hours free from police work for dinner and a movie. As the sun rose over the Arch, they were still talking.

A chilled six-pack of Budweiser was in the fridge. The doorbell rang. The clock read ten past six. She opened it to Malachi's smiling face and the smell of fresh pizza.

"Whatever you brought, it smells divine," she said, leading him to the kitchen.

"One St. Louis-style pizza and gooey butter cake from Gooey Louie's for your last night in our fine city," Malachi declared, kissing Linda's cheek.

They moved in tandem—Linda pulling plates from the shelves and Malachi setting the oven on low.

Malachi helped himself to two Budweisers, placing the bottles on the counter. He found the opener in a drawer and handed Linda a beer. "Here's to the perseverance of good old-fashioned police work."

Bottles clinked as they drank to their victory. "As much as I want to get home, I am really going to miss you. Sure, there will be the trials, but that's part of our jobs," Linda said wistfully.

Malachi grinned and clasped Linda's hands in his. "I say we give a long-distance relationship a chance and see where the journey takes us. I have vacation coming, and I've always wanted to see for myself what the 'Go Big Red' madness is all about."

She was delighted at the suggestion. "It would be fantastic to *see* a game for once." Her face clouded. "But we're both committed to our careers. Are we fooling ourselves we can make this relationship work?"

"We'll take it slow," he said.

Linda wrapped her arms around Malachi's muscular neck, tilting her face up to his. "It's a deal," she smiled. He pulled her close, engaging in their first kiss of this unexpected romantic interlude.

65

September 9, 2010
Potosi Correctional Center, Mineral Point, Missouri

Today was the last day of Pamela Jane Watts's earthly existence, and the remaining moments crept by. Never had she believed she would actually be looking forward to her execution, but she had nothing more to live for. Thoughts kept churning in her head. *I was so damned close to disappearing for good.* Pamela sat in her solitary cell, glaring at the drab walls, two distinct voices arguing in her head. *Nearly got away with it all. I should've killed Ray. But I hesitated.*

And she knew why.

She'd fallen for him. Unlike Darryl or Gregory, Ray exuded charisma, which had drawn her toward his magnetic presence. *I was an idiot.*

Four trials in three and one-half years jumbled together in her head—lawyers, cops, judges, families of victims, and juries made up of her peers with faces too numerous and nondescript to remember. The worst part was finding herself on death row, a fate her legal team genuinely believed they could avoid. Pamela recalled four judges separately sentencing her to death, her own stunned reaction and that of her lawyers. She heard guards whispering among themselves over newspaper accounts: Pamela Watts is the sixth woman on death row in Missouri and the first in Nebraska. *A very elite group,* she reflected sarcastically. Her legal team made numerous appeals, giving her a sliver of optimism. And then the appeals ran out. There was still a minute chance the Missouri governor would grant a last-minute reprieve, but she wasn't just a heinous murderer, Pamela Watts was a *child killer.*

The authorities in Nebraska had decided to try her for the murders of Gregory and the children at the same time. Her legal advisors were blunt. *You are the most vilified woman in the country, Pamela. Don't expect a miracle; people want to see you pay for your sins.* She rolled her stiff shoulders against the wall. *None of this would have happened if Gregory hadn't been hell-bent on being a savior in Africa. He completely upended my plan. Insisting missionary work would strengthen our marriage. Didn't even fucking ask me. He was suddenly the "head of the household." Said I couldn't question his authority. Bullshit. I should have recognized he was becoming an arrogant prick and left sooner.* A frustrated sigh emerged from deep within her lungs.

Her attention roamed to Jacob and Elizabeth. If Gregory had just died as she'd intended, she would simply have left the children sleeping in their beds. But Jacob woke to find his father stumbling over packing boxes. When she slammed the wooden baseball bat repeatedly against her husband's skull, the blood splattered over the floor and walls; her son had witnessed it all. *Why is Daddy bleeding?* She threw a blanket over Gregory's body. *Daddy's just resting, sweetheart.*

She had to think fast, so she had mixed crushed Ambien into chocolate milk for both children as a special treat. She remembered waiting for their breathing to grow labored and then, under the muted glow of a full moon, finished digging their graves in the garden. She could never accept them as her blood and bone anyway.

Her shoulders slumped further against the cool cement wall. During the prior three days, prison guards had observed her every move in the sparsely furnished cell containing a mattress, a toilet, a sink, and a Bible, which she'd stuffed under the mattress. When she was issued a special dark prison jumpsuit, she had thought, *An outfit to die for.* That thought almost made her laugh out loud.

Three hours prior to the execution, she had ordered her last meal from the prison menu. When it arrived, she had little appetite for it. She was allowed to watch TV and tried focusing on the programs. Oprah and some PBS documentary distracted Pamela for a while, but her mind kept wandering over the mistakes that had led her here. *I should have let Ray overdose. But no, I couldn't resist his passion.* She was permitted to talk with her legal team but declined. There was nothing left to say, unless the governor called. *I'd rather spend these last aware moments in silence, making everyone try and guess what I'm thinking. They won't have a clue.*

There was one tiny, positive action that she had managed to keep secret. The DA in Minneapolis had decided not to press charges in the deaths of her adoptive parents—due to lack of evidence. A smirk curled her lips. There was satisfaction in knowing that the ignorant, fat couple who loved calling her "our precious adopted daughter Pammy" had died by her hand. *I hated them. They always had to include the word "adopted," like they were my redeemers. The fire had been a tragic accident. No one will ever know the truth.*

She twisted white curls around her fingers and sneered. Linda Turner, that fucking cop from Nebraska who wouldn't quit searching for her, testified at every trial. Pamela sat stiffly forward, still twisting her hair. *She'll no doubt be present to view my final moments, and that damn Detective Johnson, too.* During one of the trials, Pamela thought she'd overheard chatter that the two had gotten married. *To hell with them.*

The entrance to her cell buzzed, the steel door gliding open. *In less than fifteen minutes, I'll be dead.* The humiliation of enduring a cavity search for contraband would be her last, making death almost a reprieve. Her hands cuffed in front of her torso, three guards escorted her to the death chamber, walls the color of urine. Pamela was strapped to cotton-padded planks, arms splayed outward like Jesus on the cross. She closed her eyes, trying not to visibly laugh at the irony. Needles pricked both her arms as the first intravenous solution dripped into her veins. *I wonder if Ray will be here to say a last good-bye.*

A curtain rose in front of a Plexiglas window, exposing unfamiliar faces. Most of them she knew were reporters, documenting this *momentous occasion.* No sign of Ray. *Maybe he wasn't invited. Too bad. At least he would have prayed for me.* She recognized two or three witnesses from their trial testimony, and a few others who had read victim impact statements. The prison chaplain, attired in a collar and black clothing, inquired, "Do you have any last words, Ms. Watts?"

The movement of her shaking head was deliberate against the board. *I'm not saying another fucking word.* Her gaze returned to the assembled group, landing on Linda Turner's expressionless features, the captain's blue eyes almost boring into her. Detective Johnson stood close by. Pamela focused her gaze directly on Linda's face.

The first drug, an anesthetic, was meant to relax her. She forced her eyes to stay wide open. Within minutes, her muscles grew rigid and paralyzed; her heartbeat waned. The yellow room began fading from Pamela's view, her lips curved into a lifeless smile.

Acknowledgments

I first began transforming *Salvation Station* from a screenplay into a novel with the assistance of Margo Dill in her WOW! Women On Writing course, "Writing a Novel with a Writing Coach." She helped me shape what became a first draft, and then skillfully edited it. I am grateful for her ongoing support and friendship as we work together on new projects.

I also wish to thank Georges Ugeux, who provided a valuable and friendly critique of my manuscript in 2017. From our meeting in New York City that fall, I was able to view the work with fresh eyes. I took the book in a slightly different direction, strengthening Linda's story and cutting 25,000 words. Revision truly is the heart of writing.

I am also indebted to Chris Olsen and Stef Tschida, who have encouraged and supported me throughout this process. When I began questioning myself, they were my cheerleading squad, rallying me to overcome obstacles and move forward.

Finally, I am thankful for She Writes Press and their commitment to creating and nurturing a community of women writers.

About the Author

© Grupa Portrait Studio

Kathryn Schleich has been a writer for thirty years. Her most recent publications include the short story "Reckless Acts" featured in *After Effects: A Zimbell House Anthology* in August 2017, and her story "Grand Slam" published in the *Acentos Review* in May 2017. She is the author of two editions of the book *Hollywood and Catholic Women: Virgins, Whores, Mothers, and Other Images*, which evolved from her master's thesis. Her guest posts have been featured on the Women On Writing blog, *The Muffin*, and she writes for the Amherst H. Wilder Foundation's volunteer newsletter.

When she's not writing, Kathryn is likely volunteering in the education and arts communities in the Twin Cities where she lives. Friends, family, good food, wine, and traveling fill her life. *Salvation Station* is her first novel.

SELECTED TITLES FROM SHE WRITES PRESS

She Writes Press is an independent publishing company founded to serve women writers everywhere. Visit us at www.shewritespress.com.

Last Seen by J. L. Doucette $16.95, 978-1-63152-202-4
When a traumatized reporter goes missing in the Wyoming wilderness, the therapist who knows her secrets is drawn into the investigation— and she comes face-to-face with terrifying answers regarding her own difficult past.

On a Quiet Street: A Dr. Pepper Hunt Mystery by J. L. Doucette
$16.95, 978-1-63152-537-7
A funeral takes the place of a wedding when a woman is strangled just days before her wedding to a district attorney—and Pepper, whose former patient happens to be the brother of the victim, is soon drawn into the investigation.

Cut: An Organ Transplant Murder Mystery by Amy S. Peele
$16.95, 978-1631521843
When Sarah Golden, a well-respected transplant nurse, and her best friend, Jackie, get tangled up in the corrupt world of organ transplants, they find themselves on a sometimes fun, sometimes dangerous roller coaster ride through lifestyles of the rich and famous . . . one from which they may not escape with their lives.

Murder Under The Bridge: A Palestine Mystery by Kate Raphael
$16.95, 978-1-63152-960-3
Rania, a Palestinian police detective with a young son, meets cheeky Jewish-American feminist Chloe at an Israeli checkpoint—and soon becomes embroiled in a murder case that implicates te highest echelons of the Israeli military.

Water On the Moon by Jean P. Moore $16.95, 978-1-938314-61-2
When her home is destroyed in a freak accident, Lidia Raven, a divorced mother of two, is plunged into a mystery that involves her entire family.